Ke

"Love goes far beyond when you call the grave."
— Edgar Cayce

Edward M Wolfe

Kendra

EDWARD M WOLFE

This is a work of fiction. All of the characters, organizations, events and locations portrayed in this story are either products of the author's imagination or used fictitiously.

ISBN: 150011748X

© 2014 by Edward M Wolfe
Cover design by Shaelee Michelle Wolfe

All Rights Reserved

Dedicated to everyone who has ever loved, and anyone who has ever lost.

Special thanks to my amazing and invaluable beta readers – I can't thank you enough; to my daughter for being a sounding board from beginning to end, and for the cover design; to Clay Grogan and Ray Odoala; and most of all, to everyone who reads my books. A writer is nothing without readers.

One

Keith was sitting in a Starbucks on a Saturday morning trying not to stare at the unhappy goddess two tables away. She was staring intently at her laptop screen, occasionally pounding the keys and always looking like she was two seconds away from throwing it through the large glass windows. He felt for her – whatever her problem was, but he also had to keep himself from laughing. She was just so damned cute in her anger and frustration. He really couldn't take his eyes off of her.

Twice she looked his way before he could avert his gaze and caught him looking at her. He tried for a pleasant, friendly smile. Just a guy drinking a Frappuccino and reading a book; not a stalker or a creep, but definitely someone who knows and appreciates extraordinary beauty when he sees it.

To get a rein on his fascination with her, he reminded himself that he knew nothing about her as a person. Beauty on the outside is often nothing more than a pretty wrapper concealing a big mess on the inside; in fact, that was the case more often than not, as far as he was concerned. He hoped to meet someone someday who was just pleasantly average on the outside but very sweet and well-developed on the inside. At 23, he'd had his share of beauty queens already and it had always been a disaster. He was practically convinced that physical beauty was a mental handicap. It subverted survival instincts and engendered an entitlement mentality.

As with any man, Keith was genetically predisposed to seek out and pursue the most attractive of the female species. But he was determined to impose some intelligent evolution on his natural impulses. The frustrated beauty working on her laptop was nothing but a very pleasant visual stimulant; like a bed of roses at dawn, or a sunset on the beach. There was no reason to assume she was even worth talking to, and he was not even trying to think of a way to approach her.

He almost told himself that the odds were 50/50 that she was not worthy of getting to know, but actually, he reconsidered, the odds are worse than that. There's a good chance that she expects things to be given to her rather than earned; her car was probably a gift from her parents, and she probably had a good paying job that she got because the interviewer was a male, and so on. It was always like that.

Keith didn't like it that super attractive people often got a free ride in life, but it was the way it was. He'd seen it all his life. He even acknowledged that his own good looks had worked in his favor at times. At his current job as an I.T. Manager, he was very young to have that position and he was certain that he had beaten the more qualified competitor for the job because although the guy had a Master's degree in Information Technology, he looked like a typical geek with no social skills.

Keith chanced another look at the beautiful young woman and now she was sitting with her arms crossed and practically pouting at the screen. Oh, she was adorable. Keith wondered if she had a specific problem with writing a story or maybe programming an applet, or was it the computer itself that was defeating her. Maybe he should find out. If it was the computer, then he could probably make her problem go away like magic.

Most people didn't have the first clue when it came to their computers. They didn't even think they could learn anything about them because they relegated all things computer-ish to some mystically confusing realm of the Technologically Impossible to Understand. Even if it meant reading a simple error message with no more knowledge necessary to understand the problem than a grasp of basic English. He was constantly being called to user's desks only to watch them finally read what was on their screen when he arrived and only then realize they didn't need him after all.

Should he ask if she needed help? No, he told himself. Don't even think it. He saw a less attractive girl over to his right. She looked physically fit and was reading a book. He told himself to forget about the stunning brunette and consider the girl who might actually have some intellect since she wasn't drop-dead gorgeous, and she liked to read something other than Facebook, which could be a really good sign. Although it was possible too that she was reading something ridiculous. He couldn't see the title, so he couldn't pass judgment.

As he was thinking these things, he smelled something delicious and intoxicating in the air and it seemed to be coming from his left. He turned his head, and there she was, standing in front of him. His first thought was to say something complimentary about her perfume or whatever it was that smelled so good. But before he could think of anything, she interrupted his thoughts.

"I hate to bother you, but I was wondering if you might know anything about computers. I'm in a terrible bind – trying to meet a deadline – and my computer is making my life hell right now. I *really* need help."

Perfect, he thought. *Too* perfect. Almost like fate, or destiny. He looked in her eyes for only a second before he knew that he would do anything for her. All of his thoughts of self-restraint and making an informed choice about the type of woman he should date and avoiding the super sexy types evaporated like steam from a coffee cup.

"Well, possibly. What's happening with it?" he asked nonchalantly.

"Is it okay if I sit down?" She glanced at the empty chair opposite him.

"Sure."

"Just a second. I'll be right back." She went and grabbed her laptop and her coffee and came back to his table, setting her stuff down before pulling out the chair. She sat and rotated the laptop so the screen faced him. "See that? That's what's happening. The screen is white and the blue circle is just spinning and I can't do anything. I have to get this article in to my editor in…" She looked at her cell phone. "…In the next 22 minutes. Normally if my computer locks up, I'll just turn it off, and then when I turn it on again, it's fine, but I can't lose this article. If I do, I'll probably lose my job along with it."

Keith was loving this. She was a perfectly beautiful damsel in distress. Her well-being and livelihood were threatened by a technological beast, and slaying such beasts was his specialty.

She got up and came over to his side of the table, standing so close to him, her left arm was touching his right arm. She leaned down and pressed the touchpad's left-mouse button several times, demonstrating to him that the computer was unresponsive.

"See?"

"Yep." Keith could barely talk with her standing so close to him, bathing him in her scent. He felt like he could just close his eyes, breathe deeply and ponder for a few years the difficulty of explaining to another human what he was feeling right now. He mentally slapped himself to snap out of the enchantment that was taking his mind away like a black hole. "Let me try something."

He tapped a key, typed a word, then moused over to the top of the window that appeared in front of her Word document. He clicked once on an item in a list, then clicked a button. Moused back up to the top of the window, clicked a word, causing a small menu to appear, then he typed another word and pressed the Enter key, then pushed the laptop back a few inches and leaned back in his chair. The entire sequence took him less than 20 seconds.

Kendra watched him and realized she couldn't have asked a more qualified person for help. And what were the odds that the best looking guy in the Starbucks was also a computer wizard? He started tapping on keys and she nearly panicked when she saw her taskbar disappear. She was certain that he had done something to make the computer shutdown, even though she had just told him she could *not* lose this document. Her job depended on it. But then he tapped, moused, and typed some more and the taskbar came back and now Word no longer appeared washed out and the spinning blue circle became a white arrow again, and lo and behold, the cursor was blinking, and that meant she could resume writing, and possibly even finish before her deadline lapsed.

"How did you do that?" She smiled brightly and Keith was sure he'd never seen anyone more radiantly beautiful. He was so grateful that something so simple could generate such pure happiness in another human and cause such a beautiful person to glow with relief that her former nightmare was not even a concern anymore.

"I could tell you, and I will sometime if you're really interested, but you've got less than twenty minutes to get your article to your editor. You better get to work." He spun her computer back around so it faced the empty chair across from him. He picked up his coffee, leaned back and took a sip, looking at her laptop over the rim of his cup and raising his eyebrows as if to say, "Get to work."

"Thank you so much!" She bent down and kissed him on his lips with supreme gratitude for being her savior. She had only meant to make it a quick peck, but as soon as their lips touched, something came over her. She put her left hand on the back of his head and pressed her lips harder onto his, and held his head in place with her hand so it wasn't pushed backwards from the force of her kiss. She pulled away from him and resumed breathing. "Thank you!"

Keith couldn't talk. His brain was buzzing and he couldn't feel his body, but he somehow managed to smile, then he pointed at her laptop.

"Oh, right!" She quickly sat down and began typing after looking at the page for a few seconds to bring her mind back to where it was when the computer had froze on her. As she typed, she periodically looked over the top of the screen for quick glances at Keith. Every time she did so, he was looking right back at her. She found it hard to stay focused but managed to finish her article with several minutes to spare.

She opened her web browser and was just about to compose an email when her phone rang. She looked at it, then looked at Keith and flashed a mock grimace.

"Hello, this is Kendra.

Yes, I was just emailing it to you right now.

Um, yeah. I'm not too far away, actually. I'll be there in about five minutes.

Okay. See you then."

She ended the call and made a funny face at her phone as if something weird had just happened. She used the touchpad to save her document and closed the lid.

"I guess I won't be emailing my article. I have to deliver it in person." She frowned as she picked up her laptop and her coffee. She stepped around the table to Keith's side and bent down, giving him a quick kiss on his lips. "Thank you again, so much. You have no idea…"

She rushed out the door and walked quickly into the parking lot. Keith turned his chair to watch her go, unable to believe she was leaving him there, caught in the spell she had cast on him. He watched her walk to a convertible red Miata. She got in. The brake lights flared and the white reverse lights came on. She backed up, turning to the right, positioning her car to exit to the left. When her car was parallel to the front of the Starbucks, she turned and looked at Keith.

From thirty yards away, their eyes met. She mouthed the word, "Bye" and her teeth came down on her bottom lip as she sucked in a breath, then she shifted into first gear and drove away.

Keith stared at the spot where she had just been, still seeing her there in his mind's eye. He recalled the name she spoke when she answered her phone.

"Kendra," he said aloud. He took a deep breath and sighed like a man who had just finished a task that had taken years to complete.

Two

Keith was well aware of the fact that Kendra had just driven off without giving him any contact information, or even her last name. He was also aware of how odd it was that he wasn't concerned about it at all. Ordinarily, meeting a woman like this and then not having a way to contact her would have driven him crazy. He'd be very anxious about how he'd ever see her again.

But not this time. He felt a calm serenity, certain that he'd see Kendra again. He didn't know how, but he knew it would happen. He didn't hope it, and he wasn't fantasizing. He just knew and didn't question it.

He thought about her all week at work, and at home while cooking, while walking his Golden Retriever, Laci, while showering, and as he lay in bed falling asleep. She dominated his thoughts like a post-dated check made out to him for a million dollars.

When the following Saturday finally came around, he woke up knowing he'd be spending the morning at Starbucks. It was the most likely place to find her. He finished his morning routine and started a load of laundry, then took Laci for a walk before heading to the Starbucks where he'd met her the previous Saturday.

Although he felt certain that he'd meet her again, he didn't know if it would be today. He just hoped it would be, and it was most likely that they'd run into each other again in the same place where they'd met, on the same day of the week.

He got his regular Frappuccino and sat at his regular table and tried reading the paperback he'd brought with him, but he found that he couldn't get into the story. He hadn't been able to read all week. Each time he tried, usually before going to sleep, he couldn't focus on the story. He couldn't supplant the real world with the fictional one in the book. His thoughts kept drifting to Kendra. He'd see her face and that fabulous smile that lit him up inside like an insane Christmas tree.

After a few minutes, he couldn't stand sitting with his back to the door so he switched to the seat that Kendra had sat in. Now he could see when anyone was approaching the door, and he could see part of the parking lot. He kept an eye out for a red Miata, waiting for her to pull in. He was in a happy state of anticipation – for a while. Then he finished his drink, tried reading again, got another drink, and finished that one. Then he started thinking about the time. What time had she been here last week? How long should he wait? Would it be tacky to leave a note with the barista? Would they even give it to her, or would they be reluctant to aid in something that might look like creepy stalking behavior?

He finally and reluctantly decided to leave. Maybe it just wasn't meant to be today. He went to his car and delayed his departure by gathering up trash and putting it in a bag he still had in the car from Office Depot where he had purchased a flash drive a few days before. He found receipts, straw wrappers and miscellaneous things he hadn't even realized were on the floor of his car and put them in the bag. He walked slowly back to the entrance to deposit the bag in the trash receptacle, giving Kendra one last chance to show up before he actually left.

But she didn't.

The following Saturday was a repeat of the first one in which she didn't show. Keith's feeling of certainty began to be edged out by self-doubt and anxiety. Had he just imagined the connection he was so sure they shared? Was his feeling that they were fated to be together really nothing more than his belief in something he desired and wished was true?

Maybe he needed to find her another way. Maybe coming back to Starbucks and just waiting for her to show up was akin to waiting for his dream girl to be delivered on a silver platter. Maybe what he really needed to do was work a bit harder for something that was worth so much. He had to *earn* his future with her.

He only knew three things about her. Her name, the type of car she drove, and that she wrote. What had she said about her writing? Keith tried to remember the reference she had made. He remembered her saying that she had a deadline and she was writing an article. She got a phone call from her editor. So she could be a staff writer for a magazine or a newspaper.

He picked up his phone and did a Google search for "article by Kendra." Most of the search results that came back were about a Playboy playmate named Kendra. He wanted articles *by* Kendra – not *about*. He changed his query to "written by Kendra" and got better results, but they were mostly authors of books and none of them were even in Tulsa or seemed to have anything to do with *his* Kendra.

He was discouraged and disheartened after barely a few minutes of searching. He didn't know how he could possibly find her with what he knew about her. He gave her less time to show up on this Saturday than the one before, and employed no stalling tactics when he went to his car to leave. He tried to fight a sinking depression that was trying to come over him, but it wasn't a depression born of negative thinking. He was feeling it in his solar plexus. It seemed to be a physical feeling and he didn't know what that meant. It made him doubt himself even more and he began to think he had been a fool, "knowing" that he and Kendra would be together.

He didn't *know* anything. He should never trust his feelings when it came to a beautiful woman. Beauty just fogs the male mind. Primal desire takes over and chemicals flood the brain. In his case, he had managed to translate the chemical endorphin high into something that he believed was his destiny. What a fool he'd been.

He stopped thinking about Kendra and focused once again on the routine things in his life. He paid more attention to Laci and resumed reading voraciously. He treated himself to a Kindle, which he'd had mixed feelings about since he'd been a paper book lover since he'd started reading as a child. He discovered that there was a time and place for both types of books and he was glad that he bought it.

Over the course of the next week, he found that the Kindle opened up a whole world of books to him, and the ease with which he could obtain them was a delight. He had loved going to the library and to Barnes & Noble, and he still would, but the ability to browse online, purchase a book with a single click, and then be reading it within seconds was just great.

On the next Saturday, he brought his Kindle with him to Starbucks. This time he was just going for his normal Saturday routine; indulging himself in a Frappuccino and leisure time with his favorite activity. He barely even thought of Kendra and he sat in his normal seat with his back to the door. He didn't even think anything of it when he felt someone tap on his shoulder.

Three

Keith smelled her before he saw her and he was already smiling when he turned around to look at her.

"Hello, beautiful."

She was smiling too. Kendra was tempted to kiss him, but decided to wait before acting again on what she felt about him. It was crazy enough that she had already kissed him. She could see that Keith was happy to see her, but the feelings she had were so crazy, she *couldn't* act on them. She needed some external confirmation first that this was really happening, and not just in her head.

"Were you saving this seat for me?"

Keith laughed and said, "Yes. For three weeks now."

"What's so funny?" she asked as she sat down.

"A really bad joke."

"I wanna hear it," she said, still smiling.

"Ah… you don't. It's pretty gross."

"Okay, now you have to tell me."

"Oh God, I'm gonna regret this, but okay. What did the single male fly say to the lady fly after landing next to her in a bar?" Keith paused. Kendra looked at him and raised her eyebrows. "Excuse me, is this stool taken?"

Keith shook his head in regret as he delivered the punch-line. Kendra squinted her eyes shut and grimaced, baring her teeth.

"I told you," he said. "It's pretty gross."

They both laughed. Then she said, "Wow, you really know how to make an impression on a girl."

"Uh! That's not fair. You made me!"

She laughed again and without even thinking, put her hand on top of his.

"I know. I'm just teasing. How have you been?"

Keith turned his hand over so their palms were touching and he gripped her hand.

"I've been good. A little impatient, but still good. How 'bout you?"

"I've been good, and busy, and eager to get back to Tulsa. My plane just landed 30 minutes ago."

"You have a plane? Wow."

"Oh, shut up," she said, slapping his hand with her free hand. "You know what I mean."

"If it just landed, that means you pretty much came straight here." Keith smiled like a fool.

"I did. I was hoping you'd be here. I didn't have any way to reach you and I've been kicking myself for not getting your number when we met."

"I've been sitting right here waiting for you – for three weeks. I haven't moved an inch. And now I'm afraid I'm going to need to go home and shower and eat, get some sleep; you know, all the things I've been neglecting."

Kendra laughed and smiled. She was getting some confirmation at least. Keith definitely liked her. She was glad that at least that much between them was mutual. But she still wasn't sure about the other part – her crazy thoughts – that strange feeling that she had met her next boyfriend the day she had met Keith, and possibly her *last* boyfriend. She didn't want to think the word "soulmate" yet, but there it was.

"I take it that means you were thinking of me?"

"Like a guy with a one-track mind."

"Good. I hope I'm the only one you were thinking about."

"Let's see. I met the most beautiful woman I've ever seen. She kissed me out of the blue before I even knew her name. Then she disappeared. And *then*, right after that, I met you."

Kendra laughed again. "I'm going to kiss you again if you don't stop making me laugh."

"A guy walks into a bar…"

She giggled. "Okay, enough. I have a serious question."

"Okay. Shoot."

"Why didn't you ask for my number before I left?"

"You left rather suddenly, and it actually never even occurred to me."

Kendra's seemingly permanent smile finally faded. She lowered her eyelids a little and bit her bottom lip. "It didn't occur to you?"

"No, I don't mean that how it sounds. I mean, yeah, you did leave suddenly, but… I don't know how to say this, or if I should, but I had a feeling that it was okay that I didn't have your number."

"What do you mean?" she asked, curious but hopeful.

"Well, I just had this feeling."

"Go on…" she prompted.

"I felt like I didn't have to worry about getting your number." She could see that he had more on his mind but was reluctant to say it. She suspected they felt the same way.

"You mean like, you knew we'd see each other again, so there was no urgency or concern?"

"Yeah. Exactly like that." Way more than that, he thought, but he wasn't going to reveal that much. Not so soon. It was never a good idea to tell a girl how excited you were about her in the beginning. She'd immediately assume you were desperate and clingy.

"How often do you come here?"

"Usually every Saturday. About the only time I don't come in on a Saturday morning is when I have a veterinarian appointment."

"You go to a vet?"

Keith laughed. "My dog can't drive. And since I work all week, I usually make her vet appointments for Saturdays."

"How long have you been coming here on Saturdays?"

"Um… since I moved to Tulsa, which was about a year ago."

"In all that time, you only saw me here once. What made you think we'd meet up again?"

She looked straight into his eyes and waited as he looked away from her, hesitating to answer her direct question. He took a breath, blew it out and slapped his hands down on the small table between them, appearing to have arrived at a decision, for better or worse.

"Okay, I'm just going to say this and hope you don't freak out."

"Wait!" She startled Keith into silence. "May I have some of your Frappuccino?" He smiled and slid it across the table. She picked it up and brought the straw to her mouth. "Go on."

"Okay. I wasn't worried about getting your number because I knew I'd see you again. And you're right. It didn't make sense to assume that I'd see you here when I'd never seen you here before, but I felt certain that I'd see you somewhere, and that…" Keith paused at the part he didn't want to reveal, but decided he would just do it. If he was right, there was no reason not to. "…And that, we would end up being more than friends." He squinted as if bracing for a blow; wondering if he had just blown it with her.

Her lips formed a closed mouth smile around the straw she was sucking. She aimed the tip of the straw around the bottom of the cup, slurping up slushy coffee. She focused only on what she was doing and didn't respond to what Keith had just said. He was starting to regret that he'd said so much, so soon.

"Well?" he asked.

"I'm sorry. Did you say something?" She tried to keep a straight face, but failed instantly and laughed. Keith laughed with her. She handed him back the nearly empty cup.

"So, what do you think?" He tried to get the last remnants of his Frappuccino through his straw.

"I'm relieved to know that I'm not crazy."

"Really?" he asked, biting on the straw.

"Yes. I felt the exact same way. I just knew we'd find each other and... you know... date, or something. I knew it the way I know my name is Kendra."

Keith's shoulders came down with the release of tension he hadn't known he was feeling. He felt like he could breathe more deeply and freely.

"So where were you for the last three weeks? You know, you could've come in on any Saturday and found me here."

"I would have, but I was on assignment in Iraq. I had to cover the elections. And like I told you, my plane just landed and I came straight here. Trust me, most people want to go home after a long international flight. But here I am."

They smiled at each other, both of them buzzing with a happiness that was compounded by the fact that their feelings were mutual.

"You must be exhausted." Keith looked concerned.

"I am. I'd love to go to sleep right now."

"Don't let me keep you. But let's trade numbers this time. I don't want to wait for another chance encounter; no matter how certain we are that we'll meet up again."

"How about you drive me home? I'm so tired, I don't trust myself to drive."

Keith drove, following Kendra's directions until they arrived at a small white duplex. He walked her to the front door, looking forward to giving her a goodbye kiss. She took her keys out of her purse and unlocked the door.

"Come on," she said, stepping inside. Keith followed her in, excited, but also feeling intrusive. She turned to the right at the end of the entrance a few feet away. Keith followed her down a short hall and into a room that turned out to be her bedroom.

Kendra flopped down on the bed with an exaggerated sigh. Her feet were hanging off the end of the bed and she pushed off one shoe with the tip of the other, then had trouble doing the same on the other foot. Keith stepped over and helped, dropping the shoe on the floor next to the first one. He stood there feeling awkward, not sure what he should do, or not do.

"I'm going to take a nap. Do you want to stay a while?"

Keith had never been invited to hang out with a sleeping person before. He thought it was strange, and wonderful.

"I'd love to," he said, allowing himself to fall forward, flopping down on the bed next to her.

"Good. I just need a few hours. I'd love it if you're here when I wake up. You can watch TV, play video games, cook; do whatever you want." She rolled on to her side, facing him. She looked sleepy and content.

Keith moved close to her, kissed her softly and said, "I'll just wait right here."

Four

Keith watched the rapid movement beneath her eyelids. As she dreamed, he had to convince himself that she was the only one doing so. Even with Kendra having revealed that she too felt an odd and fateful attraction, he was still impressed with how strange it was to be lying on her bed and watching her sleep when he really didn't know her at all.

Adding to the surreal feeling from lying on a virtual stranger's bed was the unfamiliarity of where he was. Keith was tempted to get up and get a little more acquainted with her by checking out the rest of her apartment, but he thought that seemed too weird. He felt like he was in a wonderfully strange dream. He didn't want it to morph into feeling like he was a cat-burglar, slinking around a sleeping woman's house.

He lay there watching Kendra breathe and felt like he was gazing at someone with whom he was completely and hopelessly in love. This was the strangest thing. He felt like he'd always been with her—she just hadn't been present yet. He didn't feel that they had just come together; he felt like they had just reunited. Was this how people felt when they said they had found their soulmates? Kendra did not feel like a stranger to him. He didn't think they needed many long conversations to get to know each other. It was more like they only needed to talk to fill in the blanks since they'd last seen each other.

Feeling immersed in the inexplicable familiarity he felt with her, he reached out and very lightly caressed her hair. She felt perfect to him. Everything about her was beautiful to him and just right; even her imperfections. He felt like he had arrived someplace he hadn't known he was waiting to reach his entire life.

Three hours passed in what felt like only moments to him. Kendra stirred in her sleep with a faint smile on her lips. She stretched out languorously; her fingers hitting the headboard, causing her to open her eyes. She saw Keith smiling at her and her own slight smile grew and spread to her eyes.

"You're here," she said, and bit her lower lip.

"Of course. There's nowhere I'd rather be." Keith leaned over and kissed her gently on her lips.

"Mmm." She put an arm around him and pulled him closer.

They kissed each other softly and repeatedly, smiling and gazing into each other's eyes. Keith ran his fingers through her hair and held her head gently as he just barely nibbled her bottom lip. In his mind, he was yelling, "I love you, Kendra!" but he didn't dare say it out loud. He felt that things were already past the point of anything remotely normal and he feared breaking the spell with classic early relationship blunders.

"Are you hungry?" she asked him.

"I don't know."

She laughed at his reply. "I'm hungry. Come with me." She rolled over and got off the bed. Keith got up and walked around to her side. She took his hand and led him to the kitchen where together, they made a late breakfast, kissing and embracing at every opportunity they could find. After eating, Kendra said she wanted to take a shower.

"I'll wait for you," Keith said.

"Um… I think it would be better if you didn't," Kendra replied in a serious tone.

Keith panicked inside. Had this just been a dream? Was it over now? How could this be? Nothing in his life had ever felt more perfect or more right.

"If you don't join me, I'm going to be very upset." Kendra laughed and ran toward her bedroom.

Keith felt like melting into a puddle on her linoleum floor as relief washed over him. She ran past him and he decided she needed to be spanked for teasing him like that.

They spent most of that day at Kendra's, then spent the night at Keith's so he could take care of Laci. On Sunday night he told her he'd call in sick in the morning so he could spend the day with her, but she told him she had things to take care of after being away, and she had to leave again in a few days. But he could come over after work on Monday.

Each time Kendra would return from an assignment, they spent as much time together as possible. Things went on for several weeks this way. Keith felt like his life was a rollercoaster of incredible highs followed by lonely lows.

One night when she came home from Kuwait, Kendra looked unhappy when Keith walked into her house. She was sitting on the couch with her head down, picking invisible lint off of her yoga pants. She didn't run to greet him as she usually did. She looked at him and he saw that her eyes were watering.

"What's wrong, babe?" Keith came over and kneeled in front of her.

"I can't do this anymore, Keith."

He knew it. It had been too good to be true. His heart plunged into ice-water. He had trouble breathing, but managed to say, "What do you mean?"

"Our relationship isn't working. I'm away too much, and—"

"But it is! I really, really like you, Kendra. Don't do this to us."

"You didn't let me finish."

"I don't want you to finish. You're wrong. Our relationship is working great. I love it."

"I love *you*, Keith!"

His brain froze. She loved him? And she wanted to break up? He couldn't think.

"I don't…" He was going to say 'understand' but the word felt insufficient. He couldn't grasp, comprehend, make sense of… he struggled to find the right words.

"You don't love me?"

"Kendra, I've known you for about a month, and I've never loved anyone or anything more in my life."

She wrapped her arms around him and cried. Keith was more confused than ever. But she loved him. That was good. She was holding him. That was good. He didn't want to say anything more for fear of turning things bad somehow. She finally pulled away and looked at him.

"I'm so glad you love me. I was so scared you wouldn't."

"Kendra, I've loved you since the day I met you."

She slapped his arm and asked, "Then why haven't you said anything?"

"I didn't want to scare you away. Wouldn't you have freaked out if I had told you I loved you right after we met?"

"Yes. Of course I would've."

They both laughed.

"Okay, then! I was right in not telling you."

"But you could've told me five minutes later, and that would've been fine."

They laughed again and kissed.

"So, are we okay now?"

"No," she said, pouting.

"What else is wrong?"

"What I tried to tell you earlier but you interrupted me."

"That our relationship isn't working?"

"Yes."

"Oh God. I wonder why lesbian couples don't self-destruct."

"What is that supposed to mean?"

"Women are impossible to understand. Impossibility squared should defy some law of physics. What's wrong with our relationship if we both love each other?"

"I don't mean our relationship, I mean being together."

"Oh. That clears up everything," he said, shaking his head.

"Keith, we lose too much time that we could be spending together by living in separate houses. There! I said it."

"You want to live together?"

"Yes."

"Thank God! I couldn't wait, but I've just been waiting so you didn't think I was rushing things."

"I spend so much time away, when I'm here, I want as much time with you as possible."

"What are you waiting for? Start packing!"

— ∞ —

Living together felt natural to them despite the short time they'd known each other. The only problem Kendra had was with her parents. They strongly disapproved of unwedded cohabitation on religious grounds. Kendra did not share her parents' religious convictions, despite their lifelong efforts to instill their beliefs in her. When Kendra visited with her mother and told her she had moved in to Keith's, she made it very clear with her how she felt.

"Your real objection isn't that we walk around under the same roof, Mother. It's that we have *sex* without being married. So would it really make any difference to you if I kept my apartment and we had sex anyway? Obviously it wouldn't, so I don't want to hear about us living together. That's nothing but a euphemism. If you're going to complain about how I live my life, at least be honest about it."

Her mother was accustomed to her daughter's directness, but had never been able to counter it. Confrontations with Kendra usually resulted in Joanne just changing the subject to neutral territory until the next visit when she'd inevitably make a disapproving remark about "people living together out of wedlock."

Keith and Kendra had nothing against marriage, but neither of them saw a need for it. They were in love and committed to each other. They had no children and didn't plan on any for the time being, so they didn't see what benefit there would be in binding themselves to each other with a legal contract. They were happy together whenever they had the chance to be together. That was enough for them. They considered themselves married on a spiritual level anyway, and when the time came where they'd get tangible benefits from actually being married, they agreed that they'd do it then.

As time went on, Kendra made Keith's house into *their* house by making small changes whenever she was back in Tulsa for more than a few days. The first thing she insisted on was the addition of plants; the larger, the better. She started with Dwarf Date Palms, then a few hanging plants. The first time Keith came home to find the plants bringing his formerly boring house to life, he was delighted.

"You like?" she asked him.

"I love it. It makes a huge difference. I wish I'd thought of this a long time ago."

"Good. There's more things I want to do that I think you'll also like."

"Great. I'll sign a blank check and you can do anything you want."

"You mean, literally?"

"Yeah. I trust your taste. I really like the feel of the house with these plants."

"I mean about the blank check. Did you win the lottery today?"

"No, that was last year. I've haven't been quite as lucky this year. All I did so far was meet you."

"Oh yeah?" she asked. "I'm having a run of bad luck too. Only one Saudi prince so far has asked me to marry him."

"Really?"

She came closer to him and put her index fingers through the belt loops on the front of his Levi's and pulled, closing the distance between them.

"So what happened?"

"Well…" she started, then kissed him seductively. "I had been weighing the pros and cons of only going outside wrapped in a black sheet with a space cut out for my eyes when I met a guy in Tulsa with a really adorable dog."

"Yeah? Then what?"

"I chose the dog."

They laughed while kissing and made their way to the bedroom.

Later he gave her a signed blank check.

"You were serious," she said.

"I still am."

She raised one corner of her upper lip and squinted an eye at him as she cocked her head.

"An actual blank check. Really? You want me to spend as much as I want making our house nicer?"

"Yes."

"Keith, I don't mean to butt into your business, but you're an I.T. manager, only two years older than me. Did you really win the lottery?"

"No. My father died a little over a year ago and he left me some money. Not a ton, but if I lived conservatively, I could go several years without working. So don't worry about spending too much at Bed, Bath & Beyond, or whatever."

She put her arms around him and talked with her lips close to his, which she loved doing.

"I'm sorry about your dad."

"It's okay. He's probably happier now."

Kendra frowned.

"That's sad."

"How could being happy be sad?" Keith asked, laughing.

"Because he died!"

"But if he's alive somewhere, then I really do think he's happier. My mother made him miserable. So wherever he is now, I'm sure he's better off."

"I hope so."

Kendra spent two weeks in the Middle East reporting on Israel's ground war with Hamas. Keith was worried about her the entire time. He was glued to news of the war, fearing that all of the countries surrounding Israel were going to see this as their chance to finally rid themselves of their mortal enemy.

Finally she came home and Keith wished she would never leave again. He was at his lowest low due to her two week absence, and her return made him happier than he'd ever been. He longed for a stable life with her always home in Tulsa, and never in danger.

They had sex as soon as she came home, and then again after they'd eaten dinner and walked Laci. Lying in bed, holding hands, Kendra said, "I have bad news."

"I don't believe you."

"No, really, babe. I have to leave tomorrow."

"What? You just got back."

"I know. My boss called while you were in the shower. They're pulling the troops out of Iraq. That's really big news, Keith. He wants several reporters there to cover multiple angles."

"And one of them just has to be you? Can't you tell him you need time off, or you're sick or something so you can get out of it?"

"But I don't want to get out of it. This is historic. It's the official ending of an American war. I want to be there and see it and report on it."

"But this isn't even a real war. It's not like we've been fighting the military forces of Iraq all this time. A *real* war is over when you conquer the enemy government, or they surrender. We won the 'war' in three weeks. Since then, we've just being 'fighting terrorism' which is a joke. You can't win a war on terrorists. As long one person wants to attack us, the 'war' isn't over."

"Yeah, but aside from all of that. It's still the official ending of what's going down in history as a war, and I want to be a part of it. I only get to do 'man on the street stuff' since I have the least experience, but still, it's pretty great that I'm getting sent to another big event."

"I just hate that you're always in the Middle East. Can't you get assigned to things at home? Or Texas, at least?"

"Keith, I love working in the Middle East. You know that."

"I know, but I just don't understand. It's really dangerous, and there's nothing there but desert and uncivilized warring factions."

Kendra shook her head and smiled sadly.

"It's funny that you say uncivilized when the birth of civilization was in the Middle East."

"You mean the Garden of Eden?"

"That was there too, but I'm talking about ancient Sumeria."

"Tell me about it later. I'm losing precious time with you." Keith rolled over on top of her, brushed her hair away from her face and peppered her with kisses.

She giggled and asked, "Again? Already?"

"At least one more time tonight. And before you get ready in the morning."

She laughed and started kissing him back.

— ∞ —

A few weeks later Keith dreamed he was in a museum during an earthquake. Everything he saw was moving; shaking back and forth, up and down, but nothing was falling over or breaking. Paintings held their positions on walls and in glass display cases. Sculptures rocked and jostled but didn't tip over. Glass cases designed to preserve historical documents wavered but did not crack. Keith felt as though everything in the museum was on the verge of destruction, the vibrations were so strong. Then he began to realize that he was in bed. The dream faded out and reality faded in – but the shaking and vibrating was not going away as the dream was replaced by conscious thought. That's when he concluded that a real earthquake had caused him to dream of an earthquake.

He opened his eyes and looked at the lamp on his bedside table. It was sitting perfectly still and yet Keith could still feel the earthquake. He looked over at his desk and neither his computer monitor nor his speakers appeared to be moving at all. There was half a bottle of Dasani water on his desk and the water inside was perfectly still, and yet Keith could feel his whole body still warbling. Warbling? He wasn't sure why he thought of that word, and was even less sure he knew what it meant. Don't birds warble?

Being of a logical mind, he tried to theorize why it was that he could feel the vibrations and not see anything else vibrating. He considered an unlikely possibility; perhaps he and everything else were vibrating at the same rate and thus everything appeared to be still. Like two people looking at each other close-up through car windows, each travelling at the exact same speed – neither would perceive motion in themselves or the other if they could see no other stationary objects for motion reference.

The vibrations started to lessen and fade. Keith imagined the earthquake moving away and causing other people and things to vibrate as it moved along the fault line. Even now with the vibrations very faint, he still felt like he was warbling, only much less so than before. More gently.

He thought again about that word and the sensation that was almost gone now and tried to identify what it was similar to and why the word warbling came to his mind. He recalled himself as an adolescent with a rectangular sheet of metal about two feet wide by one and a half feet long. He had held it with his fingers on the edges and shook it rapidly back and forth and it made an unusual sound – warbling.

Yeah, he thought. My whole damned body was warbling. He knew there were two different kinds of earthquakes – those that rocked and those that rolled – now he wondered if there was a third type that warbled.

Five

Keith looked at the clock next to the lamp beside his bed and saw that he was up nearly an hour before his alarm was set to go off, but he didn't feel tired as he usually did after only six hours of sleep. Ordinarily, he'd hit snooze several times and then rush to work, stressed the whole way there that he'd be late.

He had stayed up so late talking to Kendra the night before that he was certain he'd sleep through his alarm this morning. She was in Iraq, eight hours ahead of him and had called him at 1am when he was getting ready for bed. If it had been anyone else calling, he wouldn't have answered, or if he had, it would have been to tell them what time it was and how rude they were – unless it was an emergency, of course.

But with Kendra, he didn't care what time she called. If they didn't talk at odd hours, they wouldn't talk much at all when she was on assignment. She said she'd be home in two days, but only for a week, then she'd be going to D.C. to cover the up-coming elections.

Keith hated that she spent so much time away, but he wondered if her time away played any part in the sustained passion they felt when they were together. Or was it just the special connection they had felt since the first time they'd seen each other? They'd been together for several months now and Keith felt just as excited about being with her now as he did in the beginning. Each time Kendra was home felt like a honeymoon. They would stay up late talking like they had the first night they ever spent together, and they made love like it was the first time, every time.

Then she'd be gone again. Sometimes she'd leave for a week, and other times, like now, for weeks at a time. When she called early this morning, she was excited about getting a short tour of the Iraq Museum International just before she had called. She apologized for waking him. He told her it was fine. He'd rather talk to her than sleep or anything, really. Kendra told him she had seen cuneiform tablets that were thousands of years old and a reporter from Reuters said that some of them contained proof of aliens on earth at the dawn of civilization. She didn't have time to see what he was talking about though since they'd been rushed through the museum, but from what he had said, it sounded pretty fascinating and she hoped to look into it more if she could manage a proper visit to the museum before heading home.

The Reuters guy suggested she should look for a book by a guy named Zecharia Sitchin; something about twelve planets. It would explain everything, she said, speaking in a rush as she always did when she called from the Middle East. She hoped she could get something to read on the plane, but she doubted Baghdad International would be very well stocked in the ancient aliens department. She said she'd be lucky if she could pick up something by Danielle Steele.

And then she said her (self-imposed) time limit was up and she had to go to keep her cell phone bill down and she loved him and she'd see him soon. And then the rushing whirlwind of excitement and enthusiasm and the soft, lovely voice of a lover so far away that she might as well be make-believe was gone and he held the silent phone to his ear not wanting to let this tenuous connection to her fall away – not just yet. He felt a little out of breath and his heart beat a little faster than usual. He kissed the air and whispered, I love you too, wishing she would have at least let him say it back before she hung up.

As the momentary high he got from talking to Kendra faded, he flopped down on his bed and wished once again that she would just use her AP phone to call him and spend longer than five minutes with him. It irritated him that she would only use her work phone for work-related calls. As if the AP would really care if she spent ten minutes talking to her fiancé on a company-provided cell phone. They wouldn't even know. Sure, her boss was a penny-pinching, tight-wad, but Keith doubted he analyzed her cell phone records for personal calls. Well, on second thought, maybe he did.

He felt guilty for feeling irritated at Kendra and dismissed the subject from his mind. Thoughts of conserving cellular minutes were instantly replaced with thoughts of Kendra describing what she'd seen and been told about the relics in the Iraqi museum. He had tried to imagine ancient statues and ancient tablets as he fell asleep.

Now, thinking about Kendra's phone call as he tried to reach his back with a soapy washcloth, he understood why he'd dreamed about being in a museum. That was the last thing on his mind before he fell asleep. He wondered why he hadn't dreamed of Kendra instead. Given the choice, he would have much rather dreamed of Kendra than museum artifacts. He tried to recall the dream he'd had before waking, but nothing came to his mind. The dream was wiped away clean and all that remained was the memory of the unusual earthquake. He hadn't even known that Tulsa had earthquake faults. He'd have to check that out on Wikipedia today.

What *was* today? He turned off the hot and cold faucets and pushed the glass shower door open and reached for a fluffy white towel on the rack next to the shower. Ah, Wednesday. He smiled as he pushed his face into the fresh-smelling towel, then moved it up to his hair where he vigorously towel-dried his short, dark hair. He was still smiling as he moved the towel around the rest of his body, absorbing and wiping away water drops. He felt a little silly with the big grin on his face that wouldn't go away. But who could blame him, he asked himself. Kendra was coming home in two days.

Six

Before getting into the shower, Keith hit the power button on his desktop computer, and started a pot of coffee. Now he sat at his desk with a large steaming cup and his unread email on the screen before him. First, he rapidly scanned the column that showed the names of people who had sent him email, looking for Kendra's name. There she was - the thirteenth new message in a list of twenty-two new messages. He clicked on the subject line "Look!" and the message loaded. There was only one line.

"What do you think of this?"

There was a paperclip icon on the right side of the message with a file named, DCS00145.JPG. He hoped it was a picture of her. It wasn't. After he clicked the paperclip, and assured Windows that it had his permission to open the attachment, the image loaded in his default image viewer. It was apparently a picture she had taken in the museum. The photo was of a long-haired, bearded man wearing a helmet, and on his back were two sets of wings. One set of wings was folded downward and the other set was standing up. He was holding something in his hand that could have been a pine cone or perhaps some kind of bread. Keith had no idea and didn't know what Kendra expected him to think of it.

He closed the image and looked at the email from her again to make sure she hadn't written anything else. She hadn't. There was just the one line. Hmm. He resolved to ask her later and went back to his inbox and looked to see if there was anything else that demanded his immediate attention. There wasn't. Just the routine stuff he received every morning. Forwarded jokes, videos, and political messages from a few friends. Urgent messages informing him that he had a limited time to take advantage of great sales at various retailers. He almost decided to take up the offer from a bookseller to save 30% on a variety of titles, but they were for best-sellers and the book he wanted to surprise Kendra with was probably not a best-seller. If it had been, he was sure he would have heard of it before, but he had never heard the name Zecharia Sitchin. He decided he'd stop at a bookstore after work and see if they had anything, and he wondered what it would cost to overnight something to Iraq, or if it was even possible. It'd probably cost a fortune to send Kendra the book in time to read it on her long flight home, but he'd do it if he could.

He went to an international shipping company's website and went through the motions of preparing a shipment selecting a 1 lb package from Tulsa to Baghdad. The estimated delivery date was a week from today. For the fastest possible shipping time, he was instructed to call a toll free number. He decided he wouldn't have time anyway with Kendra being eight hours ahead of him.

He changed mental gears and clicked the Home icon on his browser which loaded Google's search page in approximately no time at all. He typed "Tulsa earthquake" and pressed enter. Over a hundred thousand results, but nothing from today. He clicked the News link which transferred the same search query into a search that would yield results from news publication websites. Nothing there. He thought an earthquake in Tulsa would be newsworthy. *Maybe they're just slow here.* He closed his browser and shut down the computer. He whistled loudly for Laci so she would hear him from wherever she was in the house. She surprised him by crawling out from under his desk.

"You wanna walk?"

She answered by wagging her tail and then took off running toward the front door. He put his running shoes on and grabbed her leash from a hook by the door when he caught up with her. He connected the leash and opened the door, then paused, wondering if he should go back and grab his cell phone. Laci decided for him by tugging on her leash, pulling Keith through the doorway. He knew Laci would think the walk was cancelled if he brought her back in and went to his desk for his cell phone. Not wanting to disappoint her, he pulled the door shut, ran down the steps and began a slow jog with Laci taking the lead.

His cell phone vibrated on his desk causing it to turn a little to the right with each vibration. His phone made contact with his keys, and the keys vibrated along with the phone making a small jingling sound. Kendra was texting him.

Stuck in Baghdad for another week.   :(XOXO

Seven

Keith's phone continued to beep every thirty seconds to remind him that he had an unviewed message, using up the last bit of charge left in the lithium ion battery. Halfway through his walk with Laci, the phone warned that the charge was critically low by turning the battery icon red and flashing it off and on, as well as adding additional beeps to those that were timed to remind him of the unread message from Kendra.

Ninety minutes later Keith was sitting at his desk at work responding to an email from an overly enthused vendor of time-keeping software when Jared walked into his office saying, "Dude! What's up with your phone? I've been texting you for over a half hour."

Keith said, "Sorry, man. I must've left it silenced. What's going on?" He reached into his pocket and pulled out his phone.

"Little Miss Muffet is complaining that her system is "going crazy" again and I can't deal with her. I'm already on Ronald's shitlist, and if she complains that I failed once again to get her PC running the way she *thinks* it should, then he's gonna seriously think about firing me."

"Fuck!"

"Dude, it's cool if you don't wanna do it! She just doesn't complain as much if you work on it. If she wasn't doing 'the Ronald,' she'd be in *your* pants."

"My phone is dead, dammit. I could've been missing calls for the last hour. I don't mind looking at Katie's PC – but it's a waste of time. She's not gonna be happy until she has a computer exactly like Ronald's – if not newer and better."

"Totally. There's nothing wrong with her box except it's not as good as Ronald's. And that's why I can't "fix" it. There's nothing to fix! She drives me crazy." Jared changed his voice to a high-pitched whine, "Ronald, Jared screwed up my computer again. How am I supposed to get any work done when he doesn't know what he's doing and is incapable of fixing my computer for me?" He turned and leaned out of the doorway from Keith's office and looked both directions before turning back to Keith and saying, "I wish she'd just die or something. Ya know? My life would be so much better. It'd be almost perfect, actually. All I'd need is a raise."

The whole time Jared was talking, Keith was looking all around his desk, under his desk, beside it, inside of drawers and on shelves.

"Dammit! Where's my charger?"

"Haven't seen it, bro. Sorry. But someone around here probably has one you can use. I'll see if I can find one for you."

"Thanks," Keith responded, now pawing through a drawer filled with Ethernet cables and miscellaneous computer parts.

"I don't mean to bug, but any chance you could go see Katie? She asked for help about 40 minutes ago. That's why I was texting you."

"Yeah, sure," Keith said, still distracted by his missing phone charger. "Did she fill out a trouble ticket?"

"Dude. Does she ever?"

"Fine. I'll submit one for her then head over. If you find a Dash charger, please bring it to me in the CAD pen."

"No problem, dude. I'll start sniffin' around right now."

Jared left the office and Keith looked under his desk again for the missing charger, then finally gave up and created a trouble ticket in Katie's name. He didn't know the nature of her complaint so he classified it as General Technical Help and marked it Not Urgent and checked the box next to "Send a copy to myself." He believed that if he created her tickets for her and did so in a way that wasn't how she herself would've filled them out, she would eventually take the time to do it herself – as everyone else did. Ronald included.

For the most part, Keith loved his job. He was the I.T. Administrator for Colton Design, a specialty company of top-notch designers with clients who manufactured everything from toasters to cars of the future. When someone wanted something completely new and innovative – not just a knock-off or slight variation on an existing product, they called Colton. The designing was all done on computers, and for Colton's designers to be productive, they had to have zero down-time on their network, their desktops and their laptops. Keeping the designers, and thus Colton happy was Keith's responsibility. Although his title was I.T. Administrator, he was practically the entire I.T. department – except for Jared who was the sole technician who worked under him.

Keith liked Jared and felt he was efficient most of the time, but he was a bit spacey and forgetful – usually at the worst times. Keith suspected that Jared might have enjoyed a little too much pot in his lifetime. Being a libertarian, Keith couldn't care less what people did in their own time, but if they did it on the job, that was different. Jared could smoke pot until he couldn't add two plus two for all Keith cared, but if he ever caught him stoned at work, he'd fire him.

After running some diagnostics on Katie's computer and finding nothing at all wrong with it, as he'd expected, he pulled a USB drive out of his pocket and stuck it in the port on the side of her monitor.

"What's that?" she asked him, sounding a little alarmed.

"It's a USB drive," he answered, managing to not sound at all sarcastic.

"I *know* it's a USB drive, but what's it for? What are you gonna *do*?"

"Well, it turns out that you've got a particularly nasty virus that has evaded our enterprise threat detection system so I need to run a specialized scan on your system to catch this thing and remove it."

Katie's mouth dropped open. "I have a virus? I didn't do anything! Someone must've been using my computer when I wasn't here!"

"You're right. I found one of the temp contractors at your desk when you were out sick the other day."

Katie clenched her teeth and squinted her eyes and was about to say something when Keith interrupted her, "*And* I made him move to another workstation. I told him this one was off-limits and if he was caught at it again, he'd surely be dismissed from whatever project he was working on since the user of this workstation enjoys a special relationship with the owner of the company."

Katie appeared satisfied that her space was defended in her absence and that a lowly contractor was made aware of her special status. "Thank you," she said. "How long will this take? Do you know? I'm working against a deadline on the TM3 interior design and I'm behind already because of this stupid computer."

"It normally takes close to an hour, but I'm gonna tweak the heuristics for you to cut the time in half and still catch this bug, so you should be ready to roll in about 30 minutes."

Katie took a deep breath and let out a big sigh with which she managed to communicate what a huge inconvenience this was but also accepting that it had to be done, so she would endure it, all without saying a word.

"I appreciate you speeding this up. I'll be back in a half hour." She walked out of the CAD pen and turned right. She could be heading to Ronald's office, or the break room. Keith figured it was 50-50 either way.

He loaded a file onto her desktop and executed it. He clicked OK on the warnings and her screen turned blue. Dots started to form a line across the top of the screen. Keith had about 15 minutes before the software would finish its task so he went to find Jared, and he hoped, a charger for his dead phone.

Eight

When Keith failed to find Jared in his office, he started asking around. One of the girls from the accounting department said she'd seen him in the electronics shop a few minutes ago. Keith headed in that direction, walking down the long hall that ran the length of the building. Taking this route meant he'd have to pass the doorway to every department in the building except Fabrications, which was in the warehouse on the other side of the building.

He made it three fourths of the way across the building when he almost ran into Tom coming out of his office. Tom was the Director of Operations and the person to whom Keith reported. He was shorter than Keith by about 8 inches, thin, muscular, bald and wore an eye-patch with a skull and crossbones on it. Nobody knew what was wrong with Tom's eye, if anything. No one asked. It could be missing. It could be nothing. But it was probably *something* because Tom wore the patch every day and Keith figured that was a bit too much for mere quirkiness.

"Perfect," Tom said. "You got my text."

"Actually, no. My phone's dead and I'm –"

"What happened to your charger?" Tom interrupted.

"Well, it was in my office yesterday but someone –"

"Okay," Tom interrupted again. "Here's what I need. I bought the new Office suite – the software is on my desk. Install that on my laptop, but don't remove the old Office suite – I need to still be able to save documents for people using the old suite."

"You'll still be able to do that with new software. You don't need to keep the old one."

Tom's eyelid lowered just a tad and he stared at Keith for a few seconds. "Keep the old one, just in case. Also, I think I might have a virus. Check my laptop and make sure it's clean. I'm due in a meeting in 2 minutes. I'll be back in an hour and a half. Is that enough time?"

"Sure," Keith answered.

"Good." Tom walked away, heading toward the conference room and executive offices. He stopped about five feet away and turned around to face Keith. "Shut my door. I don't want anyone interrupting you while you work on my laptop. Thanks." Tom turned back the other way and began walking.

Keith had no doubt that Tom's mind had shifted gears immediately to the meeting he was about to attend as soon as the word "thanks" left his lips, almost as an afterthought. As if Tom was an asocial alien who had just remembered at the last second that to be semi-human he should thank someone for compliance with his orders and so he tacked the word on at the end, just in time to almost make it sound like he meant it.

Keith shut the door to Tom's office and sat down at Tom's desk and took a deep breath before starting on the tasks Tom had assigned him. He really wanted to find out if Jared had located a charger for him. He could go hours and hours without talking to or hearing from Kendra with little or no problem. But the thought of *not being able* to hear from her was eating away at him. He reminded himself that she had to be asleep right now and wouldn't even be awake to write to him or call him for at least five hours.

Keith installed the software on Tom's laptop as quickly as he could, which wasn't saying much since he mostly sat there impatiently watching an installation progress bar with a slowly incrementing percentage at the far end of it. Once the Office suite was installed, he launched the antivirus application on Tom's laptop, checked for updates, downloaded an update, and then executed a full system scan. Now with an even longer and boring wait before him, he decided to go check on Jared. He left Tom's office, shutting the door behind him and headed once again toward Electronics.

As soon as he opened the door to the shop, he looked around the room and spotted Jared's hair hanging down in front of his face as he focused on something in front of him on the workshop table. Keith called out, "Jared!" His long-haired assistant jerked his head up and smiled. Keith took that as a sign that Jared had found a charger, but for some reason, instead of bringing it to him, he decided to continue working on something that probably had nothing to do with I.T.

Keith walked around the large workshop table that was loaded with circuit boards and appliance modules, small plastic bins with electronic parts that Keith hoped he would never be able to identify, soldering irons, other tools he didn't have names for, and several technicians seated at both sides of the workbench focused on their work like starved android diners at an electronics buffet.

Keith approached Jared and asked, "Did you find one?"

"Not exactly, but I got the next best thing."

"And just what *is* the 'next best thing' to a charger that would work with my phone?"

"How about a charger that wasn't designed to work with your phone, but will now?" Jared smiled, very pleased with himself. He had been sent on a mission, and facing the likelihood of failure, he resolved to succeed no matter what it took. And now he put the finishing touch on the fruit of his labor. "Just a sec. I'm almost done." Jared wrapped several loops of electrical tape around some wires he had just spliced together. "Viola!" he exclaimed.

"What is *that*?"

"It's just a deliberate way of screwing up the word voilà - cuz it sounds funny."

"No - that!" Keith said, pointing at the frankencharger in Jared's hand.

"Oh! It's a modified phone charger – modified to charge a T-Mobile Dash, bro! Gimme your phone."

"Are you sure this is going to work? I see that you added the right tip, but what about voltage or amps or whatever?"

"Already taken care of. That's what took so long. I had to look up the right amperage, but I found out that the adapter doesn't push the amps, the phone pulls, so nothin' to worry about. Let me see your phone and I'll have you charged up in no time. "

"Are you absolutely sure this is going to work?"

"Dude. I fully schooled myself on this. Trust me."

Keith reached into his pocket and slowly withdrew his phone. He looked at Jared and maintained eye contact with him as he slowly handed over the phone. He felt a little guilty for feeling doubt, fear and suspicion without the faintest stirrings of gratitude. Jared had gone to a lot of effort, even "schooling" himself on amperage to make a charger for him.

"Okay" he said, as he reluctantly let Jared take the phone out of his hand.

Jared plugged the adapter into a power-strip on the workbench and peeled back the rubber cover of the micro-USB port. He inserted the tip and waited to see the display indicate that the phone was charging. Jared was smiling and couldn't wait to see that his modified charger worked, which would also mean that Keith would have a spare now after he found his real charger. He was pretty pleased that he could do something to show Keith that he really was a valuable guy to have around.

Both men stared at the phone's display. They saw the battery symbol appear and start to cycle – filling with green then blinking off, then starting over again. Jared smiled big, showing his teeth, looking at Keith and waiting to see Keith's joyous reaction.

Keith asked "What's that smell?" with alarm in his voice.

"Dude, it's an electronics shop. It always smells like that in here."

"No, it smells like something is burning."

Both of them immediately looked at the adapter and saw a small wisp of smoke rising from the black plastic.

"Shit!"

"Fuck!"

They both reached for the phone at the same time. Jared got it first, grabbing the phone with his left hand and the tip of the charger with his right. As soon as he picked it up, he threw it back down again. "Ow, fuck! Fuck! Fuck!"

"God dammit!" Keith went around Jared to get to where the phone had landed. When Jared tossed the phone, it hit a large spool of heavy-gauge wire and bounced to the right.

"Hey, what are you guys doing over there?" another technician asked after smelling the unmistakable odor of burning electronics.

Keith grabbed the charger cord and yanked it, afraid to actually touch the tip or the phone as Jared had. At first, the phone came with the cord, flying up off the table and into the air, then the tip came free of the port and the phone sailed a few feet then dropped to the concrete floor. When the phone fell, Keith let go of the cord, not sure if it actually felt hot to the touch or if he was imagining it. He stood staring at his phone lying on the ground. His teeth were clenched and he was breathing hard. He was struggling to control himself and not lash out at Jared who was only trying to help. He kept telling himself that. *He was only trying to help.*

Finally, in order to determine how angry he should be at Jared, Keith bent down to determine the fate of the phone, if possible. He'd dropped it before and it had never done any damage. But now he feared it might be fried. He reached for it and tapped it with an index finger to see if it was hot. It was warm. He picked it up and turned it over. The screen was cracked. Keith took a deep breath. Now he was really pissed, but it was his fault the screen was cracked. Or was it? If the damned thing hadn't been smoking, he wouldn't have had to yank it away from the goddamned frankencharger.

Instinctively, he pulled the phone up to his face and sniffed. It smelled just like the smoke that was still lingering in the air. He pressed the power button and nothing happened. He pressed it and held it. Still nothing.

"FUCK!" he yelled, and threw the phone at the far wall where it impacted with a metal locker and broke into multiple pieces. In order to not kill Jared, Keith quickly walked around the workbench table, opened the door, walked through it and then tried to slam it shut but the hydraulic door closer resisted his effort and closed the door slowly and almost inaudibly as it was designed to do.

Nine

Keith's first opportunity to call T-Mobile's customer support line was during his lunch break. He didn't usually take an actual break; he would just eat some fast food while continuing to work, but this situation demanded that he take some time for himself. He looked up the number online and called it from his desk phone. He listened closely to the menu options that 'may have changed,' which he thought was incredibly stupid – as if people called so often they memorized the options and now couldn't rely on what they'd memorized.

It took an exasperatingly long time to finally reach a human, which was making Keith even more angry and impatient. When the human voice finally came on, thanking him for calling T-Mobile support and telling him in an accent he could barely understand that he was speaking to Susan, he responded by saying, "Right. And my name is Genghis Kahn."

"How may I provide with superior customer service today, Genghis Kahn?"

"I was kidding. My name is Keith, and I need my phone replaced as soon as possible."

"I will be happy to assist you with that today, Genghis Kahn. Can I start by getting your ten digit phone number, beginning with the area code first, please?"

He repeated that his name was Keith and then gave her his phone number.

"I am sorry, sir. Is your name Genghis Keith or Genghis Kahn?"

"Would you just forget that I ever said Genghis Kahn and look up my damned account where you'll see my name on your damned screen?"

"Sir, I will have to ask you to please refrain from using abusive language in order for me to be able to assist you today."

"You're really starting to piss me off. Oh, I'm sorry. Is 'piss' abusive?"

The representative said something Keith couldn't understand. Her accent was becoming more pronounced as she was becoming upset with Keith.

"I don't know what you said, but have you looked up my account yet? Can we just get on with this? I need my *friggin'* phone replaced!"

"I will be happy to assist you today, Mr. Kahn, but I am going to ask one more to refrain from using abusive language so I will be able to assist you."

"Oh, for God's sake. Are you saying that 'friggin' is abusive now? Let me speak to your goddamned supervisor. Better yet, get me a manager who speaks English as their first language. I'm sick of this shit!"

"I will be happy to locate a native English-speaking customer service manager for you. Please hold, Mr. Khan."

To Keith it sounded like, "Ah whale bay hoppy to low-cat a nattof ainglash-spicking costaimer sairveece monager fair you."

"Thank God!" Keith exclaimed, and then the background noise of the call-center where Susan was located was replaced by silence, a few beeps and then a dial tone.

He slammed his phone down and cursed at "Susan." He took a deep breath and called the number again. He got through the automated voice response system more quickly this time and finally reached a co-worker of Susan's with the same weird accent who said his name was Steve.

"Hi, *Steve*. My name is Keith Erikson. My phone has stopped working and I need to make an insurance claim to have it replaced. Can you assist me with this without delay? I don't have a lot of time."

Steve assured Keith that he would be happy to assist and asked for Keith's phone number. He looked up the account and asked Keith his first and last name although Keith had already provided his full name, then proceeded to verify security information just in case it was a burglar or unauthorized Good Samaritan who was trying to get Keith's broken phone replaced for him.

After jumping through the initial hoops, Steve wanted to perform diagnostics on the phone. Keith told him that was impossible as the phone did not work and he could not turn it on. Steve asked him to remove the battery and to wait fifteen seconds before replacing it. Keith did as he was instructed, knowing it was a waste of time. He told himself to stay calm and go through the motions.

He replaced the battery after fifteen seconds, then put the back cover on and pressed the power button. He informed Steve that the phone would not turn on. Steve asked him if he had pressed the power button on the top-right side of the phone. Keith responded, "Being that there's only *one* power button - that was the one I pressed."

Steve told him that all of T-Mobile's phones only had one power button, so this wasn't unusual.

Keith told Steve that he knew there was only one power button and that this wasn't in dispute. He was just frustrated at being asked if he pushed the power button "on the top-right corner of the phone" as if he didn't know where it was after using it for nearly two years, and there wasn't any other power button he could've possibly pushed.

"I'm sorry, sir. Are you saying that you cannot find the phone's power button?"

"How could I possibly be saying that? I just told you I pressed the power button and that I've been using this phone for close to two goddamned years. Can we just replace the damned thing and be done with this?"

And now Steve was compelled to give Keith the warning about abusive language. Keith was ready to scream with impatience and frustration but said calmly, "I'm sorry, Steve. I'm having a bad day and I just want to be able to use my phone. What else do we need to do before you can replace it?"

Steve had Keith press and hold the power button for fifteen seconds. Next he asked Keith to plug the phone into its charger. Keith responded that he did not have the charger with him. Steve suggested that Keith needed to charge the battery and if the phone still did not work after he had a chance to charge it, he could resume trouble-shooting on a subsequent call to customer service by using a case number that Steve would give him and which would remain open for 24 hours.

Keith explained that the reason he didn't have the charger was because it started smoking and he threw it away, so he'd already tried charging it and it was apparently the charger that broke the phone. Could he just have the phone replaced?

Steve asked Keith to read the product I.D. number from the charger to verify that he was using the correct charger.

Keith said, "I'll call you back," and hung up the phone.

He took a walk around the building to calm himself down and then went back to his office and called customer support again. He very calmly told the representative that his phone didn't work and that he didn't know why. He patiently and robotically pretended to go through all of the trouble-shooting steps, including plugging the phone into an imaginary charger until he was finally told that they would have to send him a replacement.

He asked for the quickest shipping possible and confirmed his willingness to pay for overnight shipping. He was told that it was too late to ship today so it would have to ship tomorrow and would take two actual days before he received a replacement phone. He was asked if this was okay. Of course it was not okay, but what choice did he have? He calmly indicated that this would be fine.

At least he'd be getting his phone the day Kendra was coming home. He just hoped he got it and could complete activation before she called him with her flight info and arrival time so he could pick her up.

It was beyond frustrating, but he was mentally exhausted from his day at work and his three calls to customer service, and he had resigned himself to being without a phone for the next two days.

He sent her an email letting her know that his phone was broken and being replaced and asked her to send her flight info via email as soon as she knew it.

Ten

Mahmud had just recently entered his sixteenth and final year. As of today, it was a certainty that he would soon die. Two weeks ago when he had awoken in the hospital, the first thing he did was ask about Amira. They had been together when the drone came and rained death and destruction down upon his village. As soon as they heard the shouted warnings that a drone was coming, Amira insisted that they run. Mahmud countered that they should take cover where they were.

Her family's house where they were enjoying a pleasant visit under the watchful eye of Amira's mother and aunt was a two-level structure. Mahmud felt that this would give them extra protection. If the house was hit by a rocket or bomb, perhaps it would only hit the upper level and they could maintain relative safety on the lower level.

The one thing they agreed on then was to not be on the second floor where they were, so they ran down the stairs together. Amira went first and just as she reached the bottom of the stairs, the house was rocked by an explosion. The concussion caused Amira to fall and Mahmud to lose his footing and come tumbling down after her. He couldn't have been unconscious for more than a few seconds but when he opened his eyes, Amira was gone. The front door to the house was standing open.

He got to his feet, intending to run out after her and bring her back to the relative safety of her home when another explosion occurred right outside the house. He had just made it to the doorway when the explosion sent him flying back into the house, through the main room and into the wall on the far side. This time, he lay unconscious for a considerable period of time.

When he awoke in the hospital and asked where Amira was, his brother Muhammed looked at him with sadness in his eyes and slowly turned his head from side to side. Mahmud wanted to deny what his brother was wordlessly telling him. He wanted to be back where he was before the drone attack – happy, safe, and in love, looking forward to the rest of his life with Amira.

He wished for the past and flirted with denial for a few seconds, and then he changed. He changed so completely that as far as he was concerned the Mahmud that woke up this morning would not be the same Mahmud that went to bed that night. He became a being of pure anger and hatred. He felt the emotions wash over him as though he were being coated by them like hot wax pouring over his entire body.

And with these feelings came a singular thought, a purpose, an obsession – his new reason for being – the remainder of his life would be dedicated to revenge. He knew only one thing with absolute certainty right now – Americans would die for this.

He didn't know who, how many, or when, but he had no doubt that there would be retribution. His life was over. The most precious thing in his world had been violently taken away from him and he vowed to himself and to Allah that the same fate would be visited upon those responsible – tenfold, if at all possible.

When Mahmud first arrived at the training camp and told the commander, Fariq, that he wanted to be a *jihadi*, he was not believed. He lacked the passion that Fariq normally saw in new recruits. Mahmud was also unknown by those who attended the nearby mosques. He also had arrived at the camp without a Qur'an or a prayer mat. The commander doubted that Mahmud even conducted *salah*. How could he, without a prayer mat?

Fariq had seen the empty hate in the boy's eyes; the cold fire burning within him. He'd seen it before. It was no secret that Mahmud was there for revenge. But that was okay. There was always a need for warriors, and it was up to Allah to judge the warrior's heart. The Qur'an said that Allah is with those who do right. That was enough for Fariq to accept Mahmud into the camp and begin training him to die as a *fedayeen*.

Each day, Fariq relentlessly ran Mahmud and the other recruits through the rigorous training routines in the scorching sun. At night, they listened to lectures and studied the Qur'an. After a few weeks of getting in shape and learning basic combat, they began training on how a suicide vest was built, how to detonate it, things that might go wrong with the detonator, and how to repair it. They practiced concealing it under their clothing and acting without suspicion while wearing a dummy vest and running errands in the nearby village.

When the day came for Mahmud to make the ultimate sacrifice, he awoke at sunrise and went outside, walking barefooted on the cool desert sand. He watched the sun cresting over the horizon. The beauty of the morning brought to his mind the beauty of Amira. He felt a mixture of emotions: love, grief, anger, anticipation and gratitude. Today he would avenge his true love. He thanked Allah for blessing him with such a beautiful day for a *mujahid* to die.

Eleven

Kendra wasn't thrilled about having to stay in Baghdad another week, but she wasn't too upset about it either. After being told she had to stay longer, she was also told that she could have the next day off before starting her next assignment. That took the edge off the blow. Now she'd be able to visit the museum again, and this time she could take as much time as she wanted – sort of.

She reached over to pick up the phone on the stand next to the bed and dialed Keith's number from memory. She was surprised she remembered it. She normally did nothing more than touch the picture of his face on her phone's home screen, then touched, "Call mobile."

She listened to the phone ringing in her ear and smiled up at the ceiling, anticipating the sound of his voice. She knew he'd be unhappy about her extra week in Iraq and so she was prepared to make him as happy as she could. The phone eventually stopped ringing and she heard Keith's voicemail greeting.

"Leave a message if you want to, but it's not necessary. I can see that you called."

"Hey, sweetheart. I guess you're asleep. I was hoping you'd be awake so I could tell you what I'd be doing if I was there with you right now. But I guess you'll just have to find out later. I'll try calling again when the sun is up in Tulsa. I'm going back to the museum I told you about. I can't wait. I also can't wait to see you and kiss your yummy lips. Mmmmm. I love you, baby! Talk later…"

She hung up the phone and frowned. She was sure she would've had an hour or so to talk to Keith before he went to sleep. It was only 11pm in Tulsa and Keith usually didn't get in bed till midnight. She stretched, reaching her arms backward and arching her back up from the mattress. She yawned and shook her head. She was tempted to just lie there a while and possibly fall back to sleep, but she changed her mind and sprung out of bed. She adjusted the band of her light grey sweat pants so the knotted string was directly below her navel. She grabbed the bottom of her white A-shirt and pulled it down over her pants so it was no longer bunched up under her breasts. She took a deep breath and began her morning exercise routine, starting by placing one leg on the bed and bending over until her face almost touched her leg.

— ∞ —

After Mahmud watched the sunrise, he went to the mosque for morning prayers. He found it hard to concentrate on even the simple task of ablution and he couldn't remember how many *rak'ahs* he had said, or how many he had committed to saying. All he could think about was that he was going to die today. Everyone died, but they didn't know when it was going to happen. Mahmud knew when and where he was going to die; today, in Baghdad. It was the strangest thing to him that he knew those two facts, and he was unsettled by that knowledge. He wanted to die, because he wanted revenge, but he was terrified too. He imagined his body being blown apart and pieces of himself flying in every direction.

Every *mujahid* was still required to perform their morning chores after breakfast, even on the day of their strike against the infidels. After morning prayers, Mahmud went to breakfast where he pushed his food around and thought about dying. He wondered if it would be easy to find Amira when he reached paradise.

The other *mujahideen* talked about how they were going to keep their 72 virgins busy day and night. Mahmud pretended that he was as excited as they were about the non-stop orgy they envisioned as soon as their sacrifice was made. He hoped Allah would not be offended when he revealed to Him the truth - he only wanted one virgin.

After breakfast, the *mujahideen* went their separate ways to perform their morning chores. Mahmud went to feed the goats, walking as though he was in a dream. Nothing felt real to him. Not the goats that gathered at the gate as he approached, nor the ground he walked on. He felt like a ghost performing the actions of a human. His body was there and it was going through the motions, but he did not feel like it had anything to do with him. It was a strange feeling he had never felt before. He thought ahead to when he would die and found that he had much less concern about it now than he did this morning. With nothing feeling real to him, his pending death didn't feel real either.

— ∞ —

After Kendra finished stretching, she showered and dressed. She did not put on makeup or style her hair. She and her co-workers had been briefed on local customs and things they should and shouldn't do before they came to Iraq. The official word was that visitors to Muslim countries were not expected to follow local customs or adhere to religious requirements, but it would be best not to draw additional attention to themselves, or risk offending anyone as much as they could prevent it.

She took the elevator down to the lobby and found Scott, her photographer, sitting on a sofa, reading a newspaper. "So... You still intent on going back to the museum?" he asked her.

She smiled. "Yes! I'm really looking forward to it."

Scott shook his head a little. "We *could* spend the whole day boating, but if you insist..."

"But Scott, just think about how amazing the artifacts are in this museum. Thousands of years old, going all the way back to Sumeria! Don't you have the slightest interest in any of it?"

"What's so exciting about Sumerian artifacts? I don't see the point in looking at old pottery, ya know?"

"Oh, I could smack you! Pottery? Old pottery? Did you look at *anything* when we went through last time? I know we didn't have much time, but you had to notice the statues, the tablets, the drawings. Did you know that Sumeria was the first civilized country in the world?"

Scott lowered his voice. "Excuse my political incorrectness, but if you ask me, these people *still* aren't civilized. If they were, we wouldn't be here." He looked around the lobby to see if anyone might have heard him.

"I mean *literally* civilized. They had a written language. They kept records of their financial transactions. They wrote about history as they knew it. I find that astounding! The people with the first written records ever – historical people – and they wrote about what was history to *them*. Oh, I can't believe this doesn't interest you! Just wait. You'll see…"

Scott smiled at her. He loved her enthusiasm and her passion. She was a beautiful creature and he loved working with her. He only wished she was single; their partnership might've been perfect if she wasn't in love with some computer geek in Tulsa. But that was life. Maybe someday she'd realize that Scott was the better man for her. "Come on. Let's go see your ancient pottery," he teased.

She gave him a playfully mean look, squinting her eyes and pursing her lips. They walked out of the hotel, laughing as they exited. He almost reached for her hand as they went, but he caught himself just in time.

Twelve

Katie didn't have a virus. Tom didn't either. But someone did, and Keith was grateful for it. He was kept busy throughout most of the day identifying and isolating infected machines, then quickly cleaning them and getting them back in production. If he hadn't been so busy disinfecting computers and keeping the network secure, he would've been going crazy not being in touch with Kendra. He hadn't gone this long without at least a text message from her since the day they had met. If she hadn't checked her email, she'd be wondering why he wasn't texting back. But he knew she hadn't checked her email yet (and she rarely did when she was on a foreign assignment) since she hadn't sent a reply.

Jared worked extra hard, trying to make up for frying Keith's phone the day before. Keith didn't want to be mad at him, but he still was. If it wasn't for Jared, he'd be texting Kendra, and he would've possibly talked to her before going to sleep last night. Instead, he fell asleep thinking about her. Then he awoke a short time later when Laci barked a warning at what was probably nothing more than someone walking past the house.

That's when the weird thing happened again. Keith had only been asleep for less than a half hour when Laci's bark woke him, and it was like he was in an earthquake again. He warbled for about a minute and a half. He tried to feel where exactly he was feeling the sensation, but it was everywhere and nowhere at the same time. Then it slowly subsided just as it had the first time, and then it was as if it had never happened. He was simply lying in bed awake. And then, maybe because he'd taken an unintentional nap, he couldn't sleep. So he thought about Kendra. And he thought about Jared destroying his phone.

"You still mad, bro?"

Keith was startled by Jared's voice. He was alone in Ronald's office, which faced the windows, rather than the door and hadn't seen or heard Jared enter.

"What's up? Did you finish running the update status on every computer?"

"Yeah. That's why I need your help. Three PCs need updates, but they keep failing. I keep waking the agents, but nothing happens. What do I do?"

"Did you look at them in person and try manual updates?"

"Well… no."

Keith swiveled back around to Ronald's computer and closed several windows before spinning back around to face Jared. "Any reason why not?"

"Well, you said to do the update scan and make sure all the PCs were up to date, so I did that and came to tell you the results." Jared wrinkled his brows, concerned that he had somehow followed instructions exactly and yet had still not done his job properly. He berated himself internally for not taking initiative and doing what he knew Keith would have told him to do next. "Sorry, bro. I should've thought of that. My head's just not in the right place today."

"It's fine. You did what I asked you to do."

Jared heard an additional phrase tacked on in his mind, "…and nothing more." He felt like a total fuck-up since he miscalculated the voltage pull from the transformer and turned Keith's phone into a piece of burnt, plastic shit. He wanted to offer Keith money to cover the cost of the expedited shipping on his replacement phone, but he didn't know how to bring it up without sounding like a total dildo.

"Who didn't get the new DAT files?"

"The shipping dude, the accounting lady in the other building, and Katie.

"I'll take care of Katie's. Can you handle the other two?"

"Yeah. No problem." Jared felt there was an insult in being asked if he could *handle* the other two computers. He knew it. Keith thought he was a fuck-up now, even at simple tasks that anyone could do.

As they walked down the hall, Jared turned left to head toward the warehouse and Keith went a bit further down the hall before also turning left into the CAD pen. When Keith entered, he saw Katie hunched over a legal pad, doodling.

"Hi, Katie."

She jerked her head up and looked at him annoyed. "What? I'm trying to work."

"I need to get on your computer for a minute. You know about the virus that hit us yesterday?"

"You said my computer was clean. I didn't do it! I wasn't even here. You said someone was on my computer. I don't believe this shit."

Keith waited for her to finish with her assumptions, her guilt, and her drama.

"I just need to update the anti-virus definition files on your computer to make sure it's aware of the latest threats."

"Why didn't you do that yesterday? I can't keep having my work interrupted, you know."

"That's fine. I won't bother you. I'll let Ronald know that after yesterday's outbreak, every machine but yours is up to date because you were busy working and couldn't be interrupted. I'm sure he'll understand that yours is the only one now that poses a threat to every other computer on the network."

"I just don't get why you didn't already do it, Keith. You were working on it yesterday. Geez."

"We have a system that does it automatically, Katie. I didn't know that yours failed to get the update."

"So you *are* saying I'm the one that got everyone infected!" She stood up, holding the legal pad against her chest defensively.

"Of all the computers in this place, I'm certain that yours was not the one that infected the others. And just so you know, I would've been done with what I needed to do already in fraction of the time that we've already spent talking about it."

"Fine! Do what you need to do, then get the hell out of here. I'm working through my lunch break and you're kinda fucking that up for me."

Keith didn't know what that was supposed to mean, but he had stopped trying to make sense of Katie's volatile emotions long ago. As she walked out from behind her desk, she stumbled over her shoes that were sitting between her chair and the right side of her desk and fell toward Keith.

Keith caught her and held her for a few seconds to give her a chance to stabilize herself. She looked into his eyes and saw him looking at hers. She dropped her legal pad as she wrapped her arms around him and started crying. Keith slowly moved his hands from her upper arms where he had caught her and put them around her, hugging her back. He wasn't sure if she would be comforted by that, or attack him, but since she was crying and hugging him, it seemed like the appropriate thing to do – even if she *was* crazy.

"Don't worry, Katie. I'll be done in just one minute and I'll be out of your hair."

Speaking of hair, he could smell hers. It was nice. He wondered what kind of shampoo and conditioner she used. Then he thought of Kendra's hair and how great she always smelled, and he wondered where she was now and what she was doing.

"He hates me. I just know he does! And I don't know what to do anymore." Katie sobbed into Keith's shirt.

"Who hates you?"

"Ronald does! He went to lunch with that Barbie-doll bitch from Zoro. I wasn't invited, so I know it's not about business. Not at all. He likes her better than me. I'll never look as good as she does. She's so skinny and beautiful. I hate her!" Katie burst into sobs and put her head against Keith's chest again.

"Katie, you look fine." Keith tried to console her even as he was feeling awkward about the situation.

"Do you think I look good?" She looked up at him, needing him to say she did. He could see the need in her eyes. He didn't even like her as a person and now here he was with his arms around her, looking into her eyes and telling her she was attractive.

"Of course you do."

She smiled and raised herself up on her toes to kiss him. Keith was startled frozen for a second, then as he felt her lips on his with her tears getting on his face, he was repulsed and stepped backwards.

"Katie, I have a fiancé I love, who I'm deeply in love with."

The look on her face changed from hope and interest to pure hatred and pain.

"Just fix my damn computer and get out of here. I hate you. You're all the same!" She stepped around him and left the CAD pen. Keith took a deep breath and sat down at her desk, updated the anti-virus files, then quickly made his way back to his office, hoping he wouldn't see her in the hall – or ever again, if he could manage it – but he knew that was impossible.

Thirteen

When Keith opened the door to his office, he found Jared sitting there, waiting patiently.

"Did you get those two updated?" he asked Jared.

"Yeah, bro. All taken care of. Thanks for doing psycho-bitch's computer. I hate going near her."

"Do me a favor, alright, Jared?"

"Sure, bro. What do you need?"

"I'd prefer it if you just referred to her as Katie from now on."

Jared moved his head back, surprised and confused. "Okay... sure. I can do that. It's just... well, you know how she is."

"I'm afraid I know more than I wanted to. And the truth is, she *is* screwed up in the head, but that's not a reason to ridicule her or despise her any more than you would look down upon someone who was physically disabled. You know what I mean?"

Jared wrinkled his eyebrows and chewed the inside of his cheek as he gave this unexpected viewpoint his consideration. Slowly, he started to nod. "I see what you mean. Like being crazy isn't her choice. It's just something she's afflicted with, or something. Right?"

"Well, to get real specific, I'd probably say it's due to a long series of choices she's made over the course of her life, but the point is that she doesn't know that because she wasn't aware of the future harm she was doing to herself accumulatively, so now she's screwed up and having a hard time with life as a result of the less than capable state she's groomed herself into becoming."

"Woah! Dude. Slow down. I'd need a bong hit and some time to meditate on that. You're getting way intense here with the psychology. What's going on, anyway? Are you like, going out with her now?"

Keith had no idea why he'd said what he did or where his thoughts were coming from. He just felt that he somehow understood her and her problems more than he ever would have thought possible. He didn't know why, and he wasn't inclined to give it any thought. It just was.

"Of course I'm not dating her. You know how I feel about Kendra. There's not a woman in the world I'd rather be with than Kendra. I just think we need to show a little compassion and understanding. Katie's down. Let's not kick her. Okay?"

"Sure, bro. I'm sorry. I'm just kinda surprised. I thought you hated her almost as much as I do. Or did, I mean."

"I don't hate her. She's difficult at times – most of the time. Okay, she's *always* difficult…" Both of them laughed and then Keith continued. "I just feel like she's so messed up, she could probably use a little understanding and niceness in her world."

"That's totally righteous, bro. Yeah. I see where you're comin' from. I can do that."

"One more thing. I'm not mad at you about the phone. I forgive you for destroying it, and I really appreciate the effort that you made to try to fix it for me. Thank you."

Jared realized his mouth was hanging open and so he closed it, then he pressed his lips together and pulled them inward so that he looked as though he had no lips. He nodded as he got up from Keith's guest chair and started walking to the door. He walked through the doorway and spoke without turning around.

"Thanks, man."

Keith saw Jared wipe at the corner of one eye with his sleeve as he slowly walked from Keith's office. He felt much better about Jared and Katie than he had when he came in this morning. He clicked his mouse a few times and looked at his screen. The day was half done and he still had no email from Kendra.

"Talk to me, babe," he said aloud.

He thought again about calling her from his office phone, but there was no way he wanted to explain the following month why he'd made personal calls to Iraq on company phones.

He took a deep breath, then blew it out. He clicked on a tab on his taskbar to change screens so he could see if anyone had submitted a trouble ticket now that the virus problem was completely resolved.

Fourteen

Mahmud was carrying a live chicken tied to the end of a stick as he walked toward the open market in downtown Baghdad. His cover story was that he was going to sell the chicken. He had been told before he left the training compound that no one would stop a kid on his way to the market. So far, no one had. He had walked past British and American troops and they barely even glanced as he went by. He could have easily killed them. After reaching the market, he was to discard the chicken and continue walking toward the commercial district where the big luxury hotels were. That's where he would have the greatest chance of killing the most American civilians possible. Once he was close, he needed to scan the area and find the biggest crowd. If there was no crowd at any of the hotels, he was to keep himself occupied with childish activities so that he would not draw undue attention to himself.

Mahmud reached the market place and saw a vendor eyeing his chicken. He was supposed to discard it, but now he thought, why not sell it and buy something to enjoy as his last meal, or treat, rather, since he was thinking of how nice it would be to have some *mann al-sama*. After all, he was about to die, so didn't he deserve to have one last thing to eat? He wondered if he would be able to eat the tasty 'manna from heaven' every day after his mission was complete and he was reunited with Amira in the afterlife.

— ∞ —

Kendra was finally making progress with Scott as she explained to him the origin and significance of many of the Sumerian artifacts she showed him. He was actually asking questions on his own now and making his own discoveries and calling her over to look at things he had found.

"Kendra!" he called out. "Come and look at this!"

She left the display of a stone carving about the *Epic of Gilgamesh* and came over to see Scott's latest discovery.

"Oh, you found the code of law."

"I can't believe all this shit! They even had *laws* written down. I wouldn't be surprised if they had courts too."

"I believe they did, and they kept records of the trials and the outcomes," she replied.

"I never knew that there was an actual civilization thousands of years ago. By now, the people here should be the most advanced civilization on earth. It all started here, and yet, now look at them. What the hell happened?"

"War happened, as it always does. I hate to leave here, but we've already gone past my time limit. It's time to go boating now," she said softly.

"No, no. This place is amazing. Let's just forget the boating and stay here."

"Really? You'd do that for me?" she asked.

"Hell, no! I'm doing it for me," he said, laughing. "I'm learning all kinds of shit. I feel like I'm more aware of the world and what's gone on in it than I ever was before."

Kendra smiled. She loved that Scott had taken such a keen interest in something she was so passionate about. She felt that many of the world's mysteries were somehow tied to this museum and this city and country. She would never forgive her own military for not securing this museum during the Iraqi invasion, allowing priceless artifacts to be looted like common merchandise. Many other ancient pieces were destroyed by the looters as they were thrown to the ground and shattered as the looters considered them worthless because they held no gold or gems.

"I'm glad you like it, Scott. Just think, this morning you thought it was nothing but ancient pottery."

"How was I supposed to know that these people had a written language, musical composition, law, schools, written records and who knows what else? And they had all that thousands of years before Jesus even. I don't remember anything about this from when I was in school."

"I don't either."

"What the hell happened to this region? If you had asked me before today, I would've thought their history was nothing but warfare."

"I think that's what happened to them," Kendra replied. "But I can't say for sure. I'm just learning about all this myself."

"Thanks for bringing me here, Kendra. I feel enriched. Boating would've just been some mindless fun, but this... I'm blown away."

Kendra smiled at him, delighted. She hoped that Keith would have the same reaction. Thinking of Keith made her think of the time. It was 3pm here, making it 7am the previous day in Tulsa. It was a good time to call.

"Excuse me a minute, Scott." She walked down the corridor while touching Keith's face on her phone's home screen, then placing the phone to her ear. After several rings, she frowned when she heard Keith's voicemail greeting again.

"Hi, babe. I'm a little worried that I haven't heard from you. Text me and tell me you love me. I love you! Bye-bye."

— ∞ —

Mahmud dipped his hands into a fountain in front of the luxury hotel where he'd been lingering to rinse the stickiness of the *mann al-sama* away. He was waiting for a large group of people to appear so he could approach and detonate his vest bomb, but so far there had only been individuals, or two or three people coming or going.

He sat facing traffic in a way that enabled him to glance to his right to see the hotel entrance where the vehicles would pick up and drop off hotel guests. After an hour of sitting and thinking about paradise and Amira, he finally saw what he'd been waiting for. Several vans were gathered at the same time.

Although he still felt like he was in a dream, his heart-rate began to increase as he got up and began walking toward the hotel entrance. He felt flushed and dizzy. The time had come; he was about to end his short life. It was time to avenge Amira. He was going to inflict a blow on the Americans that would be worse than the one they had inflicted on him and his village. He hoped they would reconsider their presence in his country and go away, forever.

He was now close enough to read the names on the vans. UPI, Reuters and AP. He didn't know what the names meant, but some of the men were carrying large cameras so he thought they might be reporters from America or Britain. He hoped that they were because he reasoned that their deaths would get even more coverage than just regular tourists.

He could hear their conversations now as they lingered at the entrance, reluctant to go in. Some of them were complaining about the curfew that was imposed on them. They were being treated like children who could not go out and have a good time after dark.

"I remember when I had to be in when the streetlights came on," one of the infidels said, and laughed as if he thought he was so funny.

As Mahmud came closer, a few of them looked at him. They were not alarmed, but they were curious about his approach, or about him, as if he were an interesting specimen just because he was an Iraqi. If only they knew that he was a j*ihadi* as well.

"Hello there. Can we help you?"

When one of them spoke to him, the rest of them turned to look at him. He reached through the hole in his vest pocket to the detonator that was taped to his stomach. His thumb was on the trigger and he was about to shout out a praise for Allah when a woman turned and looked at him. She had Amira's eyes. When he saw her, he felt his heart melt inside and a painful lump instantly formed in his throat.

He shook his head at the man who had offered to help him and continued walking past the group and past their vans and around the rest of the driveway until he was back at the street, where he turned and kept walking as if he was out for a late afternoon stroll. Once he was out of sight and had less incentive to restrain his emotions, he couldn't hold back anymore, and he cried, thinking of Amira and his grief, and his love for her.

Fifteen

Keith couldn't wait to fall asleep and wake up to the day that Kendra was coming home. After checking his email and still finding no messages from her, he took Laci for her last potty outing and went to bed. He lay there and thought about Kendra. He ached to be with her. He had never minded being alone before, but since meeting her and falling in love with her, being alone was becoming unbearable because it meant she wasn't there with him.

Alone used to mean being by himself, but now it was defined as the absence of Kendra. He wondered how long she would be able to stay home before being sent away again. He really wished she would take a permanent assignment somewhere in the city, or even the state, but he knew how much she loved to travel and learn about the world, so he would never ask her to stop doing what she loved.

He knew she missed him just as much when she was away, so he didn't feel hurt by her failure to think of not traveling any more. It was an opportunity that she couldn't pass up, and she endured their separations as he did, with longing in her heart to be with him.

Keith started to drift off to sleep, thinking of her and feeling his intense love for her. He reached a state where he wasn't asleep yet, but neither was he awake, and he became mildly aware of a floating sensation. He felt as if he was sleeping in the air instead of on his bed, but he didn't focus on the feeling. As he was feeling this, he saw mental imagery like a movie playing in his mind's eye; almost like a dream, except he wasn't asleep yet. But he was very close.

In his almost-dream, he was floating at the entrance of what might've been a large hotel. There was a portico, white vans and a small crowd of people. Kendra was in the crowd with her photographer, Scott. Keith wasn't happy about Scott being so close to her. He suspected that Scott wanted more than friendship from her. He couldn't blame him though. She was beautiful, intelligent, vivacious, positive and compassionate. She was the most amazing person he had ever met.

He watched a young Iraqi boy coming toward the group of people. He looked intense. He stared at the crowd as he approached, but then his eyes changed and became wet. Keith felt the pain of loss as he watched the boy walk past him. Then the boy was gone and the feeling of grief was gone too. Someone slammed a door shut on one of the vans and Keith opened his eyes, feeling as if he had just stepped off the end of a sidewalk without knowing he had reached the street.

Chills ran from his head down his body and then the warbling began. Keith felt like he was not quite properly situated inside his own skin. It occurred to him that this could explain the weird vibrational sensation. What if he was partly in his body and partly out of it and was able to feel himself in both places at the same time?

He had heard of people who claimed to have left their bodies during near-death experiences, like during car crashes or during surgeries. As the vibrational warbling subsided, he wondered if it was possible to actually go out of one's body, and if so, could it happen when one *wasn't* in a near-death situation?

He started to reach for his phone on the nightstand to see if Kendra had texted and then he remembered he didn't have a phone. Not until tomorrow. He took a deep breath and told himself to be patient. He'd survive not talking to Kendra for one more night. Tomorrow he'd have his phone and he'd have the love of his life in his arms. He smiled as he imagined how great it was going to feel when he had his arms around her. Nothing in the world felt as good as holding her. His entire mind, body and soul relaxed and rejoiced and he felt like everything in the world was perfect just the way it was.

Sixteen

Kendra awoke and repeated the same routine as the day before except she got up earlier today. She and Scott, along with most of the other journalists were on assignment this Saturday morning to report on the troop withdrawals. Today was the first day of the beginning of the end of the Iraq war. She was so glad to have something positive to report on for a change.

After calling Keith and once again reaching his voicemail, she exercised, showered and met with Scott in the lobby, where once again, he was sitting on the sofa reading a newspaper.

"Good morning, beautiful. You ready to work your tiny butt off today?" He glanced down her body as he said this, then brought his eyes back up to meet hers. Kendra had hoped after the time they had shared yesterday at the museum that he might see her less as a sex object and more of a friend. After all, they had bonded, hadn't they? But apparently, that had the opposite effect on Scott. He appeared to be more sexually interested in her than usual. She was disappointed.

"Yeah. I just need to grab a muffin or something," she said, glancing back toward the dining room.

"Okay. I'm gonna go outside and have a smoke. I'll see you out there." Scott headed toward the exit, and Kendra went the opposite direction.

Reporters were gathered outside in front of the hotel, waiting for their company vans to take them to their assignments. Some of them were smoking. Some of them were talking. Scott continued reading his newspaper as he waited for Kendra to join him.

Mahmud saw the same group of people gathering this morning that he had seen the night before. After failing to complete his mission, he slept in an alleyway behind some pallets, feeling ashamed. He knew he had disgraced himself and his family, as well as Fariq, but he was most ashamed of having let down Amira. He should be with her right now in paradise as a martyr.

But despite his failure, Allah was giving him a second chance. He could still accomplish the very thing he had failed to do the night before with the same targets. He looked at the crowd gathered in front of the hotel and realized he was blessed even more today. The reason for his failure would not happen again this time. The woman with Amira's eyes was not among the group of infidels.

He made his way toward them, determined this time to not lose his resolve. He shoved his hands inside his vest pockets and walked with his head down. He was just a young man, going where he needed to go.

As he came close to the group of men and women, a few of them looked his way and possibly remembered him from the night before and found him less interesting this time. He had snubbed their offer of assistance last night and now as he approached, no one asked if he needed help. He looked like he was heading somewhere with purpose and not in need of assistance, unlike last night.

He reached the group and acted like he was heading into the hotel as if he was an employee, or someone who had a reason to be entering the hotel. He thought of Amira as he placed his thumb on the trigger so that she would be the last thought that occupied his mind. Although it was common for a *jihadi* to shout the *takbir* before giving up his life, they were not instructed to do so and without thinking, Mahmud modified it to reflect his greatest desire and the true reason for his sacrifice.

"*Amira hy akbar!*" he shouted, and as he pressed the button, the last thing he saw was the woman with the beautiful eyes; the same mysterious dark and lovely eyes as Amira, coming toward the lobby door and looking right at him.

The vest exploded and Mahmud felt no pain as his body was blown apart like a human claymore, sending pieces of himself along with ball-bearings and nails from his vest in all directions, penetrating flesh, breaking glass windows and doors and damaging everything in the path of the shrapnel.

Mahmud's spirit began traveling toward Amira automatically since she was the focus of his thoughts, but he did not know that was where he was going. He only knew he was in motion, and he was confused about where he was and what was happening. He thought his body was sailing through the air, alive and airborne from the blast.

He couldn't believe that he was still conscious after the explosion. Just as he began to make out a landscaped area in the distance and a sense that he was nearing Amira, he began to wonder if he had failed at dying once again. The combination of his change of thoughts and a repelling energy from the park-like place in front of him caused a change in his direction and he found himself heading off to another place. The sense of coming closer to Amira faded away and he felt depressed and even more confused about what was happening.

As he was pulled toward a dark, stormy vortex he thought of the carnage that he had caused. He saw the ripped limbs, mangled torsos and blood splattered everywhere. He became painfully aware that he was the same as those responsible for Amira's death. He too had caused horrible pain and anguish for the loved ones of innocents. He was consumed with self-hatred and a burning desire to undo what he had done. He could not take control of his mind and free himself of the images and the guilty thoughts.

He began to tumble and turn erratically as if he were caught in a never-ending ocean wave, submerged and drowning in regret, grief and darkness.

Seventeen

Keith awoke with a terrible feeling of having witnessed a disaster or some form of death and destruction. He knew he had dreamed something and it had to do with Kendra, but he couldn't remember what the dream was about. Whatever it was, it left a dark residue in his mind and a feeling of dread and anxiety that he couldn't shake. He was so glad it was Friday and she would finally be home today.

He got out of bed and checked his email again, certain that there'd be a message from her telling him what time her flight would arrive. By now she had to know that there was a problem with his phone and she would resort to email. But still, there was nothing in his inbox except the usual spam, and notices informing him that he had missed popular stories on Facebook.

He went to work intending to leave early so he could be home when his phone arrived. He wanted to activate the new phone as soon as possible so he wouldn't miss Kendra's call from the airport. She had probably already sent him a text telling him what flight she was on and her arrival time. He'd know as soon as he activated it.

Fridays were pretty relaxed at Colton Design. Not a lot of work got done; longer than usual lunches were taken, and weekends got off to an early start as people left before the end of the day, and some people just took the whole day off. Keith had no doubt that he could leave about three hours early and be home when his phone was delivered or shortly thereafter. He should have had it sent to his office, but he was so frustrated, he hadn't thought of that at the time.

He had very little to do, so time was passing slowly for him. Jared had taken the day off, so he had one less distraction that he could've used to pass the time. After he had checked the server status and the backup tapes, which were all fine, he looked at the bandwidth throughput to see if anyone was slowing the network down, even though he'd received no complaints. No one was streaming any audio or video.

Everything was fine and he found himself wishing for a catastrophic system failure somewhere so he'd have something to occupy his mind. He wanted to leave now and sit on his porch to wait for the delivery truck with his new cell phone in it. He launched Firefox and clicked on the News link from the Google home page. The top story was a suicide bombing in Iraq.

"So much for the war being over," he said to himself, and felt thankful that Kendra wasn't there. Her flight would take about 14 hours, so she would have left sometime yesterday. He clicked on the bombing headline and heard a knock on his office door before it swung open.

"Could you step into Ronald's office for a moment?" Tom asked, and walked away without waiting for an answer.

Keith was glad he'd finally have something to do. He got up and went across the hall and walked into Ronald's office without knocking and saw that he was on the phone. Tom had just sat down in one of the chairs in front of his desk. Both of them looked at Ronald's back, waiting for him to hang up and turn around. Keith looked at Tom. Tom noticed that Keith had looked at him, so he pulled the corners of his mouth into a smile that lasted a full half second before he released it and returned to his normal stony, emotionless state.

Ronald was laughing and telling someone that he couldn't wait. It was a great idea. He was looking forward to it.

"Absolutely." Ronald spun around in his chair and looked right at Keith. "I'll even make sure we have tech support on hand, so nothing can go wrong. It'll be just like being in the office – except completely different." He laughed some more, louder and longer this time.

Finally, he hung up. Keith was getting impatient and wanted something to do. Ronald turned back to face him with a big smile on his tanned face.

"Tomorrow's your lucky day. Your presence is required on my yacht."

All Keith could think of was that he was indeed lucky, but not because of anything to do with a yacht. He planned to spend the entire day alternating between being in bed with Kendra and cooking for her whenever she was awake and hungry. She'd need to recover from the jet lag, and he couldn't think of a better way to do that than to lounge around in bed with her all day. He was *very* lucky.

"Thank you, sir, but I've actually got plans for tomorrow. My fiancé is coming home from Iraq tonight."

"Great. She's invited too, but this isn't a social invitation. You'll be on the clock and I trust you won't let her be a distraction in the event that you're professional expertise is needed. If nothing goes wrong, then you two get to enjoy being out on the ocean for the day. Either way, you're going to love the catering."

Keith felt the world shrinking around him. He didn't want to be on a yacht with Kendra tomorrow. She didn't even like going out on the ocean. She didn't mind rivers, but she had gone deep-sea fishing in California once hoping to spot dolphins and she got sick and vomited and swore she'd never go out on a boat like that again.

"I appreciate that, sir, but would it be okay if I had Jared take my place? I'm sure he'd love it, being an ex-surfer and all…"

Ronald shook his head.

"This is business, Keith. I need someone professional. Appearance is everything. It's fine if you want Spicoli working in your department – I trust you to handle M.I.S. for my company – but I need *you* for this meeting. That's settled."

The second he finished, he turned to Tom who immediately began speaking as if Keith was no longer in the room. The two of them started discussing the deal they hoped to close tomorrow. Keith left Ronald's office and returned to his own a few feet away. *M.I.S. Nobody calls I.T. "M.I.S." anymore.* He wanted to slam his door like an angry teenager, but he resisted the urge and plopped down in his office chair.

What luck! He would barely get to spend any time with Kendra tonight and then he'd have to be away from her all day tomorrow, waiting for a computer to break down in the middle of the damned ocean. Sometimes he really hated his job.

He got back up and went over to Ronald's office and knocked on the open door.

"Excuse me."

Ronald looked at Keith expectantly. Tom stopped talking and swiveled his head toward Keith with no expression.

"Two questions. You said we'd be on the ocean. Did you mean the lake?"

"My yacht is moored in South Padre. In the ocean."

"Oh." Great, Keith thought. Even more time away from Kendra, flying to Texas and back. Could things get any worse? "Since I'm going to be working tomorrow and everything here is perfectly fine with no open tickets, would you mind if I left early today?

"Is Jared here in case someone needs something?" Ronald asked.

"Uh… actually, he took today off."

Ronald looked at Tom and Tom barely nodded his approval by moving his chin downward a quarter inch.

"Sure," Ronald said. "That will be fine. Just keep your phone handy in case something happens."

"Thank you. I will," Keith replied, and quickly departed, hoping neither of them had heard about his phone disaster. At least one thing worked out in his favor, but it was a small consolation that he'd be able to get his phone as quickly as possible and be able to deliver the bad news to Kendra without delay.

"Keith!" Ronald called out from his office.

Keith turned around and returned to Ronald's office.

"Yes?"

"On second thought, I'll need you back here in two hours. We're going to fly out to South Padre tonight so everything will be ready for an early launch tomorrow. You said your girl is flying in tonight. Were you planning on picking her up from the airport?"

"I was most definitely planning on that, *and* she's relying on me to do that."

"This should cover her cab fare," Ronald said, handing Keith a fifty dollar bill. "You can keep the change." He smiled, pleased with his own generosity and the fact that he was solving a problem for the I.T. guy for a change. Then he looked to Tom, and then back at Keith as if to ask why he was still standing there when they were clearly finished. "Two hours. Right?"

"Yeah," Keith said, and left the office.

Eighteen

Keith really hated how Ronald seemed to view anyone who wasn't as wealthy as himself as a servant-class citizen. Keith loved the autonomy of his position, and Ronald paid him well, but then there were times like this when Ronald didn't give a damn about the fact that he was a human and had his own life.

Now he had less than a two-hour window to wait at his house for his phone to arrive. He was tempted to quit, he was so angry and frustrated. He tried to calm down as he drove toward his house. Yes, this sucked. It sucked a lot. It was driving him crazy to not be able to talk to Kendra, and now he wouldn't even be able to see her tonight; nor most of tomorrow.

But tomorrow night he'd be back, and she'd be in his arms, and they'd have all of Sunday together. In fact, he decided he was taking Monday off. He was damn well going to have two full days with Kendra no matter what. He'd make sure Jared was there Monday and he was taking the day off, even if he had to lie and say he was sick.

As soon as Keith turned onto his street, he looked to see if he could spot a package on his porch from a distance. He couldn't. He confirmed there had been no delivery as he pulled into his driveway and saw absolutely nothing on his porch other than the welcome mat that Kendra had put there.

After taking Laci for a short walk, he sat on his porch, urging the delivery service to arrive. Fifteen minutes before he was to be back at work, he got in his car. It would take him twenty minutes to get to work, but he couldn't leave without his phone, so he resolved to just drive as fast as he could. It was a stupid risk to take because Ronald liked to be early to his flights, even though he flew in his own private jet. And even worse, if he got pulled over for speeding on the way there, he'd miss the flight, really pissing off Ronald.

As Keith drove away from his house, he saw in his rear-view mirror as he was turning a corner, a Fed Ex truck was turning onto his street several blocks behind him. It was the hardest thing he'd ever done to complete his turn and continue driving away from the delivery that he so desperately wanted.

He couldn't stand to think about what Kendra might think after not being able to reach him for days, and then his failure to pick her up at the airport. He'd call her when he got to the motel in Texas and hope he wasn't too late, leaving her stranded. As he drove, he imagined her calling a taxi, then coming home to an empty house. *Fuck!* He forgot to leave her a note. And he forgot to feed Laci.

He took out his frustration on his gas pedal and drove recklessly to his office. He didn't even care now if he got pulled over. He half wished that he would. Ronald might be angry enough to fire him, but at least he'd be able to go back, get his phone, pick up Kendra, feed Laci, and spend the night in the loving arms of his fiancé. That would be heaven. At the moment, his life was feeling more and more like hell.

When he pulled into the parking lot at Colton, Ronald and Tom were just coming out of the front door. Ronald visibly sighed. He wasn't pleased with Keith's sense of timing. Keith got out of his car and walked toward the company van that the two men were approaching. They were both looking at him funny. He didn't know why.

"You're traveling a bit light, aren't you, Keith?" Ronald asked.

Keith realized what the looks were for. He hadn't brought a suitcase or backpack or anything with a change of clothes.

"I'm still pretty clean. It was an easy day today so I can wear this again tomorrow." He felt stupid as soon as he'd said it. His cheeks flushed and he felt like a dopey kid. He had no toiletries or clothing appropriate for a yacht. He had nothing but whatever was in his pockets. He didn't even have a cell phone; possibly one of the few people in the city to not have a cell phone in his hand or pocket. Just he and a few homeless people; but even they probably had Obama phones.

Ronald and Tom talked to each other on the way to the airport and made no effort to include Keith in the conversation. It was the same in Ronald's Lear jet. Keith was used to it though and wasn't in the mood for small talk anyway. He just fought the overwhelming negative feelings he was drenched in and struggled to find a bright side to something.

When he arrived at his hotel room, the first thing he did was call Kendra. Her phone rang several times and then he heard the sound of her voicemail greeting. He left her a short message.

"Hey, babe! I wish I had good news, but I don't. My phone is dead. Sorry I didn't call and tell you sooner. Not only is my phone not working, but I won't be able to pick you up tonight. I'm stuck working with Ronald tomorrow and I'm in a hotel in South Padre right now using the motel phone. I'll try–"

He was cut off by the time restriction for voicemail messages. He thought of calling back to finish his sentence, but he knew she'd get his intention. Obviously, he'd try to call her the next day, one way or another.

Rather than leaving her another message, he called the front desk and requested a wake-up call. Without undressing, he flopped down on the bed and stared at the ceiling. He mentally apologized to Kendra, whom he couldn't help but visualize standing in the airport feeling forgotten by him. And hurt.

As Keith slept, he dreamed he was in an airport trying to find Kendra but without knowing which airline she was coming in on. It felt like he was in a busy mall at the peak of holiday shopping. There were retail stores to his left and his right and the space in between was so crowded with shoppers/passengers that it was difficult to see ahead of him or to even walk without constantly having to stop and wait for an opening to take a few more steps.

After what felt like a long time, he emerged from the crowd of bustling people and found himself in a narrow hall with windows on one side. It was dark outside and the light on the inside caused an image of himself and the opposite wall to reflect on the glass.

He put his face to the window and cupped his hands around his eyes to block the light. He saw a body of water with a small island illuminated by moonlight. It didn't seem odd to him that there were not runways or tarmac outside. There was a figure sitting on the tiny island. He was sure that it was Kendra. He didn't wonder why she was out there alone. His only thought was wondering how he could get to her. He was here! He was *at* the airport. He hadn't forgotten her or abandoned her.

He awoke seconds before the phone rang with his wake-up call. For a moment, his mind was still in a place where he was close to Kendra but separated from her by a body of water and a pane of glass. When he opened his eyes, the sense of separation and longing to be with her was magnified by the real distance between them, and the frustration of having to spend the day on a boat without even knowing when he'd be free to go home and be with her.

Nineteen

Keith got up and took a shower, then got dressed again in the clothes he had just taken off. He started to berate himself for being so mindless that he didn't even think of bringing anything for an overnight trip, and he hadn't fed Laci. He stopped himself right after he started and told himself to think positive. Everything would be fine.

So what if he was wearing yesterday's clothes? Laci would be fine. Dogs didn't die after one day of no food. It was harder to reassure himself about Kendra, but even that situation would work itself out. He'd explain what had happened to his phone and how he couldn't be at the airport, no matter how much he had wanted to be. She'd understand and life would be beautiful. He couldn't wait to see her. He had no idea how long this day would be. He hoped it would be short.

He took the elevator down to the lobby and grabbed a continental breakfast. When he got back to his room, a light on his phone was blinking. He had a message. Had Kendra called him? He picked up the handset, his heart beating fast. When the message played, it was from Tom, telling him to meet down in the lobby in ten minutes. The message had no timestamp so Keith didn't know when ten minutes would be. He glanced around the room while finishing off his cinnamon roll. He had brought nothing with him so he had nothing to worry about leaving behind. This was going to be his easiest checkout ever.

Half an hour later, Tom drove the three of them to the nearby marina and they boarded Tom's yacht. Keith realized that he should've brought his laptop with him. If he didn't need it for technical reasons, he could've used it to read a book or to keep himself occupied some other way while waiting to be needed by someone. Tom's client showed up within minutes and the four of them headed out to sea.

No one needed any technical assistance all morning and no one talked to Keith except to tell him when it was time for lunch. Catered food had already been brought on board that morning before they boarded and was kept hot down below. Keith took advantage of the opportunity to speak to Ronald.

"Ronald, do you have any books on the boat? Anything at all would be great. I'm bored to death here."

Ronald took offense at Keith's statement. He should be grateful that he was on Ronald's boat and spending the day on the ocean.

"No, I don't have any books on the boat, Keith. Why would I? This is a *boat*."

Ronald looked at him as if he was a complete idiot, and Keith felt like he was a complete idiot for asking someone as shallow as Ronald if he had any books. Keith served himself a plate after the others finished serving themselves. He took his plate and a bottle of Fiji water back to the deck chair where he had spent the day so far.

After the men finished eating, Ronald and the client smoked cigars. Keith wished they would just finish the meeting and be done with it. But now the meeting wouldn't even resume until the damned cigars were finished. He felt like this day was never going to end, and having nothing to do but stare at the ocean and think about Kendra was making time pass painfully slow.

Keith felt the boat slowing down and dreaded the idea of being parked out here miles from land. He dreaded the thought that once the meeting concluded, only then would they make the return trip. The boat came to a stop and he felt it bump into something. Oh no! he thought. Now what? If they bumped into another boat, would they have to wait for the Coast Guard to come out and write up a report, dragging this day out even longer? He got up and walked to the side and as he got clear of the cabin, he was pleasantly surprised to see that they had docked. They were already back. He couldn't believe it. Was this phase of his nightmare actually at an end?

Ronald, Tom, and the client he'd never been introduced to came out of the cabin and walked toward the ramp. They were all smiling so Keith assumed they had a deal. Hooray. He just wanted off this damned boat and to be back in Tulsa.

The flight back took less time than the pilot estimated, and that further lifted Keith's spirits. He walked over to the van and waited. He wished he had driven his own car to the airport. He stood there watching Ronald and Tom *slowly* make their way to the van. He wanted to scream at them to hurry up, but he maintained a neutral expression of patience and said nothing.

On the drive back to the office, Ronald spoke to him once. Tom didn't.

"How was that for a day at work, Keith? You didn't even have to work. As it turns out, we barely even used our computers. Lucky you, huh?"

"Yeah," Keith replied, wanting to strangle him from the back seat. "It was great. Thank you."

He saw Ronald in the rearview mirror, smiling, pleased with himself that he was so generous to have given one of his employees the gift of spending the day on his yacht with a delicious brisket lunch on top of it.

When the van finally came to a stop at the office parking lot, Keith couldn't get out fast enough.

"See you Monday," he said, and sprinted to his car.

As tempted as he was to race all the way home, he restrained himself and drove only five miles over the speed limit. He knew Kendra was going to be upset when he got home. He expected her to be hurt and confused, but he just hoped she wasn't angry; and if she was, he just had to explain what had happened. Kendra hated to argue, and if she was upset, she would isolate herself "for their own good" and not talk until she was sure she was in control of her emotions and could communicate and respond rationally. Keith appreciated her self-control and devotion to reasonable and peaceful communication, but he prayed she wouldn't delay him from explaining why he had failed to pick her up from the airport.

As he came down his street, he could see a small box sitting on his porch. He was surprised Kendra hadn't brought it in. He heard Laci barking as he pulled into the driveway. She knew he was home and she was excited. He went up the steps quickly, picking up the box and then reaching for the storm door. He opened it and held it open with his hip as he reached for the door. It was locked. He wondered why Kendra would leave the door locked in the middle of the day.

As he reached for his keys in his pants pocket, he realized what must've happened. When Kendra got home last night, she entered the house through the garage and never saw the package. Or maybe she was so angry, she just got in her car and left. Maybe she wasn't even here.

He opened the door and Laci came running out, briefly undecided between whether she should jump up on Keith or run into the yard to relieve herself. She decided to wait a bit longer and chose jumping on Keith first.

"Down, girl!" Keith said, stepping into the house and holding the storm door open for her to go outside if she wanted to. She did. Keith set the box from T-Mobile on a table in the foyer and looked for signs of Kendra being home as he walked toward the inner garage door. The house was too quiet and everything looked as he had left it yesterday so he wanted to see if her car was there. When he opened the door to the garage, he had to unlock it first; further evidence that she wasn't home. He fully expected to see an empty space in the garage, but he was glad when he saw Kendra's red Miata sitting there. Great! She *was* home. She was probably just sleeping.

He kicked off his shoes so he'd be more silent as he walked to his bedroom. He didn't want to wake her if she was asleep. The door to their room was open. He stepped into the room quietly and found their bed empty. He checked the other two rooms. One was used as a guest room and the other was used primarily by Kendra as a home office. Both were empty.

Twenty

Keith couldn't open the box from T-Mobile fast enough. But first he had to get through the packing tape. He took the box to the kitchen and pulled a steak knife out of the silverware drawer. It occurred to him that a knife without a serrated edge would've been better, but he didn't care. It got the job done. He took the phone out of the smaller box that was inside the larger box along with a battery, owner's manual, USB cord, warranty info, charger and Styrofoam.

He put the battery in, replaced the cover and pressed the power button. He willed the phone to boot up quickly. He needed to talk to Kendra as soon as he could. When the phone finally made it to the home screen, the status at the top indicated that there was no SIM card.

"Oh, for God's sake!" Keith yelled.

They hadn't mentioned anything about the SIM card when he talked to customer service, and he hadn't thought about it after the phone fried and he stormed out of the electronics shop. He put the phone in his pocket and grabbed the charger. He went to the front door and opened it. Laci was sitting there, wagging her tail and panting at him with what could only be described as a smile on her face. He couldn't believe he left her in the front yard, which was unfenced.

Keith opened the storm door and she bolted in and started jumping on him.

"I love you too, sweetheart, but I have to leave. Shit!"

He went back into the kitchen and filled her food and water bowls.

"There you go."

Laci went straight for the water. Keith felt like a bad dog owner as he headed out of the house and got in his car. Back at his office, he went to the electronics shop first. His phone wasn't on the ground where it had landed when he threw it several days ago. He looked in the trash bin. That was stupid. The cleaning service emptied all of the trash bins nightly.

He sunk into a sitting position on the shop floor and dropped his head in his hands. This was unbelievable. Now he'd have to call T-Mobile and tell them he needed a replacement SIM card. *Jesus.* Well, at least Kendra was back in the States. He just didn't know where she was. *Screw it,* he thought. *I'm buying a pre-paid cell phone. I have to talk to her.*

He remembered that he had the phone with him when he called to get it replaced and went through the motions of troubleshooting the problem. He ran to his office and looked around. The phone was nowhere. Okay. Time to go to Walmart for a cheap disposable.

As he headed back to the exit, he passed Jared's office and had a thought. He entered the small office and looked around. Sure enough; there was his broken phone, sitting on a shelf next to the frankencharger. Keith smiled.

"Thank you, Jared!"

Keith was aware of the irony of now being filled with gratitude for Jared having retrieved his phone, while it was also Jared's fault that he was in this phone predicament in the first place. He easily could've just gone out and bought a phone charger when he noticed he'd forgotten his. Why hadn't he thought of that in the beginning? He couldn't believe that the same ability to immerse himself in a technical problem also made him act like an idiot sometimes with non-technical problems.

He took the SIM card out of the burnt phone, wondering if it too was fried. He put it in the new phone and the symbol that had indicated he was missing a SIM card went away. The card was still good! He went to his address book and it was empty. He assumed that the phone needed to initialize with the card already in place in order to populate the address book, so he turned it off, then turned it back on. After it booted, he looked at the address book again and all of his contacts were there. He pressed Kendra's name which appeared at the top alphabetically because he had entered it as _Kendra. He held the phone to his ear as he walked to the front door and out to his car. He reached her voicemail again.

"Kendra, I'm so sorry about last night. Please call me back. I'm dying to see you. I just now got my phone turned on – like seconds ago – I hope you're not mad. I haven't even –" Time ran out. He was going to say that he hadn't checked his text messages or voicemail yet. It pissed him off that Kendra's phone service limited voicemail message duration.

He got in his car and put the key in the ignition without starting it. He looked at his phone and saw that he had voicemail. He switched screens and hit play on the first message from Kendra. She sounded cute and sexy. She told him she was going to the museum. He smiled at the sound of her voice. The next message was from an engineer who needed support. Keith saved that one and went to the next one from Kendra. She said she was worried that she hadn't heard from him. The next two messages were from Jared; one apologizing about the charger episode and another saying that he'd be out sick Friday.

Where was Kendra??

He looked at his text messages and scrolled thru the small list until he saw one from Kendra dating back to Wednesday.

Stuck in Baghdad for another week. :(XOXO

"What?!" Keith yelled out. "Oh my god. She's still in Iraq for another week? Oh geez!"

He was extremely relieved to know that he hadn't left her stranded at the airport, and the mystery of the empty house was now solved, but he was sadly disappointed that he wasn't going to be seeing her as soon as he had thought. He could feel depression beginning to descend over him.

He gave himself a small pep talk, reminding himself that everything was much better now than it was an hour ago. He had a phone again – praise the gods – and he knew where Kendra was. She could have easily been dispatched to Iraq for this long to begin with. She'd been sent places for longer than this, so it wasn't the end of the world, and all things considered, life was pretty much back to normal. As soon as one of them reached the other, he'd find out exactly when she was flying back, and in the meantime, he could now talk to her again late at night or early in the morning.

Keith started the car and headed for home, trying to remember the things he had planned to do this weekend before it became a saga about a lost phone and an unexpected day on the ocean. He turned on the stereo, thinking that some music would make him feel like things were fully back to normal.

The radio was broadcasting a commercial and Keith just left it on that station. He didn't want to search for something to listen to. He'd take whatever came on. After the commercials, there was a news report. The top story was an update about the recent suicide bombing in Iraq. Eleven people were killed; two of them were injured and in critical condition. No further information was available at this time. The reporter went on to the next story, but Keith's mind was stuck on the first. He remembered the relief he had felt when he first saw the news about the bombing. He had thought Kendra was on a plane at the time so he wasn't worried.

He told himself that the odds were against one person you knew in Iraq actually being one of eleven who were killed, so he tried not to think about it. But it would continue to bother him until he spoke to her. When he got home, he petted Laci for a minute then went to his room and looked up news on the bombing. One unconfirmed report said that the victims might have been journalists. Keith's heart started beating hard when he read that. That absolutely increased the chances that she could've been one of the killed or injured. He did additional searches for more news but couldn't find any additional information.

He called Kendra's mother on his cell phone. She answered on the first ring.

"Hi Joanne. This is Keith. I was –"

"Hello Keith! How *are* you?" He could hear her big smile coming through the phone and could see her southern belle hat in his mind.

"Joanne, have you spoken to Kendra lately?"

"Well, no, not for a few days. You two aren't fighting are you?"

"Not at all. Do you remember what day you talked to her?" There was several seconds of silence before she replied.

"It was Wednesday. I remember because I had just come back from the Harmony in Marriage bible study, and that's on Wednesdays."

"That's the last I heard from her too. I was hoping you'd heard from her more recently."

"What's the matter, Keith?"

"I'm not sure. I'm just worried because she's in Iraq and there was a suicide bombing yesterday. I'm kinda freaked out, knowing that she's there and some people were killed but the media doesn't have much information on it yet, and so…"

"Keith, I'm certain Kendra is just fine. Don't you worry about a thing."

"But we don't *know* if she's fine. That's why I'm trying to find out for sure."

"Well, *I* know for sure. I prayed for her safety the day she left the country. So I *know* the good Lord is watching over her."

Keith wanted to ask if the good Lord was watching over the eleven people who died in the attack, or the two who were in the hospital fighting for their lives. Why did people assume that God would protect their loved ones when tens of thousands of people died every day despite people praying for them? But he never voiced his opinion about religion with believers, especially not with Kendra's parents. There was no point in upsetting them and there was even less point in arguing with them. Keith had learned from his mother that a person's beliefs transcended reason and logic, rendering reasonable discussion impossible.

"I sure hope so, Joanne. If you hear from her, please let me know and I'll do the same for you."

"Thank you, Keith. And God bless you."

"Uh, thanks. Bye-bye." He ended the call feeling no better than before. He wished he could assume that an almighty being was watching over Kendra. But he had no reason to assume such a thing, so he'd continue to pursue facts, and hope to discover one that indicated she was not in the bombing. He needed information, not faith or wishful thinking.

Twenty-one

Keith sent text messages to the friends he and Kendra had in common, asking if they'd heard from her since Wednesday. Those who replied said that they hadn't. Fear and anxiety were beginning to consume him. He paced back and forth in his room. He made several trips to the kitchen only to turn around and come back to his room again where he didn't know what to do when he got there.

"Okay. I need to get a grip," he told himself, aware that he was starting to become irrational and letting fear take over his mind. He walked over to his bed and sat down. He reviewed the only facts that he had. There was a bombing in Iraq. Kendra is in Iraq. When he broke it down into two simple statements, he laughed out loud at the silliness of his fear. It was unfounded on anything other than location. Surely he had no reason to be worried. Iraq is a huge country.

But then, he thought, on the negative side... Despite Iraq's size, very little of it is populated, and even less of the populated square mileage is targeted by suicide bombers. A bombing would only take place in a city where there were things to blow up, not just sand and rocks. So that narrows things down a lot. The odds were very good that a suicide bombing would've been in Baghdad, and that's where Kendra was sent.

Not only was she in the most likely place for a bombing, if she *had been* hurt or killed, he would be unable to reach her. So far, neither he nor anyone who knew her had heard from her since Wednesday. She is also an American, which would make her a preferred target of a Muslim extremist. Keith didn't know if being an American journalist made her an even better target. He was pretty sure that suicide bombers didn't observe any Geneva Convention rules against attacking non-combatants like medics and reporters. In fact, their primary targets were more often than not, completely innocent people; that's how they created terror.

His attempt to get a grip wasn't working. He had convinced himself that she was definitely at risk of having been mortally wounded or killed. He went back to his computer and checked the news again. Still nothing new. He tried calling Kendra's cell and got her voicemail again. He took a series of deep breaths so as to calm his body. Calming his mind wasn't working yet and he needed to start somewhere. He got the phone charger he had put on his desk earlier and plugged it in to an outlet near his nightstand. He made a mental note to buy two more chargers each for his phone and for Kendra's.

He sat back down on his bed and took off his shoes. He got comfortable lying on his back with his eyes closed and began focusing on his breath and attempting to stop his internal monologue. Every few seconds he would begin a new thought, but then he would catch himself and just let it go unfinished. He visualized himself lying on the bottom of a pool. In his relaxation method, he viewed his thoughts as being made of air and thus they could not stay on the bottom of the pool with him unless he held them there. Since his intention was to clear his mind, he let each thought go, visualizing it as a bubble drifting up to the surface of the water.

> *Did Kendra mention what her assignment...*
> *Where was the last bombing in...*
> *'The good Lord is watching over...'*
> *If I had bought a charger as soon...*
> *Kendra, baby, where are you??*
> *Maybe she's covering the...*
> *They could be on stricter curfews after...*

Keith continued releasing each thought as soon as he could after he started thinking it until his mind was finally still. Now he began work on his body. He could feel the tension everywhere he placed his attention. He engaged in a physical relaxation process and allowed himself verbal thoughts to aid in the process. He started at the top of his body, stating silently, "I am relaxing my scalp," and took a deep breath. He imagined his scalp muscles relaxing and becoming languid with exhaustion. He continued this process all the way down his body until he was visualizing his toes drooping at the end of his feet in total relaxation.

He was glad to discover that he was still able to completely relax himself in a way that he hadn't done for a while. Since he'd met Kendra he'd been so happy and relaxed about life that he hadn't needed to calm himself. Now he needed it badly and it still took a conscious intention to not resume the internal worry monologue.

He focused on the silence of his mind and the relaxation of his body. He wished he had put on some relaxation music to help him focus on remaining in this state. He didn't want to get up though and start over so he just resolved to keep a strong intention on remaining calm and at peace. Several minutes later he felt the warbling begin.

Twenty-two

When Keith woke up, he looked around, disoriented and desperate. He didn't know where he was for a few seconds and he needed Kendra. He saw that he was lying on his bed and he was alone. It didn't make sense to him. He had just been with her moments ago. It hadn't felt like a dream at all. It couldn't have been, his mind insisted as he absorbed the painfully harsh reality that there was no one in the room with him but Laci.

He thought back to the night before. He had been lying in bed trying to calm his mind before he had a panic-attack from worrying about the possibility that Kendra may have been hurt in Iraq. As he reached a relaxed state, he began to drift off while maintaining conscious awareness of his body and his bed. Then he felt like he was floating and drifting upwards. Up and up until he imagined he was going right up through his ceiling and then he was above his house where his upward motion finally stopped.

Although he was weightless, he slowly turned around and viewed his neighborhood in all 360 degrees. He saw the lights from the pedestrian bridge that crossed the Arkansas river and he was attracted to them. He felt himself swiftly moving in that direction with his speed increasing the further he traveled. He was flying so fast he was sure he'd fly right past the bridge, but as he came near it and saw the place where he and Kendra had recently stood and held each other, he suddenly found himself standing in that exact spot.

He closed his eyes and listened to the sound of water rushing beneath him and felt the constant strong wind on his face and he recalled the feeling of being with Kendra and feeling her arms around him and her scent and the pure joy he experienced in her presence. When he opened his eyes, he was standing on a shore, not far from an island where a solitary figure was sitting.

"Kendra!" he yelled across the choppy water.

The figure that was kneeling in the sand, tilted her head up at the sound of his voice.

"Keith?" she asked quietly; barely above a whisper, but Keith heard her clearly as if she had spoken directly into his mind.

"Kendra, why are you there?"

"I don't know. I've been here for a while. Why are you over there?"

"I don't know. I just opened my eyes and here I was."

"But why are you still there? Don't you want to be with me?"

"I do, but I don't know how to get there."

"How did you get where you are?"

"I think I must have flown."

"Then fly to me."

That made perfect sense to Keith. He had been flying *earlier*. Why not just fly now, across the water to the island? The only problem was, he didn't know how to fly. He didn't know how he'd done it earlier. He had been floating above his house and then he found himself flying toward the bridge. So he felt that he hadn't *done* it, it just happened. And now he didn't know how to make it happen again.

"Keith!" Kendra's voice pulled him out of his thoughts and he looked directly at her. "Fly to me!" she commanded.

Without thinking, Keith took a running start and when he reached the waterline, he jumped up and spread his arms like wings and started to fly, but then he wondered if he should flap his arms or not and he dropped like a rock into the water. At first, he panicked and involuntarily took a breath. He did not choke, but breathed in the water as if it was air.

He continued sinking into the dark water that was not cold, but not warm either. He barely noticed the water touching him. He was like a heavier form of air, and he was sinking fast. Images of the bridge and flying and the island and the shore crashed into his mind and frustrated him because nothing made sense. He wanted everything to go away. He just wanted to be with Kendra. Now!

In an instant he was standing before her on the sand. She got up from her kneeling position on the sand and wrapped her arms around him. He returned her embrace and felt all of the world slip away as he let himself become lost in her love. He could stand here forever, just holding her. He needed nothing else in life but her love.

She broke the spell by asking, "Where are we, Keith? I've been all alone and I don't know where I am."

Something was crowding the edge of his mind. Something from the world that seemed so far away right now. Danger. Fear. Worry.

"I was so afraid that something happened to you. I'm so glad to see you're okay!"

"Something did happen to me. I'm on an island near a deserted beach and I don't know how I got here or how long I've been here."

"I was afraid you might've been hurt… or killed."

Kendra drew back a step and looked at him with fear in her eyes.

"There was a bombing where you were, and I couldn't reach you."

When Kendra heard the word "bombing" she began to remember something bad, and then she vanished.

Keith looked around the small island. Kendra was gone. What just happened?

"Kendra!" he yelled as loud as he could and opened his eyes. He was lying in bed, disoriented and desperate to find her again.

Twenty-three

Keith's heart was beating fast and he was breathing hard. This was unlike any dream he'd ever had. He was *there*! He *felt* Kendra. He couldn't explain it to himself, but it wasn't like being with someone in a dream. It felt the way it did when he was actually with her. He could feel her and smell her and sense her energy. They were *together*. What did that mean?

He swung his feet off the bed and sat for a few seconds. His cell phone rang and vibrated on the wooden surface of his nightstand. He grabbed it and looked at the display.

Joanne Hodges

Kendra's mother. He touched the word **Answer**, and put the phone to his ear.

"Joanne?"

There was no response for a few seconds but Keith could hear her crying.

"Joanne, what's wrong? What's happened to Kendra?"

"I'm sorry, Keith. The Associated Press just called me." Her voice caught and she inhaled sharply and held her breath for a few seconds before she spoke again. "Kendra was hurt in that bombing we talked about."

"How bad? She's okay, right?" He immediately recalled reading the news story that said the two survivors were in critical condition. But that could've been wrong. Reporters often got information wrong in the rush to report something as soon as they could, before they'd confirmed anything.

Joanne lost her composure and resumed crying.

"Joanne, please answer me."

"Let me call you back, Keith," she said, and hung up.

There was no way Keith was going to be able to wait. He looked in his phone's address book and touched the listing that read **Kendra – Office**. When no one answered, he was presented with the options of leaving a message, using the company directory or speaking to an operator. He chose the last option. When he told the operator why he was calling, she put him on hold, then came back and transferred him to someone who didn't know him, but knew *of* him and therefore confirmed that Kendra had been hurt in a suicide bombing; she was in a hospital in Baghdad, and her present condition was unknown, but it was believed to be bad. She was very seriously hurt and her prognosis was not good.

Keith asked for the name and number of the hospital, which was given to him after a short delay. It was just after 3am in Baghdad, but it was a hospital, so he called. They weren't going to be closed. Keith was relieved that the person who answered spoke English, although heavily accented. He said he was Kendra's husband and was calling to inquire about her condition. Keith was put on hold and waited thirty-two minutes before he finally concluded that no one was coming back on the line to tell him anything.

He called Joanne and asked her what she knew. She told him nothing he hadn't already been told by the woman at the A.P. She had spoken briefly with someone at the hospital who told her that Kendra was in critical condition, but nothing more. She was going to find out the following morning if the A.P. knew the name and address of the hospital so that she and Bill could fly to Iraq as soon as possible.

"You're welcome to come with us, of course. We'll pay for the flight."

"Thank you. I'd like that. I just need to call my boss and tell him I'm taking a leave of absence. I'll call you right back."

Keith called Ronald's personal cell and told him what had happened to Kendra and asked for time off. Ronald told him to take as much time as he needed, but to make sure before he left that Jared would be there during his absence – without fail. Keith called Joanne again and told her he was free to go with her and Bill. She said she'd let him know as soon as their flight was booked, and they ended the call. He emailed Jared, saying he had to leave due to an emergency and that he was counting on him to be at work every day until he returned.

Now that he was done with obligatory communications, Keith didn't know what to do with himself. He was fighting the urge to cry and just lie down and despair. Then he thought of Laci.

She could use a walk and he could use some fresh air and some space. As he walked along the sidewalk, stopping when Laci stopped, and absent-mindedly resuming forward motion when she did, he felt like he was in a dream.

Nothing was real to him except Laci; and even she was just faintly real. He kept worrying himself until he became aware of his thoughts and told himself to stop it. Worrying was nothing but asking questions he couldn't know the answers to. Is she going to be okay? Is she going to die? Does she have all of her limbs, and will they function if she lives? Will she have brain damage? What will he do if she dies? And so on. He was doing nothing but torturing himself. He wasn't helping her or himself by worrying and asking himself these things. His father used to say, 'If you can do something about a situation, then do it - if you can't, then put your mind somewhere else until you can.' He wished his father was still alive. But even if he had been, he couldn't have done anything in this situation either. No one could, with the possible exception of the doctors. He fervently hoped the doctors in Iraq were capable.

Okay, he told himself. *No more negative, worrying thoughts.* He decided he needed to be positive. He knew that all life was energy, so maybe if he thought positive thoughts they might be helpful to her in some way. If not, and he may never know, at least he wouldn't be driving himself crazy.

He told himself that Kendra was going to be just fine. But that didn't feel like positive thinking. That felt like a stupidly false statement, or at least a statement that he didn't know the truth of. He had no idea how she was going to be. He couldn't just lie to himself and declare that the future would be good. So he decided to hope for the best. That was as positive as he could realistically get. He visualized Kendra being home and recovering and eventually being physically fit and healthy. He focused on that and made a statement dedicating his energy to that future.

Later that night, it took him a long time to fall asleep, even after doing his relaxation technique. He had control of his mind for the most part, but his body was still exhibiting signs of anxiety and unrest. After two relaxation visualizations over his entire body, he finally started to drift off.

Twenty-four

Keith was flying over the nighttime landscape of the city. He was thinking of Kendra and therefore heading toward her without knowing it, but he was also amazed at the beauty of the city at night; the alluring incongruity of the structures and lights created by men which blended in and around the trees and bodies of water provided by nature. This admiration of the view below him caused him to travel at a rate much less than the speed of thought.

As he adjusted to the view below him and the novelty started to wear off, Kendra occupied more of his thoughts and he began to see the landscape and buildings get smaller and smaller. He was now flying forward and upward, like a jet plane after takeoff when it ascends to cruising altitude. Keith did not level off as a plane would. He continued his ascent until he saw the entire country below him and both oceans, and then several continents followed by the entire globe. The view of the earth was so stunning that it displaced Kendra from his mind entirely for a moment and he stopped moving. Then Keith's mind went back to Kendra, as it always did and he found himself flying upward again toward the sight of billions of stars such as he had never seen before.

He felt Kendra's presence nearby and then suddenly she was there in front of him. She was made of tiny stars and blue-white light. She was beautiful in a brand new way. She flew toward him. He extended his arms to embrace her and she flew through him and swirled around his back and reappeared in front of him again, floating and smiling.

I'm so happy you're here. I needed you.

Her mouth did not move. She continued to smile, but he heard her voice only in his mind.

I always need you, he thought in response, and she swirled around him and through him again.

Good. I always need you too.

You can hear my thoughts, he said in his mind.

Yes.

She laughed in the same silent way that they were talking to each other.

And you can hear mine too.

He could feel her smiling as she flew away from him, increasing speed as she went, then she tumbled over and turned around and flew back to him faster than she had departed and zoomed right through him again, then she veered to the right and circled back to face him.

Why do you keep going through me? He smiled as he asked. He liked it every time she did it, but he wanted to know why she was doing it.

It feels good when we occupy the same space for a second, she replied.

It does, he agreed. *But you keep moving and doing it again. Why don't you stay in the same space with me?*

It's too intense. I can only take a little at a time.

Kendra swirled around Keith again and stopped right in front of him. If they had been in bodies, their noses would be touching. They were both smiling, feeling each other's energy radiate into each other.

Keith moved forward to kiss her. His energy body passed through hers where their lips would be. He held himself there for a few seconds, then drew back quickly.

I see what you mean. It's like an electrical charge starts to build up.

Yes. I wish I could hug you. I need to feel your arms around me. I miss you, Keith!

I don't understand. If I'm dreaming, why can't we… just hug like normal?

I don't think we're dreaming.

Her energy changed. Keith felt grief, fear and loss flowing out of her as if she was broadcasting it and he was a radio receiver. She disappeared in a flash of wispy light, heading downward. Keith followed without thinking, as if he was attached to her. The earth grew rapidly as they approached it at super-sonic speed. First it was a globe, then it was continents, then a desert with cities and then they zeroed in on one building. Kendra slowed her descent through the night sky but didn't stop when she reached the roof of the building. Keith followed her through the roof and through several floors, coming to a stop in a room where a badly injured patient lay unconscious in a hospital bed.

There I am, Kendra silently communicated to Keith.

The negative feelings he picked up from her earlier were much stronger now, like a scent filling the room. He drifted over to the bed to get a closer look at the patient. Her head was wrapped in bandages and her face was lacerated, swollen and discolored, but there was no mistaking it. That was Kendra lying in the hospital bed.

He swiveled his viewpoint back to the non-physical Kendra he had followed to this room. She was still a sparkling energy body, but the sparkling was less visible against the backdrop of the white hospital room. It was harder to see her in here, but he could feel her energy clearly.

From the suicide bombing?

Yes.

Keith needed to think. What kind of dream was this? Kendra said it wasn't a dream. Then what was it? He rotated back to the Kendra on the bed and quieted his mind, attempting to sense if he felt anything coming from her. He felt nothing. It was as if she was a stranger to him. He found that strangely sad. How could the physical presence of Kendra have no effect on him at all?

He drifted back to the dream-Kendra and instantly felt her presence just as he did when they were physically together. He suddenly thought that he understood something. The dream-Kendra was the energy essence that he normally felt coming from the physical-Kendra who was now lying in the bed. With her energy absent from her body, he now felt nothing in her physical presence.

Come with me, he thought to her, and he flew upwards, back up toward the stars. She followed right behind him.

About a mile up, she said, *Keith, come this way. It's too lonely up there.*

She took the lead and flew him back to the island where he'd seen her the night before. They couldn't feel the night air, but the impression on the island was that of a warm and peaceful night as they came to rest on the sand near a palm tree. The sky was deep purple and strange looking. Small swells washed up on the shore and turned to moonlit bubbles popping on the sand as the water retreated with the tide.

Kendra felt better here and the sadness she gave off began to diminish, but did not go away completely. Keith rested beside her, still struggling to understand everything. It almost made sense to him if he thought of Kendra as a ghost. He looked at her, wondering if that's what she was.

If I'm a ghost, then what are you? You're the only person who can see me or talk to me.

His first reaction to what she said was compassion and concern for her, and he found his energy expanding and encircling her. Kendra felt his embrace and for the first time since she found herself floating outside of her body, she felt like she was in contact with someone. Keith's embrace did not cause the overly intense feeling that they experienced when they passed through each other, temporarily occupying the same space; she was just surrounded by it, feeling Keith's love for her.

As Keith immersed himself in the feeling of being close to Kendra and enjoying the sensation the same as if he was holding her in his physical arms, his thoughts turned to her question. What was he? If she was outside her body because it was in a coma, where was he? How was he here?

Kendra wasn't thinking of anything at this moment. She was just enjoying the feeling of being with Keith and feeling his love wrapped around her. When Keith's mind became absorbed with the question of himself and his identity and how it was possible for him to be here with Kendra, he suddenly disappeared. Kendra felt like she had gone from being together with her lover in a warm bath to standing outside, naked in the cold.

Keith opened his eyes, gasped for breath and felt chills run down his body. He looked around his room, and for a few seconds, he couldn't believe that Kendra was not there with him.

Twenty-five

After Keith's heartbeat and respiration returned to normal, he thought about what he had just dreamed and whether or not it was possible for it to have been more than a dream. He remembered everything. That wasn't usually the case with his dreams. He would normally just remember the last thing before waking and a few key things here and there, but those would be forgotten by the time he was drinking his first cup of coffee. He wondered if he was going to forget all that he currently remembered about meeting with Kendra's spirit and flying with her to the hospital in Iraq and up to the stars. That had to be a dream. It was too crazy. But it felt so real.

He reached over and turned on the lamp beside his bed. He looked around at his room, somewhat dazed still and not sure why he turned on the light instead of just trying to go back to sleep. It was just after 4am. It was Sunday so he didn't have to worry about being tired all day, but there was nothing to be up for.

Suddenly he got up and went to his desk, turning on his monitor and waking his computer. He went to Google and typed: *dreams that feel real*. He got results that led him to reading about lucid dreaming wherein a person is consciously aware that they're in a dream and can take control of the dream. One study found that if a person who was lucid dreaming directed their dream to involve sexual activity, it not only felt real in the dream, but the orgasm they experienced from the dream was the physiological equivalent to the orgasms they had while awake.

Was he having lucid dreams about Kendra? According to what he was reading, lucid dreamers chose what they wanted to dream about so that they could experience anything they wanted. Keith knew that if he had a choice, he'd definitely choose to dream about Kendra, but he wasn't aware of having made any choices at all. He just found himself outside, flying around. Yes, he was lucid, but he didn't feel that he was in control of anything that was happening, other than choosing to follow Kendra and choosing to leave the hospital.

He read more and thought about the fact that lucid dreamers are not just in control of their dreams, but they *know* that they're dreaming. When he dreamed he was with Kendra, it never occurred to him that he was dreaming. Wait, he told himself. He *had* mentioned to Kendra that they were in a dream and she said that they *weren't* dreaming. That's when she took him to see her body in the hospital. This was so confusing. He didn't know what to think.

Keith didn't know what he was doing during his sleep. None of it made sense to him. All he knew was that he wanted to be back with her again. He didn't care if it was a dream, or a lucid dream or whatever. He just wanted to be with her. When they were together, nothing else mattered. He turned off his monitor and crawled back into bed. He thought about Kendra and willed himself to dream of her, or find her, or do whatever he had done earlier. After a long while, he fell asleep. If he had dreamed while he slept, he didn't remember it when he awoke a few hours later.

While he was shaving, his phone rang, but he couldn't do anything about it at the moment. When he finished, he went to his room, drying his hands by wiping them on his sweatpants. The missed call was from Joanne, and she left a voicemail. He played it back on the external speaker.

"Keith, this is Joanne. I was just able to get tickets to Baghdad. The only problem is, the flight leaves in four hours. Please call me back and let me know if you can meet us at Tulsa International in two hours. I'm very sorry for the short notice, but it's good that we can go right away. Don't you think?"

Keith's mind kicked into gear, thinking, what did he need to bring? He could pack in minutes. He could go without having a change of clothes for all he cared. But something was nagging at him. He needed something. He couldn't think. His mind was a nervous blank. He went to the kitchen and made coffee. While the coffee brewed, he opened the back door, letting Laci go out by herself instead of going on her usual morning walk.

Back in his room, he drank coffee and checked his email thinking of how great it would be if Kendra had emailed him, telling him that she had come out of the coma and was going to be fine. His email consisted of the usual junk and a reply from Jared assuring him that he would be at work every day, he had Keith's back, and he hoped everything was okay. Keith appreciated that Jared didn't even ask what the emergency was; he just gave him the reassurance that he needed.

Keith was in the shower when he realized what had been nagging at him. He needed a passport! He couldn't go to Iraq without a passport, could he? He'd only been to Canada and they didn't ask to see his passport at the border; they'd only asked where he was going and what he was going to do. That was simple. He was on his way to the arena, and he was going to see Pearl Jam and Neil Young. They had waived him through without another question. He was pretty sure though that going through airport security in Iraq was going to be much more difficult. He wondered if the airport was controlled by Iraqis or American military. Maybe he wouldn't need a passport if the military was running the airport. No, America was withdrawing its troops. They wouldn't be in charge of the airport.

"Shit!"

He'd have to call Joanne and ask her if she knew anything about passport requirements and was it even possible for him to get one in time for their flight. Could he get one at the airport? That would be the most logical place for a passport place to be, but it seemed like in movies people always went to some seedy place downtown to get a passport. Keith felt really stupid not knowing anything about this, but he'd never traveled and hadn't needed to know. But still, he told himself, he ought to be a bit more informed about things that he might need to know some day.

If he couldn't get a passport and make the flight, he'd just have to take a later one, that's all. He tried to calm himself down. Kendra was in a coma anyway. She wouldn't notice that Keith hadn't arrived with Paul and Joanne. He breathed deeply and slowly as he got dressed, trying to relax and not get all freaked out about the passport issue.

He heard his phone buzz and make the bing sound to remind him that he had a message waiting. Okay. Nothing to worry about. Joanne will know about passports because she and Bill traveled every year. He buttoned up his Levi's. and walked over to his phone. Missed call from Joanne again. Another voice message.

"Keith!" She was crying. *Oh god, now what?* "I just got off the phone with the hospital in Iraq. I wanted to find out if we could see Kendra right after we arrived. I don't know if they have visiting hours like we do or how that works over there." She paused to sniffle and blow her noise, still crying. "Kendra's gone." *What? No!* "They don't know what happened to her or where she is."

What the hell did that mean?

Twenty-six

At first, when Joanne said Kendra was gone, Keith felt like he was going to have a heart attack. He thought she meant "gone" as in dead; gone from this life. But then she said, they don't know where she is. Surely that didn't mean she had died and they had misplaced the body. It must mean that she got up and went somewhere and that's why they didn't know where she was. She just wasn't in her room. That's all. And that was great news!

It's not like Al Qaeda came in and took her away so they could finish the job. No one was worried about her identifying the bomber. She was probably wandering the halls somewhere, lost and confused about where she was. He pressed the Call Back button on his phone screen.

"Joanne, tell me what the hospital told you. How do they not know where she is?"

"Oh Keith! I'm so upset right now I could just spit. I need to know what they've done with my baby!"

"Joanne, take a deep breath and just focus for a second. Okay?"

He heard her take two deep breaths and swallow.

"Okay. I'm okay."

"Good. Now tell me what they said when you called."

"I told them my flight will arrive in Baghdad at 2:35am and asked if I would be able to visit my daughter then. They said it depended on what ward she was on and if the doctor had noted any restrictions. They asked me her name, then said they would check to see if I could visit that late." She started to lose her composure, her voice quivering.

"It's okay. Just breathe. Take a second and tell me what happened next."

"Nothing happened. I was on hold for a few minutes and then I heard a dial tone. I called right back and this time a man answered. I had to go over everything again. He told me they had no patient named Kendra Hodges in the hospital." Joanne burst into tears and continued talking but Keith could barely understand what she was saying. He understood that they had argued and that the man had hung up on her. "He was so rude, Keith! How could they lose my daughter? You can't just lose a *person* like that!"

"Joanne, I'm going to come over and we'll find out what's going on. Don't worry. Just relax and try not to upset yourself. We'll find her."

After Keith ended the call, he wondered how he could sound so calm and in control while talking to Joanne, but now his mind was so rattled and shocked, he couldn't even think. He wanted to try out scenarios in his mind to come up with an idea of what could be happening, but he couldn't even form a coherent thought. He felt like there was a wind blowing through his mind, making it impossible for him to think.

When Keith arrived at the Hodges' residence, he saw Paul in the driveway loading suitcases into the back of their Lexus SUV. Paul was retired but he looked like he was dressed for business or an important meeting. Joanne came out of the house as Keith was getting out of his car. She walked briskly toward the driveway but stopped suddenly when she saw Keith coming toward her.

"Oh, Keith! I was just going to call you on our way to come and pick you up."

Keith thought that was odd since he had just told her on the phone that he was on his way over, but he didn't say that.

"Oh." He looked at her, not understanding the change in plans.

"We're on our way to the airport. It's good that you're here. We'll get there quicker now."

"Did they find Kendra?" he asked.

"Not yet, but they will. And if they don't, then *we* will." Keith looked at Paul who nodded a greeting to him but remained silent otherwise.

"But wouldn't it make more sense to wait until they find her so we know what's going on and where she is?"

Joanne looked at him as if he had suggested that they sit around and eat bugs for a while.

"Keith, there's nothing going on, and we know exactly where she is. She's at the *hospital*." She walked over to the passenger side door and tried the handle. The door wouldn't open so she turned and looked at Paul expectantly. He looked uncertain for a few seconds and then seemed to suddenly wake up, fumbling in his pocket for the remote fob. He pulled it out, pressed a button and the locks on the front doors clunked into the unlocked position. Joanne opened her door and got in. Paul pressed the fob again and the back doors unlocked. He looked at Keith.

"I guess we're leaving now."

Keith wasn't sure what to think, but something didn't feel right to him. Logic told him that it didn't make sense to fly across the world to visit with someone whose location was currently unknown. There would be plenty time to find her though before they could get there. But still, it didn't feel right to him. He felt like something was telling him not to go.

"I'm going to stay here, Paul. I can catch a later flight – when they find her." He had almost said, '*if* they find her.' He didn't know why he'd almost said that, and he didn't know why he stopped himself.

Paul nodded and walked around the vehicle. Keith went back to his car, got in, and sat there without starting the engine. He felt like he needed to think. He also felt that he might be making an irrational decision, but he was following his instincts. He needed to process what was compelling him and what the best course of action was, but he needed time. Being told that Kendra was missing, and then being told that they were heading to the airport when he had expected to resolve the mystery first, didn't give him enough time to process anything.

He could see Paul and Joanne talking briefly and then they backed out of the driveway; the rear of their vehicle briefly coming toward his before Paul put the car in drive, and they were on their way.

Keith asked himself if he was being stupid. Aside from the worst possibility that Kendra had died, what would explain her absence from the hospital? She could've been transferred to another hospital. She could've even been transferred to another ward and someone failed to note the move in the computer system. No matter what had happened, she was still there and he was sure they'd find her by the time their plane reached Baghdad. He told himself he could still easily meet up with Paul and Joanne at the airport in time for the flight. But he sat there with no will to start the car. He felt rooted to the spot and he didn't know why.

He started feeling heavy, as if gravity was affecting him more than it should be. Suddenly he wanted to be asleep more than anything. It didn't make sense to him. He'd gotten more than enough sleep lately and he'd been doing nothing to make him tired. But he could feel his mind shutting down and something like fatigue washing over him. He reached for the lever between his seat and the door and reclined as far back as he could. He closed his eyes and stopped questioning why he felt this way. All that mattered for the moment was to be able to lie back and close his eyes. He found a relatively comfortable position and started to sink into the feeling of being pulled downward and inward. The vibrations started shortly after he closed his eyes.

Twenty-seven

Keith opened his eyes and saw a purple sky through his windshield. He was still in his car. And he wasn't alone. He looked to his right and saw Kendra sitting in the passenger seat, smiling at him. But this time, she looked like she had a real physical body. When he looked at her, she leaned toward him and wrapped her arms around him. They held each other for a long moment, feeling actual physical contact, then she pulled herself back.

"Did you hear me?"

"No, what did you say?"

"I didn't say anything, really, but I was calling for you. I wanted you to come talk to me. I can't talk to anyone else." She looked down and away.

"Why is the sky purple?"

She looked up at him. "It's violet. I was looking at the sky and I thought of my eyeshadow and the sky changed to look just like it."

"Are we dreaming?"

"I think you are. Sort of. But I'm not."

Keith thought about that for a second and quickly gave it up. It was too complicated and there was something more important on his mind.

"Where are you?"

"I'm with you, dummy," she said, and leaned over to kiss him. Kissing her was great. It felt completely real to him and was so much better than when they had the sparkling energy bodies. But he stopped and re-questioned her.

"I mean, where are you – physically? We were going to fly to Iraq but the hospital said you weren't there. Are you still…?" He couldn't finish the sentence. If she wasn't alive, he didn't want to know. Not yet. He felt so good being with her, he didn't want to ruin what might be a very short visit.

"Yes, I'm still in a coma." She looked down again; her eyelids covering most of her eyes.

"Where?" Keith asked, almost impatiently.

She opened her eyes fully, looking into his.

"I'm here… in Tulsa! Well, Broken Arrow, actually. But you know… same thing."

Keith was relieved to know that she was okay. Or rather, that she hadn't gotten worse, and she wasn't lost.

"How did you get here?"

"I flew."

"I mean, how did your body get here?"

"I know. It flew."

Keith looked at her like she'd lost her mind. It was hard enough to accept that they were seeing each other while she was in a coma and he was asleep, but now she was saying her body flew. He began to question whether he was losing his own mind. Maybe all of this meant he had gone crazy when he found out she'd been in a bombing and he was locked up somewhere in a padded room imagining all of this.

"I don't understand, Kendra. I know you can fly in the sparkly energy body, but you're saying now that your physical body can fly too?"

"On a *plane*, Keith. They flew me on a military plane from Baghdad to Tulsa. And not just me. The other people in the bombing were brought home too. We landed in Virginia, then they put me on another plane that came to Tulsa."

"Oh, good. I was starting to think that none of this was real. You *are* real, aren't you?"

She put out her palms facing up. "Do I feel real?"

Keith put his hands on top of hers.

"Yes, you do. I just don't understand this. Later, I'll open my eyes and you'll be gone and I won't know if I was just dreaming." Keith was looking at her hands as he caressed them with his thumbs.

"Look at me." Keith looked up and into her eyes. "I'm at St. Joan's hospital."

He stared at her, waiting for her to go on. She didn't.

"And…?" he asked.

"That's so you'll know this is real."

He got it finally. If she was in St. Joan's, he'd know she had really spoken to him.

As he was looking at her, he saw the scene behind her change. Her parent's house with the big trees and the vine-covered wall and the circular drive all faded to nothing and then there was water. An ocean of water and a beach appeared where the front yard should have been.

"What just happened?" He pointed at the beach behind her. She looked over her shoulder, then turned back to him, smiling.

"I was thinking how I wanted to go to the beach with you. I guess I did that."

Keith couldn't make sense of how this was "real." If she turned out to really be in St. Joan's in a coma, then she was really communicating to him and this wasn't a dream. But if the landscape and the sky could change, that meant this *was* a dream.

"I'm confused. Are you real and in my dream which is not real? I was really in my car, and I'm still in my car. So this has to be real."

"This isn't really your car."

"Huh?"

"Look at your dashboard."

He looked at it and saw a simplified version of his instrument panel. There was no tachometer, oil pressure gauge, voltmeter; all of the dimmed "idiot light" indicators were gone. He looked back at Kendra as she opened the glove compartment. It was empty and looked brand new.

"You usually have a bunch of junk in here."

"So what is this? A replica of my car?"

"That's what I think. In this dream-like place, the things are made from what's in our minds. I don't know cars really well, so my mind doesn't conjure up a very good copy. Ooh! Look at your dashboard now."

Keith looked and saw that the missing gauges and indicator lights were now there.

"You must've added those because you know what they're all for and they're clear in your mind," she said.

Keith looked at the sky and concentrated on a light blue color. The sky changed to a violet hue streaked with blue. He looked at her then back at the sky. She looked at the sky and saw what he was trying to do. The violet disappeared and the sky turned pure blue. Then a rainbow appeared.

They both laughed and turned to kiss each other. It was something they did whenever they saw a rainbow. It was one of the silly rules of their relationship. Another was to never walk up or down an escalator but to stand still holding each other and kiss until they reached the end.

"Hey, let's get out of the car." He couldn't believe he hadn't thought of it sooner.

They both got out and ran along the beach. Then running together turned into him chasing her. As they ran, their clothes changed to swim shorts for him and a bikini for her. Since this experience was real but dreamlike, he figured it would be safe to tackle her. He increased his speed until he was right behind her then dove at her back, wrapping his arms around her as they fell and rolled in the sand together, laughing and out of breath.

They came to a stop with Kendra on her back and Keith on top of her. He pulled himself into a sitting position and gazed upon her face as he caught his breath. She was so beautiful he felt that he could look at her forever. He could feel her energy as he had on their previous visits, and he was so glad they could touch this time without that overwhelming pleasure-shock feeling.

The thought of touching Kendra dominated his thoughts and he bent down and kissed her. He rolled to the side, pulling her with him, then he pulled the string of her top behind her back, undoing the loose knot. He rolled them back to where they were and he pulled her top away. The sight of her topless thrilled him as it had since the first time. He thought she was perfect in every way possible and loved her inside and out.

He kissed her while fondling her breasts with both hands. She wrapped her arms around him, running her fingers through his hair, then down his back. She hooked her thumbs under the waistband of his shorts and tugged them downward. He pulled away from her briefly to remove his shorts, then resumed kissing her, first her lips, then her neck. He kissed and sucked her neck from below her jawbone and over to her ear as she tried to pull down her bikini bottoms.

He slid off of her, allowing her to remove them all the way. Afterwards, she pushed him down and straddled him. Her hair looked wild hanging down in his face. He looked at her hair and her face then down at her full breasts and her flat stomach. He visually feasted on her. She lowered a breast to his mouth and he sucked blissfully, wrapping his arms around her and holding her there as if he never wanted her to move from that position. She lifted herself up, reached down and guided him into her as she lowered herself back down. They both gasped at the sudden overwhelming pleasure as she lowered herself all the way down, causing him to fully penetrate her.

She leaned back a ways so she could see his face.

"Do you feel that?"

He tried to talk but his voice was scratchy. He swallowed and cleared his throat. Waves were rushing through his mind, buzzing and pulsing. He was barely breathing.

"Yes," he said. "It's like my nerve endings are turned up to eleven."

She nodded agreement. They looked into each other's eyes; their feelings magnified by the knowledge that they were each experiencing the same extraordinary pleasure. She lay down on him and kissed him, marveling at how sweet and sensual it was as her tongue moved inside his mouth. Despite the intensity of the pleasure they felt, they were able to make it last a long time, and only brought themselves to a climax out of curiosity after a long time of exploring the amazing sensations of making love in this state.

"You can come inside me," she panted. He hadn't even thought of that. They had always used a condom before, but now he needn't worry about getting her pregnant.

"Okay," he said, still finding it hard to articulate anything.

He changed his intention from just luxuriating in physical pleasure to wanting to climax and reach a peak. He rolled them over so he was on top. He took hold of her hands and interlaced their fingers.

He covered her mouth with his, tasting her and drinking her in as he increased the speed and depth of his penetration.

He felt his orgasm approaching. She had already enjoyed several but he hoped she would have another with him.

I'm going to, she said in his mind. That surprised him. They hadn't talked that way the entire time they were in these physical-feeling bodies. Something was changing.

He felt his muscles contracting with pleasure, starting in his feet and climbing up his legs. His brain felt like it was numb with pleasure. His teeth hummed in vibration. The rising sensation of his climax suddenly burst upward from his thighs and into his groin and he erupted inside of her, and as he did, they flew upward, transforming into their energy bodies and swirling around each other as they climbed into the sky, through puffy white clouds and up into space where the sky was black and sparkling with billions of stars.

Twenty-eight

Keith's body jerked and he opened his eyes, startled. He felt chills run down the length of his body and he tried to catch his breath. He sat up and looked in his rear-view mirror. A man in a car parked behind him in front of the neighbor's house honked his horn, looking toward the house impatiently. Keith wanted to yell to him to get out of his car and go knock on the door. Idiot.

Knowing that people were going to be coming outside and getting in the car behind him, he felt embarrassed and wanted to leave. He reached into his pocket for his car keys and was surprised to find that his pocket was wet. He pulled his keys out, started his car and pulled away, wiping his hand on his pants.

Keith's breathing normalized as he drove slowly and thought about what he had just experienced. He had just had the most mind-blowing sex of his entire life. He thought, if that's what people in comas do, then no one needs to feel sorry for them. He felt guilty as soon as he finished the thought. He suspected that not everyone in a coma did what he and Kendra were doing – not just the sex, but the meeting, talking, and flying around together. He'd never heard of this before, and if other people were doing it, surely they'd be talking about it.

Or maybe not, he thought. Who would he tell? At first, he thought, no one. Then upon further reflection, he considered that he might tell everyone in the world. If he could confirm this was really happening, he'd want everyone to know. There was more to life than we thought there was!

Then he remembered: St. Joan's! He needed to get to the hospital and find out if Kendra was there. He increased his speed and thought about the quickest route to the hospital when he remembered that he needed to go home and change. He looked down and saw that his shirt was wet where it met the waistband of his pants.

He drove quickly to his house, his mind racing with thoughts of Kendra and what the future might hold for them. Naturally, he wanted her back with him in his regular life. But if she never came out of the coma and they continued to meet, and to even have sex, which he still couldn't believe how awesome that was, then she wouldn't really be gone or missing at all. Things would just be different; sometimes amazingly different.

When Keith walked into his house, Laci sniffed at his crotch and he pushed her face away.

"Down, girl."

He walked to the back door and ordered her outside so she could potty. He didn't know when he'd be back, but at least now he might not be taking a flight anywhere and he wouldn't need Jared to take care of her.

He went to his room to change and realized he needed to shower. He was a mess. After he quickly showered and changed, he topped off Laci's food and water and let her back inside. He squatted down and massaged her neck as she licked his face.

"You be good. I'll be back later."

He opened the curtains on his way to the door, letting the light in and making it so Laci could watch him drive away. He believed it helped to lessen her anxiety if she actually saw him drive away, rather than just having to assume that he had left since the sound of his car went away from the house.

He made his way to the Broken Arrow Expressway and turned on the radio. His mind was going in too many directions at once. He needed some music to give him something to focus on.

Fifteen minutes later Keith found visitor's parking and walked into the hospital. It was early afternoon, so there should still be a chance to visit – if Kendra was actually there. He'd have to lie of course, and say she was his wife. No. He didn't have a wedding ring. He'd say she was his sister; step-sister, to explain the different names.

He went to the information desk and said he'd like to visit Kendra Hodges, his step-sister. The woman behind the window tapped on her keyboard, found what she was looking for and asked Keith his name. He gave it to her and she said, "Room 603. The elevators are down there to your right."

He could see where the elevators were, but thanked her anyway. He was relieved that getting access to her room was so easy. He guessed that they couldn't really ask him to prove she was his step-sister. How would he? But if he had said she was his fiancé, he wouldn't have stood a chance of seeing her. Hospital rules were so stupid.

He rode an elevator to the top, emerged, and there was no sign indicating which way the numbers got higher or lower the way they would in an office building outside an elevator. He decided to go to his right and saw that the numbers were too high and getting higher. He went the other way and found room 603. The door was open.

He walked in and there she was, looking pretty much the same as she had when he saw her a few days ago when he and Kendra flew down from space. It felt crazy to think that, and to remember that, but now he knew it had really happened. Not only had he seen her bandaged exactly as she was now, but she had told him she was here. And she was. It was all real.

He sat in a chair against the wall that faced her bed. He grabbed it from underneath and slid it forward as far as he could, then he took her left hand and held it in both of his and closed his eyes. He brought her hand up to his mouth and kissed it. Holding it there, his lips brushed against her skin as he mouthed the words, "I love you."

He almost started to cry but fought the urge. He looked at her damaged body. Her right arm was in a cast that included her shoulder. She had a brace around her neck. Her legs were covered by a sheet but he could tell from the size of the bulk beneath the sheet that her legs were in casts. Her head was wrapped in gauze and she had healing cuts all over the purple and yellow skin of her face.

The woman he loved was shattered and broken; nearly killed. Practically killed, since she was in a coma and not actually doing any living now. This time he couldn't hold back and the tears flowed. Even as he cried, he tried to counter his anguish at seeing his love lying in this bed. He told himself that this wasn't her. It was only her body. She was alive, and when she was with him, she was definitely happy. He knew she wasn't always happy though. When he first found her on the island, she was very sad and alone. But now, when they were together, she was very happy and vibrant. It was like seeing her at her best.

He wondered where she was now – the real Kendra; the one he met when he was dreaming or sleeping. Was she in the room with him? He thought if she was, he should be able to feel her presence, but he didn't feel anything. She could be right next to him for all he knew. He wondered if she went into her body. Did the energy version of Kendra need sleep? He'd have to ask her these things if he could remember the next time he saw her.

He tried to reconcile the two realities in his mind. In one reality, Kendra was in a hospital bed, physically recovering from a horrible bombing. In the other reality, she was alive and able to go anywhere and do anything she wanted. One part of him was traumatized by what had happened to her, and another part of him felt jubilant and excited about the time they were able to spend together. It was very strange.

The physical part of him wanted to find out what her physical prognosis was. He got up and left the room, looking for someone who could tell him what her official condition was. Would she come out of the coma? If she did, would she be normal again with a functioning brain and body?

He approached a nurse behind a glass wall. Behind her there was a cabinet with medicine bottles and various supplies. Patient charts were on a roll-cart. She looked up as he approached.

"Hi. My name is Keith Erikson. I'm wondering if you can tell me anything about my sister's condition; Kendra Hodges?"

"Just a moment, Mr. Erikson." She typed Kendra's name and then studied the LCD monitor in front of her. She pursed her lips and just barely shook her head side to side. "I'm sorry, Mr. Erikson, but your sister was very badly wounded and is completely non-responsive in a non-active brain state. She's comatose."

"I'm aware of that, ma'am. I meant to ask, can you tell if she's getting better? Is she expected to come out of the coma?"

The nurse looked at the information on the screen again. She tapped a few keys then looked back at Keith.

"It appears that she's been in this state since she was treated by first responders. That was in Iraq." She realized as she said it that Keith already knew that she was injured in Iraq. "She has not improved or worsened according to what her doctor there observed, and from what her doctor here has seen so far." Keith could tell by her tone that she didn't think much of the medical professionals in Iraq. She practically spoke the word *doctor* with quotation marks around it.

"Thank you. Can you tell me her doctor's name and whether he's here or not? I'd like to speak to him, if possible."

She glanced at the screen for just a second. "She's being cared for by Dr. Garrison. He'll be in tomorrow. I can't say exactly what time, but he usually starts in the morning and is here all day."

"But he's not in today?"

"No, sir. He isn't in today." She looked as if she was about to say more, such as the reason why he wasn't in, but she didn't offer any additional information.

"Thank you very much. I'll try him tomorrow then." He started to walk away, then stopped and looked back at her. "What are the visiting hours here?"

"8am to 8pm."

"Thank you again."

He walked back to Kendra's room, glad that he had plenty of time to spend with her.

Then he remembered: Joanne and Paul!

Shit. He needed to call them and tell them not to get on the plane. He picked up his phone from the console tray and manipulated the screens with his thumb, selecting the phone symbol, then Recent Calls, then touching Joanne Hodges' name, then

Call Again. It rang until he heard her voicemail greeting.

"Joanne. Don't get on the plane! Kendra is *here*. I hope you haven't left yet. Call me."

He ended the call and looked at the time. He couldn't believe how much time had passed. They were already in the air. He should've thought to call them as soon as he was woken from his… dream, or whatever he had with Kendra that culminated with sex on the beach. He'd never think of the cocktail the same way again. He felt bad that the Hodges were going to fly all the way to Iraq only to turn around and fly home. But they shouldn't have gone. He tried to tell them, but Joanne wouldn't listen, and Paul acted like the two of them shared a single brain.

Twenty-nine

She was in a taxi more than halfway to the hospital before Joanne thought to turn her cell phone back on. A minute later it chimed to let her know she had voicemail. She saw that one message was from Keith and the other two were from friends; probably to let her know that Kendra was in their thoughts and prayers. She couldn't deal with Keith right now, so she dropped her phone in her purse.

At the hospital's information desk, she had a terrible time trying to communicate with the receptionist.

"Kendra Hodges," Joanne said very loudly and wiggled her fingers in the air, pantomiming typing.

"Honey, she's not deaf, and people are sleeping. There's no need to make a scene," Paul advised, placing a hand on her shoulder. Joanne glared at her husband, daring him to stop her from making a scene. This was their daughter they were talking about. She would very well make a scene – if that's what it took.

"Give me a pen and paper and I'll spell the name for you." Now she scribbled in the air with an invisible pen.

The woman behind the desk repeated something in Arabic, then struggled for a translation. "See now… no. Sun… yes." She tapped her wristwatch and looked at Joanne, pleading with her eyes for Joanne to understand.

"I don't want to see my son. I want to see my *daughter*! Do you understand me? My daughter!" Joanne yelled. Paul tried to coax her away from the front desk, but she resisted, planting herself firmly in front of the Iraqi woman. She was determined to make her understand even if it meant yelling at the top of her lungs.

The rest of the lobby was silent. The elevator dinged and the doors opened. An orderly stepped out and heard the commotion at the front desk and came over to see what was happening. He spoke to the receptionist in Arabic, then turned to the Hodges.

"She says the time for visiting begins at 9am and asks that you please return then." He looked at his watch. "Less than six hours from now."

"We just flew here from the United States to see our daughter who was nearly killed…" She was going to say "by one of your people," but stopped herself. "…By a terrorist! Please, just let us have a few moments with her," Joanne pleaded, close to tears from exhaustion and frustration.

The orderly and the receptionist spoke to each other again. The young woman's expression changed to one of sympathy and she nodded at the orderly as she spoke in Arabic.

"Okay. She will permit a brief visit, but please understand, this is…" He searched for the word he wanted, but couldn't find it, so he substituted with additional words. "...A one-time rule-breaking, not to be repeated."

Paul addressed the orderly. "Thank you, doctor. We appreciate you making an exception in this tragic case."

"Yes!" the orderly shouted, startling the Hodges. "Exception!" He now had the word he wanted, and he had been mistaken for a doctor. He was very pleased.

"Could you please tell us where she is?" Paul asked the orderly.

The orderly consulted his co-worker again, then looked at Paul. "How is your daughter's name spelled?" Paul spelled Kendra's name and the woman typed it, waited, and then typed again.

"Spell again, please?" she asked.

Paul repeated it more slowly. The woman typed a third time and shook her head, then spoke to the orderly. He looked concerned as he relayed to the Hodges. "She is not finding a patient named Kendra."

"This is the same thing I was told on the phone before we flew here, and it's ridiculous! How do you people run a hospital when you can't keep track of your patients?"

"Joanne, just calm down. Berating them isn't going to help us locate Kendra."

"I will NOT calm down. I will search every room in this hospital if I have to. If they can't find my daughter, then I will!"

"I think they would have found her by now if she was here. Perhaps she was moved to another hospital."

"I was told she was brought here."

"I know, dear. But they could've moved her since then, and that would explain why they can't seem to find what room she's in." Paul turned to the orderly. "Is there a way you can search the records for recent patients who have been transferred?"

The orderly spoke to the receptionist who tapped her keyboard again and her face lit up and she spoke rapidly to the young man. He turned back to Joanne and Paul and said, "You were correct, sir. She was transferred by American military ambulance two days ago."

"Does it say where she was taken?"

After another exchange in Arabic, he wrote down an address and handed it to Paul. "This is the address for the base that came for her."

"Thank you very much. Could you call us a taxi?"

Paul tried unsuccessfully to convince Joanne to wait until they had gotten a motel room before attempting to track down Kendra. They needed some sleep first. But she was insistent on going to the base immediately. Nothing as simple as jet-lag or lack of sleep or nutrition was going to keep her from finding her daughter.

Because it was so late, an hour passed before a taxi pulled in to the patient drop-off area, driven by a sleepy Iraqi. Once in the backseat, Paul handed the driver the piece of paper with the address written on it and the driver opened his mouth to say something, then stopped himself, shaking his head in apparent resignation. He tapped the paper, saying, "I will take you close. You walk to reach barricade."

"Can we pay you to wait? We'll need to get a hotel room after a brief visit to this address."

The driver said he would wait for 20 *dinar* an hour. Paul agreed without asking how much that was going to cost him in U.S. dollars. The cab driver turned around, smiling as he put the car in gear and headed toward the military base.

When the taxi came to a stop, the driver pointed toward the military guards at the entrance of a U.S. Forward Operating Base. He assured them he would wait, and surprised Paul by not asking for any cash in advance. Joanne was so glad to be close to finding her daughter, she didn't ask why they had to walk the last block. She suddenly stopped walking, causing Paul's arm to yank him backwards as Joanne gripped it tightly.

"Why are they pointing guns at us?" she asked, suddenly terrified.

"I'm sure it's just a precaution," Paul reassured her.

"But we're Americans!"

"Honey, they don't know what we are. They're just doing their jobs. In fact, I think it would be a good idea of we removed our coats so they can see from a distance that we're not concealing anything."

"I don't understand, Paul. What would we possibly be concealing?"

"Just hand me your coat, dear. I'm tired. I'll explain later."

Joanne did as she was asked, and the two approached the armed sentries. Paul spread his arms out to show that he was unarmed and had nothing strapped to his chest. A soldier came forward and patted down both of them while other soldiers kept their rifles trained on them.

"Paul...," Joanne started to object, but was hushed by her husband with a stern look telling her to just comply and keep quiet.

After Paul explained the reason for their visit, one of the soldiers escorted them to a building where Paul repeated the story of how they were trying to locate their lost, injured daughter. They were led to a large room that could have served as a dining hall or a conference room. There were tables and chairs, but little else.

Thirty-five minutes later, a military officer arrived and gave them the information they'd been waiting for. Kendra had been transferred to the Al-Salam Palace along with the other reporter injured in the attack.

Joanne interrupted the officer to ask why her daughter was taken to a palace. "Does that mean she's out of the coma?"

"I know nothing about her medical condition, ma'am. I'm sorry. She was taken to Al-Salam for safe transport to the airport via the subterranean tunnel below the palace."

"Why would they be taking our daughter to the airport? She needs to be in a hospital," Joanne said, desperately trying to make sense of the information the soldier was providing.

"That's why she'd be going to the airport, ma'am. So she could board a U.S. military flight to the U.S. where she can get the best medical care in the world."

"Can you tell us exactly where she is now, Corporal? I don't blame you, but it feels like we're on somewhat of a scavenger hunt to find our gravely wounded daughter and we're not sure where to go from here."

"I'm sorry, sir. I can imagine how difficult this must be for you. I was going to say that after transport to the palace, she would've gone to the U.S. on the next flight capable of providing her medical assistance en route, and she'd be state-side by now in either Walter Reed MMC, or if she had her own medical insurance, she could be in a hospital on her plan. Again, I wish I could be more specific, but there are too many variables, and this is an unfortunately unique experience where a civilian was wounded, but aided by the U.S. Army due to the nature of the incident."

Paul stood up and reached for Joanne's arm. "Thank you, Corporal. You've been very helpful."

"He has?" Joanne asked, tired and confused, and still uncertain about Kendra's whereabouts.

"Come along, Joanne," Paul said gently, walking his wife out of the room and back through the series of halls to where they had entered the complex, and then back to their taxi which was dutifully still waiting.

"Thank you for waiting," Paul said to the driver. "Please take us to a good hotel near the airport."

On the way there, Paul explained to Joanne that after they slept, she would need to call the Associated Press and find out who they used for employee medical coverage, then make another call to the insurance provider. Then they would find out where Kendra was. He didn't add that all of this should have been done before they'd ever gotten on a plane.

Thirty

When visiting hours came to an end, Keith reluctantly left Kendra, holding her hand, kissing her cheek and telling her that he would be back in the morning. He drove home slowly with his mind blank and his emotions in freefall.

Spending time in the presence of Kendra's broken and nearly lifeless body was emotionally devastating to him. He felt utterly depressed and had no information from which he could summon some hope that she would get better; that they would be together again.

And yet, he had been spending time with her every day. When he saw her in the non-physical realm, wherever or whatever that was – he couldn't believe that wasn't somehow more real than sitting next to her in the hospital. He gave up thinking about it. His mind was too tired and drained, and it was all so strange. He just drove, focusing on the road. Exhaustion and hunger settled over him as he pulled into his driveway.

He barely acknowledged Laci and her excitement when he walked in, and he forgot to let her out after verifying that she had sufficient food and water. He made a quick and easy dinner of a peanut-butter and jelly sandwich and ate it while sitting in his recliner, staring at the television without bothering to turn it on. The more he ate, the more tired he felt. More specifically, he felt like he was sinking, or as though something was pulling him downward and inward.

He put the last bite of his sandwich in his mouth and pushed the recliner back all the way, raising his feet to a more comfortable position. He closed his eyes and felt himself sinking into the center of his own being.

Almost immediately, he found himself in a dimly lit space. He couldn't see anything but he felt as if he was in a room with a table and two chairs. Kendra was in the room with him, but he couldn't see her.

"Finally!" she said. "I've been calling you."

"You have? I didn't hear anything."

"Well, not *calling* calling, but, I don't know how else to put it – like pulling at you sort of; trying to reach you. And now you're here." He could feel her smiling but still couldn't see her.

"Why can't I see you?"

"I don't know. I can see you just fine. We're sitting in a place like an interview room. It's pretty drab, but I haven't tried to change it. Do you want me to?"

"I don't see anything anyway. It doesn't matter. Maybe it's because my mind is in turmoil about a lot of things. There's so much I don't understand about what's going on. I spent the day with you at the hospital and it didn't feel like I was with you at all."

"I wasn't there until just a while ago. I was watching my parents. They're in Iraq." There was a sad tone in Kendra's voice when she said this.

"I tried to tell them not to go."

"When my mother is on a mission, there's no getting through to her. My dad is so patient and loves her so much. She'd drive anyone else crazy."

"Are you able to meet with them the way we do? Can you talk to them?"

"No. I can't reach them at all."

Keith's surroundings started to morph from a hazy grey smoky place into the vague shadings of a room with sofas and possibly a tall plant in the corner. He could see Kendra sitting in a comfortable chair, but she was like a silhouette; an outline of herself.

"I was wondering something. Do you spend time in your body? You know, like the way you were before the bombing?"

"I went into it once when I realized I was outside of it and it was terrible. I couldn't see, hear or feel anything. It felt like being buried alive, like I was in a casket underground. I feel much better like this, outside of it and free."

"Do you see or talk to anyone else?"

"Right after the explosion, I saw an Arab boy… the one who wore the bomb. We were both in the air looking down at the horrible scene below us. I can't tell you how awful it was. It was the worst thing I've ever seen."

"Did you talk to him? Ask him why he did it?"

"No. But I know why he did it. He was angry and getting revenge for the girl he loved who was killed by our military."

"How do you know that?"

"I could feel his feelings. They were just pouring out of him. He was looking down at the people who were blown apart with pieces of their bodies scattered in front of the hotel; there was blood splattered all over the vans and the walls. He was horrified by what he'd done and didn't understand why he didn't feel the satisfaction he'd expected to feel. Then he left to find his lover and I followed him. We crossed over to a different place; I don't know what to call it, but he was going to where she was, but she didn't want him there. She repelled him somehow. It's like there was a force-field he couldn't get through to reach where she was, so he went past that place and kept going somewhere else, and I didn't like the feeling. It was dark. That's when I stopped following him. I couldn't go back to the hotel. It was too terrible. The next thing I remember is sitting on the island where you found me."

"I'm so sorry, Kendra. Do you have any idea what will happen next? Can you tell if you're going to get better?"

"I don't think so, Keith. My body feels like a car with no battery. I couldn't feel anything when I was in it. I think the brain functions like a circuit board and I provide the electricity, and I'm the driver, and I can't plug in to it. I can't do anything. I think it's dead and the doctors are only making air go in and out of it - keeping it alive artificially."

"Can you leave here – this whole place and go on, like through a tunnel or something? Is there anything like a white light beckoning you like you hear about when people die?"

"Not that I know of. I feel that there's something out there somewhere, like a place I can go, but it's like I can't go there yet. There's no… I don't know how to say it… no path or doorway for me to reach it. Like it's on the other side of a river and I don't see a bridge anywhere; no way to cross over."

"Okay. So you're really you, and this isn't my imagination at all."

"The only part that's imagination is what we see. I'm really me, Keith. You should know you're not imagining me."

"I know. It's just so strange that my mind has a hard time accepting everything at face value. And it's so hard to experience losing you, but I haven't lost you yet. It's all kinda crazy in my head."

She became clearly visible then, looking into his eyes with love and sadness. They were sitting on a loveseat. He took one of her hands in his and held her, cherishing the feeling. He closed his eyes and let his mind focus entirely on the warm softness of her skin. Just being able to hold her hand felt incredible. His eyes filled with tears as he asked a question he was afraid to hear the answer to.

"Do you need to be able to go?" She knew what he meant. He wasn't referring to her leaving the room where they were.

"I don't feel like I need to, but I probably should just because I'm stuck between two worlds. There's one that I think I'm supposed to go to, but I can't find the way there, and then there's the one where you are, but I can't really be there either, except like this. I just drift around most of the time, lost and alone, until you come to me. Then I'm happy again. I don't want to leave you, Keith. Not until I know where it is I'm supposed to go."

"So there's somewhere you need to go to, but maybe the time isn't right yet?"

"Something like that, yes. That's how it feels to me."

"When the time is right, will you be able to go if they're still keeping your body alive with machines?"

"I don't know. What do you mean?"

"I'm just wondering if your body being alive is keeping you from moving on."

"It might be, but I'm not sure. Are you saying that if I died, then I'd be able to see my way to where I'm supposed to go?"

"That's what I'm wondering. Maybe your connection to your body is holding you back. Or will the way become clear when the time is right, whether your body is alive or not?"

"I have no idea. I just feel the need to be with you.

"If I could, I'd stay asleep forever to be with you always."

Thirty-one

Joanne woke up before Paul did and quietly got dressed. She did her hair without showering and got made up for the day. She took the elevator down to the lobby for breakfast and coffee in the hotel dining area. She put some fresh fruit on a plate and poured coffee, then sat at a small table with a fresh flower in a small white vase. When she set her purse in the empty chair to her right, it opened and she saw her cell phone. She hadn't touched it since silencing it at the airport.

She pulled out her phone and unlocked the screen, looking at how many missed calls and voicemail messages she had. She listened to her messages, holding her phone in one hand, and feeding herself pineapple slices with the other. The oldest message was from Keith.

"Joanne. Don't get on the plane! Kendra is here. I hope you haven't left yet. Call me."

"Oh dear," she thought and started to cry in frustration and regret. She wished she had listened to Keith when he came to their house as they were leaving for the airport. They could be with Kendra right now. But how did he know? Who told him, but didn't tell her? She dabbed at her eyes with a napkin she pulled from a metal dispenser beside the vase. It wouldn't do any good to tell Paul about this.

After she ate and finished drinking a cup of coffee, Joanne called the Associated Press, but it was just after midnight in the States so she could only leave a message at the number she had. She figured there was probably a hotline staffed twenty-four hours a day since news wasn't limited to business hours and every news agency wanted to be the first to break a big story, but rather than trying to discover such a number, she decided it would be easier to call Keith. He already knew that Kendra was there, so he could tell her everything she needed to know.

Keith was lying on a blanket in a meadow with Kendra when the sound of a phone ringing came from a picnic basket sitting a few feet away. He let go of her hand, sat up, and crawled forward. He looked inside the basket and it was empty but he could still hear the phone. He opened his eyes and saw his phone sitting on the coffee table in front of him. He pushed down with his feet on the footrest, bringing the seat into an upright position and grabbed his phone.

"Hello?" he said, after tapping Answer and then the speaker icon.

"Keith, this is Joanne. I'm sorry if I woke you."

"It's fine. Where are you?"

"We're in Baghdad. I should've listened to you. I'm sorry that I didn't."

"It's okay," he said, trying not to yawn.

"Where is Kendra? Have you seen her?"

"She's at St. Joan's. I was with her all day today."

"You were? How is she? Is she getting better?"

"She's the same. Still in a coma."

"Were you able to find out how long it will be until she wakes up?"

"Her doctor wasn't there, but he's supposed to be back in the morning. I had to say I was her brother so I could get in to see her. Don't tell them who I am when you visit."

"I won't tell them anything, Keith. Paul and I will be on the first flight back. Please let us know if anything changes, or when she wakes up."

"Okay. Sure." He yawned into the phone. "Sorry."

"I'll call you when we land. Thanks for being there for my baby." Joanne started to cry. "Goodbye, Keith."

Keith was still tired, but after going to his room and trying to sleep, he found that he couldn't. The conversation with Kendra answered some of his questions, but also spawned new ones. What happened after a person died? Where did they go? What was in between that place and where the living were? What about out-of-body experiences? How was he able to meet with her? Were OBEs known to occur with other comatose people? Had others met with comatose people the way he'd been doing with Kendra?

He felt like there was a whole world sitting right there on top of the one he lived in but he had known nothing about it his entire life. Sleeping was impossible so he got up and went to his computer and tried to find answers to some of the questions swirling around in his agitated mind.

After a few hours, he concluded that although there wasn't, and could not be any authority on the subject, there was definitely a culture of people who were quite familiar with the types of things he'd been experiencing. He couldn't find anyone who had regular out-of-body visits with someone in a coma, but there were plenty of people who claimed to regularly leave their bodies, and some of them met with others who were doing the same thing at the same time.

He found discussion groups on Yahoo devoted to the subjects of astral projecting, lucid-dreaming, and OBEs. There were plenty of books available on Amazon and Barnes & Noble on the same topics. He learned of a school in New York called the Monroe Institute that had been there since the 1970s when the founder wrote a book about his experiences, coining the term "out-of-body" to describe what occurred with him spontaneously in the late 1950s.

Keith went from knowing almost nothing, to becoming overwhelmed with the enormous quantity of data on the subject. He ordered Monroe's first book, "Adventures Beyond the Body" from Amazon because he seemed like the most analytical author on the subject, and the least New Age. He was just a regular business-man involved in radio, and then later, cable TV. He had no religious background or interest in religion, and he had approached his own experiences with skepticism and kept notes on his experiments and research.

That's all Keith wanted – to learn facts as much as possible. He didn't want to dive headfirst into a field of esoterica and read about Light-Workers and Indigo Children and raising humanity's consciousness, etc. He had never known there was a huge metaphysical culture thriving in America. He wondered if it was a by-product of the psychedelic era. The amount of information and people claiming to have knowledge was overwhelming, so he resolved to just wait for the book from Monroe and let that be a stable point from which to start his education.

The most interesting thing he'd discovered was that there were those who worked for years on having out-of-body experiences, and then there were a lesser few, like himself and Monroe who had experienced them spontaneously and didn't know what was happening. He wondered why that was, and thought about it a little as he got back in bed and drifted right to sleep.

Thirty-two

When Keith fell asleep, Kendra was there and waiting. She had watched him focusing intently on his computer, so she did not try to pull him to her. In the times when she did pull, he felt it as a sinking, tired feeling. It made him think of lying down and closing his eyes, which he associated with sleep. As soon as she saw that he had fallen asleep, she took his hands in hers and pulled him out of his body.

"Wow. What was that?" he asked her. They were still in his room where his body was sound asleep. He was in his sparkling energy body and she was too.

"I was impatient," she said, giggling. "I couldn't wait for you to come out, and I didn't want to wait until you dreamed. So I just came and got you." She looked at him like she had done something bad but fun.

"What are you so happy about?" he asked, smiling at her infectious good mood.

"After we talked, I wanted to clear my mind so I went to the ocean."

"And…?" he asked, watching her swirl around him.

"I swam with dolphins. They can see me!"

"Wow. That's great. I don't suppose they could talk to you too."

"Not exactly. Let's go someplace fun," she said, and grabbed his hand before shooting up through the ceiling and flying over the tree-tops.

"What does that mean, 'not exactly'?" he asked.

"I can feel their intentions and desires, but not words. So there's communication, but it's not with words. I'll show you…"

Everything around them turned white and fuzzy. When Keith's vision cleared, he was looking at the calm sea with a full moon shining brightly. They were standing on what he now thought of as Kendra's Island. She was slowly turning in a circle and concentrating.

"Are you –"

"Shhhh."

"They're here. Come with me," she said, diving into the water. Keith followed her with his arms stretched out before him as if he were flying like Superman. He did nothing to propel himself forward through the water; he just intended forward motion.

Kendra was much more dramatic, swimming with an undulating motion, occasionally aiming upward, breaking the surface of the water, flying several feet into the air and arching back down with a splash. Keith realized she was acting just like a dolphin. He began swimming the same way she was and doing the same air jumps.

They swam side by side, jumping together and splashing back into the water with perfect timing.

He felt the water move him forward from behind and looked back to see a team of dolphins following them. When he and Kendra flipped into the air, the dolphins did it too; all of them creating a huge splash as they came down together.

After a few minutes, Kendra stopped swimming and climbed on to the back of a dolphin. Another one swam slowly below Keith and stopped. He felt what she had described earlier about their communication; the dolphin wanted Keith to get on. He willed himself to sink down further in the water and straddled the dolphin.

She grabbed onto the dorsal fin of the dolphin she was riding and looked at Keith. He did the same and both dolphins immediately surged forward like torpedoes, gaining speed as they went. After increasing speed, the two dolphins swam upwards until Keith and Kendra were above the water, side by side. They felt themselves turning in a wide arc as the dolphins made a U-turn and headed back in the other direction. Up ahead of them, they saw the rest of the pod floating in the water, lined up in a row, two dolphins wide.

Their speed increased and suddenly they were in the air flying over the dolphins lined up beneath them. When they splashed down, the pod broke the obstacle formation and took off to setup another stunt. They continued playing for a few hours, constantly amazed at the ingenuity of the dolphins and the games they created. The dolphins communicated that they needed rest and food. Kendra thanked them and kissed the head of the one she'd been riding and they rode off, leaving their passengers close to the island.

They swam to the island then walked along the sand together holding hands until Kendra stopped in the spot she liked best. Keith's mind and energy were still racing from the exhilarating joy of playing with the dolphins. They sat together, smiling at each other, still in energy-thought form.

"Keith, think of your physical body. Not the one in bed, but think of yourself as physical. Concentrate on it. Okay?"

He did as she asked while she did the same thing. They began to morph into their physical selves, slowly taking on the appearance of being solid as they had been the day before in his car and on the beach. He opened his eyes to see her smiling at him.

"Did you have something in mind involving our bodies?" he asked.

"Yeah. I want to get physical with you," she said, and moved forward to kiss him with extreme passion, pushing him backwards onto the sand.

Neither of them had thought of clothing when they summoned their bodies, so they weren't wearing anything when they became physical. The pleasure and excitement from playing with the pod blended into a new and equally exciting pleasure as they kissed, touched, and made love in the moonlight for hours. Every touch was an expression of love and devotion. They had never been happier together.

"This is so amazing. We should be exhausted after everything we've done tonight, but I feel like I have unlimited energy," Keith said. They were lying on their sides in the sand facing each other.

"I know what you mean. But I never get tired."

"Why is the sand so soft?"

Kendra laughed. "Because it's marshmallow sand," she said, and laughed some more.

Keith pushed his finger down on the sand and it sunk down to the knuckle. He thought for a few seconds, then smiled and got up. He walked over to a palm tree and grabbed something, then did the same thing at another tree, then came back to her carrying graham crackers and Hershey bars. Scooping up some of the sand, he made S'Mores for each of them.

Kendra laughed as she ate the deliciously sweet treat. "You're not hungry, are you?"

"No," he said. "I just wanted to see if I could do that. It seems that we can do anything. Like we're only limited by our own imagination."

"You're right. I've had a lot of time to experiment and see what's possible. I can do anything I can think of."

"I have an idea," he said, then closed his eyes and concentrated.

Kendra watched as the shape and appearance of Keith began to dissolve and then a dog appeared where he was.

"How do I look?" the dog asked her.

"Like a silly dog that a child might draw," she said, bursting out in laughter. "With crayons," she added, barely able to speak, she was laughing so hard.

The dog closed its eyes and evaporated, then the energy form of Keith appeared. He looked down at himself and said, "I cleared my mind completely. Now look at me. This must be what we really look like when we're not assuming an identity based on what we perceive ourselves to be."

"Could you turn physical again? I want to do something."

"Again?" he looked at her, grinning. He reappeared as his physical self. "Okay, what?"

She moved close and kissed him.

"That's what," she said smiling at him. "Watch this." She took the remainder of the S'More she was eating and threw it upward into the air where it became a dove and flew away.

"Wow. You really have had time to experiment. This is so much more fun than 'real life.' This might sound crazy, but if I could get myself into a coma somehow, I would. Then I could be with you all the time. Isn't this better than our normal lives?"

"It's great when *you're* here. But I only get to be with you for a while. Then you wake up and I'm totally alone again."

"I'm sorry. I'd stay if I could. You know I always want to be with you. When I wake up, I'll go straight to the hospital."

Kendra frowned at him. "You don't need to do that. It doesn't do anything for me."

"I guess not. I just feel in my awake life that I should be there for you."

"You should be. But I'm here."

"I think I can be here when I'm awake too. I'm going to try something today. I won't go to the hospital when I wake up. There are people who know how to deliberately go out of their bodies without going to sleep. I should be able to do it too."

"But what about your job?"

"I'm on a leave of absence. Ronald knows you're in the hospital and said I could take as much time as I need."

"Keith, will you hold me?"

"Okay, but only for eternity. After that, I've got some errands to run."

She laughed and they wrapped their arms around each other, feeling their love for each other magnified by the physical pleasure of embracing each other.

Thirty-three

Keith woke up when Laci barked at the mailman walking up to their porch. Ordinarily, Laci barking at the mailman was something that irritated Keith. He thought it was stupid that she seemed incapable of learning that the mailman was not a threat to his or her safety. Laci was able to recognize the sound of his car approaching from down the street. Why couldn't she recognize that the mailman did nothing day after day but put envelopes in their mailbox?

But this time, he woke up from her barking and realized why she was doing it. It was an act of love. She was alerting him and protecting him. In Laci's mind this was Keith and Kendra's house and anyone who wasn't a known friend or brought inside by Keith or Kendra did not belong on the porch.

"Good girl!" Keith said, getting up from the couch. He brought in the mail, then went to the kitchen and made coffee, feeling better than he could ever remember. After walking the dog and showering, he spent the first part of the day running errands, paying bills, buying groceries and then finally mowing his lawn.

After his second shower, he decided he would try to meet with Kendra deliberately. He didn't feel the sinking-pulling feeling that usually preceded a visit with her, but he thought it was worth trying. He'd been seeing her every time he fell asleep, so maybe it would be possible by just getting into a relaxed, almost-asleep state.

After lying down, he had to calm himself because he was excited at the possibility of it actually working. He engaged in simple breathing-relaxation exercises then proceeded to the more advanced relaxation technique where he visualized every muscle in his body relaxing, becoming limp and practically melting, while maintaining an alert mind. After completing the process twice, his body was completely relaxed and he concentrated on keeping his mind focused so he didn't fall asleep

After a minute of maintaining the relaxed state he was in, he started to feel the vibrations. He marveled at the fact that he could feel it everywhere, but nowhere specific. It even felt like his mind was subject to the strange warbling feeling. He lay there keeping his mind free of distracting thoughts so he didn't lose the feeling and waited for something to happen, but nothing did. After a few minutes he felt the vibrations subsiding and fading away, leaving him lying there awake and relaxed as if he had just decided to take a break and do nothing for a while. He wasn't even tired from all of the running around he'd done that day.

Since he hadn't been to work in a week and his next check was going to reflect his absence, he got up and logged in to his company's payroll system where he scheduled all three weeks of paid vacation he had coming to him. He had bills scheduled for auto-payment and he'd rather use money from work to cover them than dipping into his savings or investment funds. He didn't know what he'd do after completing that task. He wanted to spend all the time that he possibly could with Kendra. Since he couldn't reach her in the non-physical plane, he decided he'd go sit with her in the hospital.

He suddenly remembered that he had planned on going to the hospital that morning to speak to her doctor. But since Kendra said his presence with her physical body gave her no comfort, he had completely forgotten to go. He still didn't know her official prognosis or her chances of recovery and returning to a normal life. It was late in the day, but he figured it wouldn't hurt to try seeing her doctor.

He took care of Laci's needs, then went out to his car. When he turned the key and started the engine, fatigue descended on him. Instead of putting the car in reverse, he waited a few seconds for the feeling to pass. It didn't pass. The feeling intensified and he suddenly felt exhausted.

"I've got to lie down. I feel like I'm going to pass out," he said to himself.

He turned off the car and went back inside and lay down on his bed after taking off his shoes. He closed his eyes and focused his concentration on the tired feeling. It felt like it was coming from a single spot, like a core of exhaustion that was spreading fatigue over his body like radiation.

As he focused on the source of the feeling, he felt himself sinking downward and inward. The vibrations hit him hard and fast and he felt himself pulled forward and upward. In an instant he was standing in front of Kendra who was smiling at him, so happy to see him, as usual.

"Did you do that?"

"Yes. You were about to drive to the hospital and I'd much rather have you here with me than there with my body."

"But I tried to get to you a little while ago. Why didn't you help me then?"

"Because you were trying to do it by yourself, so I just watched. After that, you were busy on your computer, so I just waited." She encircled him with her energy. "I missed you." He felt her love all around him like a force field.

"I always miss you, Kendra. I love you so much."

"I love you too. I'm so glad we can be together like this but I really wish I could hold you for real." The brightness of her energy dimmed slightly.

"Hey! Your parents are coming back. We should find out soon from your doctor how you're doing and when you'll get better."

"I'm not going to get better, Keith." Now her energy was even darker, like pinpoint lights running on weak batteries.

"Don't say that! You don't know that you won't get better."

"I want to show you something." She moved out of the room slowly and gradually increased her speed as Keith followed and kept pace with her. They flew over the city for a few minutes before Keith finally got impatient. Usually when they wanted to go somewhere, they either flew fast, or instantly translocated.

"Where are we going?"

"I'm looking for something. It's not easy to find, but I'll know it when I see it."

She slowly increased their speed and continued scanning the houses below them for a few more minutes, then finally said, "There!" and dove downward, went through a rooftop and into a house, coming to a stop in a bedroom. There was a young woman sleeping in the bed.

Keith whispered, "What are we doing here?"

"This person is out of her body. Try getting into it."

"What!?"

"Just lay down on top of her body and try to meld into it as if it was your own body."

"I'm not going to do that!"

"Keith, even if you tried, you couldn't. Watch."

Kendra's energy body tilted with her head going back and down and her feet rising up until she was floating horizontally. She drifted to the side until she was floating above the body of the young woman then started lowering herself. She came within inches of the body and stopped. The light energy on the bottom side began to glow a yellowish-white and she rose up a few inches away from the body.

"See? I can't get in. I really wish you would try it so I can demonstrate something to you."

"It feels wrong, Kendra, like trying to possess someone, or something. I don't even like the thought of it, but if it's what you want, I'll do it."

She moved out of the way and went back to standing beside the bed.

"How do I do it?" he asked.

"Just visualize yourself in the position you want to be in, then see yourself going where you want to go. It's sort of like the way you turn when you're in the air. Like when you jump on a trampoline – how do you turn your body? You just intend it and your body does it. Think of it like that."

Keith imagined himself floating horizontally the way he'd seen Kendra floating and nothing happened. Then he intended for his body to move into the position and he slowly started moving. He smiled at his success and understanding of what she meant. Once he was horizontal, he imagined himself floating to the left over the bed and he slowly positioned himself where he wanted to be.

"Now just think of yourself lowering," Kendra advised.

He started to lower himself and felt something stopping him similar to how it would feel if he was pushing one magnet toward another and unable to overcome the resistance. There was a force, but it felt natural and buoyant. He moved back over the floor and tilted himself back into an upright position.

"Okay. I felt the resistance. I couldn't descend no matter how hard I tried. She softly but firmly pushed me back up."

"Right. Now come and see this…" She took off and Keith had to focus on her to find her. He found himself standing in her hospital room a few seconds later. "Now try lowering into my body."

Keith hesitated, still not liking the idea of inhabiting any body but his own, but Kendra stood there looking at him and waiting.

"Okay," he said, resigning himself to her wishes. He didn't see the point, but if it was important to her, then it was important to him. He repeated the steps from a moment ago, turning horizontal, floating over the bed and then slowly descending toward the body beneath him.

A few seconds later, he lost all of his awareness of the room. He could no longer see anything or even sense Kendra standing near him. He felt nothing and he heard nothing. He felt claustrophobic and started to panic. He jolted himself out of Kendra's body and continued flying in the direction he was facing.

"Keith!" Kendra shouted, flying beside him.

He snapped out of his panic and stopped moving. Everything around him was black except for the sparkling shape of Kendra. "What happened?"

"Well, you went into my body and you felt how terrible it is to be inside it. Let's go to the island and talk."

The darkness around them took on shape, lighting and color; all of it subtle. They heard the sound of the ocean swells washing up on the sand. A crescent moon shined brightly in the starry sky.

"This is much better. Thank you." Keith was relieved to be in the peaceful setting of Kendra's Island. He was still shaken by the few seconds he had spent inside her comatose body. "So what did you want me to see – that being in a coma totally sucks?"

"Well, not exactly," she said, shifting her form so that she appeared to have physical density. She made herself appear in a purple bikini and she started a sunrise with warm morning rays bathing the island. Keith saw her transformation and did the same. He became solid in appearance with a pair of cut-off shorts. "I wanted you to see how you normally can't get into a person's body."

"Why not? I mean, not that I ever want to, but what stopped us?"

"I don't know. I just tried it one night out of curiosity because I could see that the person wasn't there. But I couldn't get in. It's like something protects our bodies. I think we leave behind part of our energy so the body is still technically occupied, but it just doesn't look like it is because the greater part of our energy is absent."

"Okay. That makes sense. But then why was I able to get into your body at the hospital?"

"Because there's no part of me left behind. I'm fully out and… I don't know – disconnected or something. It's like a dead shell that isn't mine anymore. There's nothing protecting my body from being inhabited by anybody at all."

"So what does that mean?"

"I think it means I'm dead," she said sadly.

"But you're clearly not dead. Your heart is still beating and you're breathing and everything."

"Yeah, but machines are making that happen. I think I'm being mechanically kept alive, so really, I'm out of the game. There's no connection between me and my body. You felt it. Didn't it feel dead to you?"

"I don't know what a dead body feels like, but yeah, I imagine that's exactly what it would be like. It's like every sensory input device I have was suddenly shut off. It freaked me out."

"Now you really understand why I have no desire to be in it and why I was so upset when you first found me here." Kendra looked down at the sand and dragged her fingers around drawing parallel lines in a circle.

"Come here," Keith said, reaching out and putting his arms around her.

They lay side by side feeling their love for each other and their sadness at the realization that she wasn't coming back to her normal life. They stayed that way for hours until once again Keith was called back by his ringing cell phone.

Thirty-four

Keith reached for his phone while his mind was still half in both worlds. He felt the tactile sensation of the cell phone in his hand while feeling the deep soul-satisfying pleasure of being close to Kendra. He opened his eyes and looked at his phone and read the words Missed Call.

It's just as well, he thought. *I hate talking to someone when my mind isn't awake.* But the call he missed was from Joanne, so he wanted to wake his mind up and call her back. She wasn't going to believe the news he had for her. His phone chimed to let him know he had a new voicemail message. He hit Play.

"Keith, this is Joanne and Paul. We just came from talking to Kendra's doctor. We need to speak with you urgently. We're going to Outback on Riverside. Meet us there if you can."

Outback? Are they celebrating good news? He touched the link for SMS/Text and typed "omw" and pressed the send icon. He was tempted to call so he could find out immediately what they wanted to talk to him about but he didn't want to be on the phone while driving there, plus Joanne had said "they" wanted to talk to him, so he didn't want to leave Paul out of the conversation by having it on a phone.

Keith told Laci he'd be back in a while as he headed out to his car. He drove quickly to the restaurant and told the greeter at the door that he was meeting with someone. She asked the name of his party and he said Hodges. The young lady escorted him to a table where Paul was sitting by himself.

"Hi Paul. Where's Joanne?"

"She's gone to the restroom. She'll be right back."

Keith was tempted to say, "So she won't be staying in there all night?" Of course people came right back from the restroom. What else would they do? But he just said, "Okay," and took a seat opposite Paul. He was anxious to learn what the urgent matter was, but did his best to engage in small talk as they waited.

"How are you two doing?" he asked.

Paul took a deep breath and looked away for a few seconds.

"Not well, Keith. This is very hard on both of us."

"I know what you mean. But I might be able to help a little with some good news. I'm hoping you have good news too."

Paul didn't respond other than to look at Keith like he was speaking a foreign language. Clearly there was nothing good about what had happened to Kendra. Keith tapped his fingers on the top of the table and looked around the restaurant at families and couples. Everyone but he and Paul seemed to be enjoying themselves and having a good time. Paul looked up with interest as Joanne approached.

Keith turned and saw her. She looked like she'd been crying. Her eyes were puffy and her eye makeup looked as if it had been recently repaired, but not very well. Paul scooted over and Joanne sat beside him.

"Thank you for coming, Keith. I know this is a bit unusual, especially under the circumstances but we've had nothing but airplane food and a continental breakfast for the last few days and we're starved."

Under the circumstances? Maybe they didn't have good news to announce. "So you saw Kendra's doctor?"

Paul looked at Joanne, letting her take over and relieved that she was back to do so. He and Keith got along okay, but rarely had much to say to each other beyond simple greetings and talk about the weather.

"Well, it wasn't her actual doctor; it was a Physician's Assistant named Dr. Harper, but that's not her *name* of course, and I suppose it's not even her proper title if she's an assistant."

Keith wanted to shout, *Who cares about the doctor's name - just get to the point!*

"Okay," he said, maintaining a neutral but interested and patient expression.

"Whatever she is, Dr. Harper said that Kendra's doctor, whose name is Davenport, is reluctant to be optimistic about her prognosis. Her score on the coma scale from Glasgow is a three, and that's apparently as low as it can be."

Joanne pursed her lips and pulled a tissue out of her purse sitting beside her. She held the tissue in her hands, folding, turning and unfolding it. Keith waited for her to continue, trying to be patient as she got to the point. He looked at her, urging her with his eyes to go on.

"With her bad scores and her imaging results, which show extensive trauma to her cerebral cortex…" Joanne looked as though she was trying very hard to recall the words used by Dr. Harper. "They think—"

"Are you folks ready to order, or would you like a few more minutes?" a cheerful server asked from beside their table, startling all of them with her silent approach.

Paul looked at Joanne for an answer. Joanne told the server they needed a few more minutes and dabbed at the corner of her eyes with the tissue.

"Okay, I'll come back in a few minutes," she said with less enthusiasm as she saw that the three of them were not having a happy conversation and the men barely acknowledged her presence.

"They think…?" Keith attempted to get Joanne back on track now that the server had moved on to assist other guests.

"They think it's very unlikely that Kendra will recover," Joanne said and finally lost the battle for composure that she'd been waging since she had left the women's restroom. "I'm sorry. Excuse me," she said, getting up and heading again to the back of the restaurant.

Keith looked solemn. That wasn't what he was expecting. He thought they had good news. Why did they want to discuss this in a restaurant with the sound of cheerful, happy people all around them? They could've eaten and then come to his house, or invited him to theirs. Or Joanne could've told him this on the phone.

Now he found that he didn't know how to feel. He was definitely saddened by this news, and yet, he knew he'd be seeing Kendra tonight without a doubt after he went to bed. If she didn't recover, he'd never have a truly physical relationship with her, but when they became physical in their meetings, it was indistinguishable from real life. All in all, he figured that he was lucky. He still had Kendra; they just had a very unique relationship now. He was sorry that Paul and Joanne didn't have time with her the way he did, but maybe he could teach them to do what he'd been doing.

"We're going to end it, Keith," Paul said abruptly, interrupting Keith's ruminations.

"End what?"

"Keeping Kendra alive with machinery. She's brain-dead with no hope of recovery, to put it bluntly without all of the medical terminology that Joanne is clinging to. Our daughter is dead." Paul spoke without emotion, except for a trace of anger as far as Keith could tell.

Keith was momentarily in shock when he realized what Paul was saying.

"You can't do that," he blurted. "She's not dead. She's very alive; more than you could possibly know."

"I think they call that denial, son. We all have to accept that Kendra was killed in Iraq. The doctors have only managed to keep her body alive by force-feeding it and pumping air into her lungs, but she's gone."

"But that's what I'm saying – she's *not* gone."

Paul started to say something but stopped when he saw Joanne approaching the table. "Let's not upset Joanne with this kind of talk," he said quickly. Joanne sat down beside Paul once again, and Keith disregarded Paul's stern gaze which implored him to not upset Joanne.

"What I have to say is not upsetting, and it's actually kind of miraculous."

Paul barely moved his head from side to side while glaring at Keith.

"What is it, Keith?"

"It's nothing, Joanne," Paul answered quickly. "I think we should just go home and eat something simple for dinner. This wasn't a good idea after all."

"I agree, Paul. I can't control myself. I thought eating in public would keep my emotions in check, but losing Kendra is just too much. I do want to hear what Keith has to say before we leave though."

"Okay, listen, you guys…" Keith started to say.

"Ah ah ah! I think it can wait until tomorrow. Come on, Joanne," Paul interrupted, sliding toward her to nudge her out of the booth. "I'm exhausted, and whatever Keith wants to say can hold till morning."

Paul continued exerting pressure from his hip onto Joanne's hip and she slid out of the booth and stood up. Paul quickly slid across the seat to join her.

"I've been talking to Kendra," Keith blurted out before Paul could whisk Joanne away. Joanne turned and looked at Keith with her mouth open. It was a few seconds before she could adjust to what Keith had just said.

"I spoke to her too, Keith, but she can't hear us. The doctor said that she has no brain function at all, so sound isn't even reaching her brain. But it can't hurt to talk to her, sweetie."

"I'm not saying that I talked to her comatose body. I've been talking to and hanging out with the real Kendra; the one who used to live inside of her body."

Joanne raised a hand to her mouth. "Oh dear," she said.

"Keith, that's enough!" Paul spat.

"You dear boy. I thought this was hard for me. I never thought about how hard it would be for you. There won't be a marriage or any children…" Joanne burst into tears again.

"Yes, it's sad that we can't do those things, Joanne, but the fact is, at least I still have Kendra. We're together every day. We talk, we kiss, we fly around and go—"

"Oh no," Joanne said, understanding the severity of Keith's grief and the toll it was taking on his sanity. She wanted to reach out to him and help him, but she was struggling with her own feelings of tremendous loss. She was ashamed to admit to herself, but she was glad that she wasn't losing her mind like Keith was. She was surprised that she wasn't. "Paul, Keith needs help. What can we do?"

"You're absolutely right, Joanne. Someone needs to get in touch with his family. Maybe you can call his mother tomorrow when you're feeling better."

"You guys aren't listening to me," Keith protested. "I don't need help and I certainly don't need my mother."

"But she's in Philadelphia, Paul," Joanne continued as if Keith wasn't there beside her. I don't think she can be of much help. I just don't have the strength right now to help him myself, but I've got to. He was going to be our son-in-law." Joanne buried her head in Paul's chest. Paul put on a fake smile for the other diners who were looking at them now as they stood next to their table.

"Let's talk about it tomorrow, dear." Paul pulled Joanne along with him toward the exit without saying goodbye to Keith.

Keith watched them walk away and turned to look at the people who were looking at him. He shrugged his shoulders.

"I don't understand what just happened. I have good news!"

Thirty-five

Keith stayed for dinner and ate a steak and baked potato by himself. Afterwards, he drove home, staying on Riverside Drive rather than getting on the freeway. He followed the path alongside the river and tried to clear his mind. They wouldn't even listen to him. He took a deep breath and blew it out.

The road curved and he looked to his left and saw a riverside restaurant where he and Kendra had their first dinner date. They had sat on the outdoor balcony that overlooked the river and provided a beautiful view of the sunset reflecting on the water.

Not far from there was the pedestrian walkway that crossed the river. He and Kendra had gone there after they ate and they stood in the middle of the bridge with the constant wind blowing their hair as they had their first real kiss.

Keith pulled into the parking lot near the bridge and parked his car. He walked to the steps and climbed them slowly, his mind flooding with images of the last time he had been here with Kendra. Her absence made him sad and he was crying by the time he reached the walkway. He walked to the center of the bridge and stood in their favorite spot. He was glad there was no one in the area. He couldn't stop crying.

He berated himself for feeling grief for her when he knew without a doubt that he would be with Kendra shortly after he got home and fell asleep. *But,* he argued with himself, *I've still lost her in my regular life, and that means I lost one future with her in exchange for another stranger one. I can still cry for what I've lost, even though I haven't lost her completely.*

Then he recalled what Paul had said. *"We're going to end it."* They wanted to take her off life support. Keith was not going to let that happen. They didn't understand. Kendra was alive! If they killed her, she'd probably lose her ability to stay in this realm and meet with him. She'd have to move on to somewhere else. For now, she was in between, and that's where he needed her to stay so he could be with her, and love her.

He would explain everything to Joanne in the morning. She would understand why they couldn't do this to Kendra, and to him. She had to understand. He knew his meetings with Kendra were strange, but they were wonderful too. They were also amazing proof of life after death. He just had to get Joanne alone, or convince Paul that his meetings with Kendra were nothing to get upset about. They should practically be celebrating. For God's sake, how many people had the ability to communicate with someone in a coma? This was a miracle, for all he knew. Maybe it was happening for a reason too. He could tell the world that people lived after they died. He could prove it somehow.

His mind whirled from the possibilities and implications. He focused on the water flowing beneath him to ground himself for a moment. He needed to get home and meet with Kendra. He had a lot to discuss with her. First, he needed Kendra to tell him something that he could use to prove to Paul and Joanne that he wasn't crazy.

— ∞ —

Joanne continued to cry as Paul drove them home. At first she cried for the loss of her daughter. Then she cried for Keith's lost mental health and the future he would have had with Kendra. Then she cried for all that she would have had after Keith and Kendra had gotten married; the wedding, baby showers, grandchildren, family holidays together, birthdays. Now it would continue to just be her and Paul, alone. She had lost her only child and all of the joy she had been looking forward to as her daughter started a family of her own. She was inconsolable.

Later when Paul came to bed after securing the house, checking all of the doors and turning off the lights, she was waiting for him.

"Paul, I think we should wait. The doctors could be wrong about this, and just imagine if they were, and Kendra never had a chance to come back to us. We can't know what God has planned."

Joanne watched Paul carefully line his feet up so that they were lined up evenly before stepping out of his slippers, then he hung his bathrobe on the hook beside the closet. She waited for him to say something. He turned down the bedcovers and got into bed, then covered himself up to his chest and smoothed out wrinkles in the sheet that folded over the outside of the comforter.

"Paul…" Joanne said, making his name into two syllables.

"Joanne, we've had this discussion and we've agreed that if it's medically impossible for her to recover, we're only prolonging the inevitable. Do we really need to go over it again?"

"But what if they're wrong? What if *we're* wrong, Paul?"

He reached over and turned off the lamp on his side of the bed. Joanne's lamp was already off. Moonlight shone through the long blinds on the sliding glass door at the far side of their room, casting striped shadows across the carpet.

"I think the only thing left is to consult Pastor Giddens. The doctors have admitted there's nothing they can do. She's in God's hands now. Let's see what the pastor has to say. Okay, dear?".

"I think that sounds like exactly the right thing to do. With God, all things are possible. If He can raise the dead, raising a poor girl in a coma wouldn't be any trouble at all. And Pastor Giddens can organize a prayer circle. Maybe he can get other congregations across the country to participate. Oh Paul, this is why I love you so much. You always think of the right thing!"

Paul grimaced inside. That wasn't at all what he'd had in mind when he suggested that they let the pastor advise them. He was thinking that the pastor could convince Joanne that it was their

Christian duty to let Kendra go; that she belonged to God now.

He didn't want to entertain the possibility of a miracle bringing his daughter back to him. Doing so would only make dealing with her loss even more difficult than it was already. The only thing crueler than life is false hope, he thought, as he closed his eyes and willed himself to sleep, thus bringing this terrible day to an end.

— ∞ —

Keith tried to think of something that he could ask Kendra so he could bring back her answer as proof that he was really in touch with her. It seemed to him that he already knew everything about her, such as her birthmark, her middle name, her mother's maiden name, where she grew up, her first boyfriend. They talked about everything when they were together. They were best friends as well as lovers. He couldn't think of anything.

He realized that he was the wrong person to even try coming up with something. She would be in a much better position to know what she hadn't told him. He was just spinning wheels, agitated about Paul saying they were going to "end this" as if Kendra was some kind of project, or bad habit. He was utterly unsettled by being informed that his fiancé's life was going to be ended. Who, in the history of man had ever had to deal with such a thing as that? Why did he have to be the first?

The thought of them terminating Kendra's life support filled him with a fearful dread. He'd already lost her once. Now that he had her back, he shouldn't have to be confronted with the threat of losing her again. He had to convince them she was alive. She was here, just as much as they were.

He lay there for a long time thinking about losing Kendra and being frustrated at wanting to see her so badly but not being able to because he was filled with anxiety. He tried his relaxation exercises a few times, but couldn't focus. After a few hours, he was finally tired enough from lying still in a dark room that he began to drift off.

The instant his body fell asleep, Kendra was there, pulling him out of his body and into her arms.

"I'm so scared, Keith. And you were taking forever!"

Keith saw Kendra before him and automatically reached for her, wanting to hold her close. His hands went through her and his body moved into hers. He realized that they were in their astral bodies and he withdrew out of her space, wondering why they didn't feel the over-stimulating charge they'd felt before when they touched in this form.

"Can we switch to physical form? I need to hold you," he said.

"Okay. Where should we go?" Keith felt the sadness emanating from her like heat from a woodstove.

"Can we just stay here?" he asked.

She nodded and closed her eyes. Keith closed his. They both focused on how they perceived themselves as physical beings and they slowly took on their normal appearance, filling in their sparkling energy bodies with solid colors and textures.

They felt the transformation at the same time and opened their eyes together and reached for each other. Kendra immediately began to cry as she held Keith as tightly as she could. Continuous thoughts of re-assurance ran through Keith's head, but he said nothing, holding her silently and wanting to never let her go.

"My parents are going to kill me," she cried, breaking the silence.

"No. They're not. I won't let them." Keith didn't know how he'd stop them, or if he even could, but he spoke from his heart, saying what he felt and what she needed to hear. "No one is going to hurt you."

They were still standing on the bed where she had pulled Keith out of his body. She bent her legs and sat and he joined her, looking into her tear-filled eyes.

"What can we do? What *should* I do? Maybe they're right and I just need to accept that my life is over." She covered her face with her hands and began crying again.

Thirty-six

The doorbell rang and Joanne put down the cinnamon rolls she had just removed from the oven. She quickly removed the oven mitt from her right hand and fluffed her hair as she rushed to answer the door. She turned to the right and glanced at herself in the mirror. Her reflection met with her approval and she pulled the door open.

"Pastor Giddens. Thank you so much for coming. Please, come in."

"Thank you, but please call me Dave."

"You know, you always tell us that, but it just doesn't feel right to call you Dave."

"How about, Pastor Dave, then?" he asked, smiling.

"Okay. Pastor Dave, it is. Please have a seat. I just took some cinnamon buns out of the oven. May I bring you one?"

"That's what that delicious smell is. Yes, I'd love one. Thank you." The pastor stepped over to the couch and sat down. He'd never been to the Hodges' home before. He stood back up when Joanne left the room so he could look more closely at the bookshelf. He was disappointed to see that they had several bibles, but they sat on a bookshelf looking shiny and new. In fact, all of their books looked as if they'd just been purchased.

He sat back down when he heard a cabinet in the kitchen bang shut. A few seconds later, Joanne appeared with a serving tray loaded with two small plates and two small glasses of milk.

"Here you go, Pastor Dave. I hope you like it."

"Oh, I'm sure I will. Thank you very much." He smiled as he reached for the pastry. "Mmm." His smile grew even bigger as he chewed. "This is heavenly."

Joanne blushed and said nothing as she bit into her own.

"Did you make these yourself?"

"Oh, no. I bought them, but I did spruce them up just a little." She was pleasantly surprised to see that the pastor had cleared his small plate already. "Would you care for another?"

"No, but thank you. That was delicious. I try not to indulge too much. Where is Paul? I understood it would be the three of us."

"Paul lost a crown this morning and went to the dentist. I'm hoping he'll be back soon, but there's no way to know, of course."

"I'm sorry to hear that. Would you prefer to get together another time when Paul can be here?"

Joanne glanced at the front door, as if hoping Paul would suddenly come through it, making rescheduling unnecessary. "As much as Paul needs to be a part of this, I just can't put off knowing something that has been eating away at me. Can we talk now, and then maybe again, another time if Paul still wants to?"

"Of course, Joanne. What is it that's eating at you?"

Joanne took a breath and willed herself to be strong and to not break down the instant she began to talk. "It's Kendra," she said, and pursed her lips, doubling her efforts to stifle her emotions.

The pastor reached out and settled a hand on top of hers. "Of course. This is a terrible thing for anyone to go through – and even worse when it involves a child. How can I help?"

Joanne was still winning the battle against her tears but reached for a tissue sticking out of the top of a box on the coffee table in front of her, not entirely confident in her ability to prevail. She closed her eyes and took a deep breath.

"Her doctor says she has no chance of recovery." Her bottom lip trembled as she took a few seconds before continuing. "If we 'keep her alive,' she'll never do more than lie in bed with a machine breathing for her. So, Paul says we need to let her go." Joanne squeezed her eyes shut for a second as she pursed her lips. She opened her eyes and blurted out the rest of her thoughts as though she had to do it before running out of time. "But isn't it possible that with prayer – and maybe with a lot of people praying – that God can do something? Doesn't God grant prayers? 'Ask and ye shall receive,' right? If we ask God for Kendra to be healed, won't we receive that?"

After voicing the thoughts and hopes she hadn't dared say to Paul, she took a deep breath and closed her eyes. She felt tears roll down her cheeks as she resisted the pain in her throat that she would have easily given in to had she been alone. She carefully blotted her cheeks with the tissue, then opened her eyes and looked at the pastor.

"Joanne. With God, all things are possible," he started.

"So she *can* be saved!"

"But not all things are His will. We can't know what He has planned for any one of us. We can only pray, and hope that the things we desire align with His will." Pastor Dave smiled slightly, trying to lighten the blow of his words which he knew were not the ones she wanted to hear.

"Excuse me for just a moment, please?"

"Of course, Joanne."

She got up and walked to the kitchen. She didn't have anything to do there, she just needed a moment by herself to process what the pastor had said. To her way of thinking, it sounded like Pastor Dave was saying that God had a plan, and if you asked Him to do something that He already planned on doing, then He'd do it. But if not, He wouldn't.

This was exactly why she hated getting too deeply into the scriptures. It was too confusing and she didn't like to feel like her mind was stuck in a complicated puzzle. She moved the remaining cinnamon rolls to a serving plate and took the baking sheet over to the sink. She walked back to the island counter in the center of the kitchen and absent-mindedly picked up a roll and started eating it.

As she chewed, she brushed the question out of her mind regarding whether or not God would answer a prayer that didn't align with His divine will. A new question had formed in her mind; one that scared her to think about. But since the pastor was here, and Paul wasn't, this was the perfect time to ask it.

She carefully wiped around her mouth with a paper towel, discarded it, and returned to the living room, determined to ask the question and to not back down. She'd gone too long in life without speaking up and saying what was on her mind. If the fate of her daughter wasn't enough to change that, then nothing was.

"Thank you for waiting, Pastor Dave. I just… needed a moment."

"I understand. And I'm sorry I'm not able to simply tell you that everything will be fine and that Kendra is guaranteed a full recovery just from the power of prayer. That must sound odd coming from someone in my position, but you might know from my sermons that I believe in telling the truth and I don't think mere platitudes are helpful when it comes to something as serious as this."

"I appreciate your honesty, Pastor. I really do. I just have one more question for you." She sat on the couch and smoothed out her slacks as she sought how to best form the question. The pastor looked at her, waiting patiently.

"If praying for Kendra doesn't bring Kendra back, what happens to her soul when we turn off her life support?"

The pastor sat up and leaned forward, taking a deep breath. He turned his head to the side, looked up and blew out his breath as if he was blowing out a candle.

"That's another tough one, I'm sorry to say."

"I have a very difficult decision to make, and if my daughter's life is over, then that still leaves her spiritual welfare to be considered. I don't recall if you or Pastor Wilson have ever talked about what happens when we die. Do we just go straight to heaven, or to hell?"

Pastor Dave stood up and began to walk around the room as he talked. "You're right. I haven't touched on this subject in any of my sermons. I try to focus on lessons that help us incorporate our beliefs into our daily lives; to make the scriptures meaningful and applicable, and not something we only think about on Sunday morning." He ran his left hand through his hair, breaking the light hold the mousse had on it. Now part of his hair hung down on his forehead and Joanne felt more at ease seeing him look more natural and less perfect.

"Well, you can certainly say that this is a situation that involves applying the scripture to real life. I need to know what I'll be doing to my daughter when I 'pull the plug,' as they say. Will I be setting her free to go to Heaven? Or will I be condemning her to Hell?"

"First, let me say this: I don't believe there is a Hell. I can explain why later, but I can assure you with my deepest conviction that you will not be sending her spirit to Hell when her physical life comes to an end."

"Excuse me, Pastor, but would you mind if we moved to the kitchen? For some reason, I'd feel much more comfortable in there. Paul and I never actually use this room."

"Sure. I understand. Can we bring the cinnamon buns?" he asked with a smile. She smiled back and picked up the tray as she stood up. They walked into the kitchen and she asked if he'd like more milk. He said he would and she poured him a glass, then they sat at the table by the windows.

"Kendra is not a believer, Pastor. She was baptized as a child, and went to services when she was young, but as soon as she said she didn't want to go anymore, we never forced her. I hope that wasn't a mistake I made that she'll pay for through eternity."

Pastor Dave shook his head as he finished chewing and swallowed. "No, I don't think you need to worry about that. I've never seen anyone become a believer by attending church against their will. And I doubt God takes much pleasure in seeing anyone dragged, kicking and screaming into His house." He took a drink of milk and wiped his mouth with a cloth napkin sitting on the placemat in front of him. "I'm sorry. These things are delicious. I can't seem to get enough of them."

Joanne beamed, pleased that he was enjoying her baking so much. "You're not married, are you?"

"No, I'm not. I should be, but I've always had this idea that I shouldn't be romantically involved with anyone from my own congregation, and yet, those are the only people I'm in contact with."

"I don't think you should worry about that. You're an attractive young man and I'm sure plenty of young ladies there would be happy to date you."

The pastor cleared his throat and his cheeks flushed. He reached for another bun just to do something with his hands. "Thank you, but let's save that conversation for another day. Getting back to your question of what happens to a person's spirit when they die…"

"Excuse me for interrupting, but now I have another question. I'm sorry."

"It's okay," he said, and bit into his pastry.

"I had asked what happens to a person's soul, but I notice that you're saying spirit. Is there a difference, or are they two different words for the same thing?"

"Oh, they're completely different. Again, I'll try to be brief, so we can try to address your concern. I know it's weighing heavily on you."

Joanne adjusted the arrangement of flowers she had put into a vase that morning.

"A spirit is like a person, but without a body," he continued. "When you join the spirit with the body, then you have a soul; a complete physical and spiritual being combined. The spirit gives the person it's animating life force, personality, character, etc. Does that make sense?"

"I suppose. But what would a person without a spirit be like?"

"Somewhat like an animal, I suppose, operating on nothing but physical needs, desires and instincts. Although, that isn't to say that animals don't have spirits. I believe they do. I just mean that a person without a spirit would lack all of the characteristics that you associate with a living person. If you've ever known twins, then you know how they're completely different people, even if they're genetic copies of each other."

"I think I understand. You're saying it's the spirit that makes the person who they are?"

"Essentially, yes. And without the spirit, they wouldn't really be anyone. At least not anyone you could relate to, or with a unique personality that you would recognize and associate with them."

"Where would you say Kendra's spirit is now?"

The pastor paused to think about that. It was something he'd never thought of. He bit his upper lip as he considered the possibilities.

"I would have to guess, and I hate to say this, and I hope it's not upsetting, but I think it would be similar to a person who has passed on."

"This whole thing is upsetting, but that's why I need to know this. It might help if I know what she's facing when she *does* pass on"

Now he was on more familiar ground and didn't hesitate to answer, becoming more animated as he spoke.

"The answer to that question depends on who you ask. According to the various religious beliefs of our time, the spirit either lies sleeping as it waits for Judgment Day, or it waits in a place called

Abraham's Bosom, or it goes to Sheol, which later became Hades, or directly to heaven if the person was saved, or it waits in a milder version of heaven or hell until Judgment Day, then goes on to the full heaven or hell after judgment."

"That is a lot of possibilities. Which one does the bible say is correct?"

"Um… all of them. That's the problem. Each belief has scripture to back it, and that's one of the reasons we have so many denominations today. Various people have focused on particular scriptures and founded religions based on their own collections and interpretations."

Joanne sighed heavily. This was not getting her anywhere. She felt none of the certainty and inner peace she'd hoped to get from pastoral counseling. She felt more like she was in Theology 101 and it was all just too much to digest. At another time she might find this to be a very interesting discussion, but right now she was in search of answers.

"Well, what do *you* believe then?"

The pastor hesitated before responding. He looked up at the kitchen ceiling; he looked at the wooden ceiling fan revolving above them and let his mind drift for a moment with the spinning blades. He made a decision and looked directly at Joanne who was waiting patiently.

"Joanne, I wouldn't normally reveal my deepest thoughts and convictions when they aren't backed up directly by scripture. As a leader of the flock, it would not be good for me to introduce questions and uncertainty to those in my charge. I need to lead and provide guidance. But in this case, I'm going to tell you what I've come to believe is true, and mind you, I can't point precisely to where in the bible my belief is supported or justified. I feel that it's a knowing that I received from the Holy Spirit"

"Okay," she said, somewhat surprised that someone who knew the bible far better than she did would have a belief that went outside of the bible, or wasn't specifically based on scripture.

"Don't worry. It's nothing crazy. It's just that I don't think of heaven and hell as actual places. I think they're more like emotional states of existence. I think a person is either spiritually with God, or they're not, regardless of any belief, or lack of beliefs. And if they are 'with God', they're in Heaven. If they're not, then the pain of that separateness from God is a form of Hell."

"I suppose that makes sense, and all of what you're saying makes sense to me, but none of it is actually… helpful. I'm sorry. That's such a terrible thing to say. I don't mean to sound so ungrateful. It's just…"

"It's okay, Joanne. I know what you mean. You're concerned with the spiritual fate of your daughter. I imagine you're wondering, if you pull that plug, are you setting your daughter's spirit free to go to heaven, or are you condemning her to hell. Right?"

"That's exactly it!"

"Okay, let's look at it from some other perspectives, rather than my personal viewpoint that most likely isn't shared by millions of people. Was Kendra baptized?"

"Yes." Now Joanne felt like she might actually get somewhere with the turn the discussion had just taken. "She was baptized at St. Bernards when she was nine weeks old."

"Okay, good. How about Confirmation?"

Joanne looked down at her hands and slowly shook her head. "No," she said quietly without looking up.

"Okay, was she ever saved or baptized as an adult, or did she ever confess her acceptance of Christ as her savior?"

Joanne began to look worried. Kendra had done none of those things. She'd stopped going to church as a teen and had always made excuses not to attend as an adult whenever Joanne had invited her.

"No," she mouthed with barely any sound.

"Hey. Don't look so glum. All hope is not lost. I've never had the pleasure of meeting Kendra, so I'm going to have to rely on your honest assessment of her, okay? Do you believe that Kendra lives her life in a way that is right by God, even without being a professed believer?"

Joanne's eyes widened and she sucked in her bottom lip as she looked at the pastor and then quickly looked away. She was thinking about Kendra living in sin with Keith and she didn't want to admit to the pastor that Kendra had not been living right by God before her accident.

"What I mean to ask is this: Is Kendra a good person who does the best she can in life with what she knows to be true? Does she have a good, loving heart?"

"Oh, absolutely! She is a lovely person, and of course I would say that; I'm her mother, but anyone who knows her would say the same. She's a very wonderful, loving, good person with a very big heart."

"Well, there you have it. If God sees in her what you see, then Kendra should, without a doubt, be going to heaven when the time comes."

"Even without being born again?" she asked, almost afraid to believe she had finally gotten the answer she had been hoping to hear.

"Even without. Can you imagine our loving Father seeing a good-hearted person doing their best to live the way He would like and then condemning them to eternal punishment for failure to abide by some system of rules that many people aren't even aware of? I can't. Christ died to redeem all of us, and he didn't say, 'I shed my blood for you, now jump through these hoops, pass through that maze, and then fill out these forms in triplicate and get in line for your membership card before you can pass through the Pearly Gates."

"So somebody good like Kendra won't be turned away by God?"

"I honestly can't believe that she would be, Joanne."

It was settled then. Joanne was at peace with the understanding that her daughter was asleep, and when she awoke in death, she'd go to heaven. She cried a combination of joyful and grieving tears as she hugged her pastor.

When Paul returned from the dentist, Joanne told him she was okay with letting Kendra go now. Paul was greatly relieved to hear it. He wanted to get on with grieving the loss of his daughter and remembering her as she was. He hated the state she was in right now; not alive, but not dead either.

Joanne called Keith and left a voice message saying she needed to speak to him in person and that it was very important. She hung up the phone, stared at it for moment and said, "I'm sorry, Keith, but it has to be done."

Thirty-seven

Kendra wouldn't stop crying when she met Keith in his room the night before. He tried consoling her by saying he wouldn't allow her parents to kill her, but it didn't help. She knew he couldn't legally stop them. He had no legal rights regarding her and she did not have a living will stating what her wishes were in the event that she ended up brain-dead.

The threat of losing their time together was depressing both of them. As cliché as it was, Keith was thinking that they'd had their whole lives ahead of them before the bombing. They had barely done anything together with the limited time they'd had to be with each other. More than half of their relationship had taken place on the phone.

There were so many things he had thought they would have time to do. Places to go and sites to see...

"Kendra!"

She lifted her head from his shoulder and looked at him.

"What?"

"Let's go somewhere. Let's go to Paris. I've always wanted to see the Eiffel Tower. Can you take us there?"

"You mean for real? Not just make it look like it's right here?"

"Yeah. For real. I want to actually see the real thing, in Paris."

"We can go there, but we won't be able to really see the real thing. It's in the physical and we're in the astral. Notice how this room isn't quite the same as it is in real life?"

"I know. We're actually making it up with our minds and memory. So what would we see of the Eiffel Tower if neither of us has a very good mental impression of it?"

"I don't know. I've learned some things wandering around like this, but there are many more things I have no clue about."

"Let's go find out!"

She hugged him and said, "I love you. Ready to switch?"

He smiled and nodded and she dissolved her thought of them having physical bodies in a physical environment. Their bodies faded away, along with the room. They stood as sparkling outlines of their former selves in empty space. There was a faint glow in the distance. Keith looked at it.

What's that?

The BOK Center, she replied.

Really? Why is it there?

Because that's where they built it.

The both laughed, then she explained that she heard him thinking about the things they wouldn't be able to do in life and that made her think of one of the things she had planned on doing.

It was going to be a surprise. I bought us tickets to see Paul McCartney. We were going to go the week after I returned from Iraq.

Can we do it now?

We can try, I guess.

Let's see how it goes, then we'll go to Paris, and who knows where after that.

She brought her sparkling energy lips to his and gave him a quick kiss which they both felt as a pleasurable electric tingle that spread throughout their energy bodies.

I love you!

I love you too!

She leaped into the air, zooming forward horizontally, and he was right behind her. When they arrived at the BOK Center, Paul was on stage with a Höfner bass guitar hanging from a strap in front of him, singing *Band on the Run*. They heard all of the instruments playing, but the stage was empty except for Paul. The stadium seats were also empty. Kendra saw this outpoint and imagined a crowd which promptly appeared, but she couldn't think of anyone in Paul's band. She imagined Linda McCartney and then she appeared on stage beside Paul tapping a tambourine. Shadowy, indistinct figures appeared playing drums, guitar and keyboard. It was the best she could do.

They stayed for several songs and thoroughly enjoyed the experience. The longer they were there, the more details filled in, making it less and less like a product of their imaginations.

One more song, Kendra said.

The band began playing Jet. During the chorus, Kendra sang along with a slight change in the lyrics.

Ah Mater - Want Keith to always love me

They laughed together and kissed, and when Paul sang, "Climb on the back and we'll go for a ride in the sky," Kendra released the physical overlay they had created and jumped up into the air, flying straight up and out through the roof of the arena and into the sky. Keith laughed, happy that she was not sad for now, and flew up after her.

They only flew for a minute over the vague landscape far below them and then Kendra thought them right to the base of the Eiffel Tower.

Whoa! What did you do? That was fast!

We don't have to actually travel the full distance. That would've taken too long and we have too much to do. After this, I want to see the pyramids in Egypt.

How did we get here though?

I just thought us here. Instead of thinking of the distance I wanted to travel, I just thought of being at the destination I wanted to be at instead.

That's awesome! We can see a lot of places tonight traveling like that.

Do you want to fly up, or climb up?

Let's fly – the slow way.

They casually floated to the upper deck of the tower and as they did so, Paris slowly lit up all around them like a city being digitally painted as they watched.

At the top, Kendra turned them physical and they kissed for a minute.

"Keith, you make me so happy, no matter how sad I get. Have I told you lately that I love you?"

"Not recently enough."

"I love you, Keith Erikson!" she shouted as loud as she could, then she kissed him very hard, holding his head from behind and pulling his face into hers, mashing their lips together. When she finally released her grip on him, he dropped to one knee, looking up at her.

"Kendra, if things change; if by some miracle, you get better—will you marry me?"

He held out his hand and she saw the most beautiful diamond ring sitting in the center of his palm.

"How did you do that?"

"You're not the only one learning how things work here. Answer the question!"

"Yes, Keith. A thousand times, yes. I'll marry you even if there is no miracle, because this is already a miracle, and I doubt I'll be so lucky that I get two of them.

"I never thought I'd be the luckiest man in two worlds, but here I am."

"Let's get married now and not worry about whether or not we can do it in real life. We might not have much time left together."

"You're right," he said, his tone turning sad.

"Don't you dare! You pulled me out of the dumps. You can't bring me back down. That's not fair."

"You're right," he said, and stood up to kiss her.

He was struggling to enjoy every second they had together and stay focused in the present without letting his thoughts drift toward what was going to happen to her soon if Joanne and Paul couldn't be persuaded to change their minds. He made a mental note to remind Kendra that he needed to know something that only she could tell him.

"How can we get married? We've never seen anybody here except for the people we made up for the concert."

"Then we'll make us a priest! But first…"

She walked to the edge of the deck, climbed up onto the rail and said, *"There are a few benefits to being in this state, you know,"* and dove off the side with her arms spread out, gliding downward, turning to the left, then to the right, enjoying the ride as she transformed from her physical body to her energy body.

When she was close to the ground, she swooped upward and flew toward Egypt. Keith suddenly appeared flying right beside her.

How'd you do that? she asked.

I just thought of where I always want to be – right beside you!

They flew for several minutes, swirling above and below each other as they went. Neither of them were able to stop smiling, then Kendra zapped them to the ground in between the paws of the Sphinx in Egypt.

Keith was staring up at the face of the giant figure when Kendra transformed them to their virtual physical state. He noticed that his clothing felt weird and looked down to see what she had done. They were both dressed in the ancient Egyptian clothing of some sort of royalty.

A man appeared before them in a strange gown that left his chest bare, but somehow had sleeves.

"Are you ready?" he asked them.

Keith turned to look at Kendra. She took his right hand in her left and said, "Yes. We are."

"Very well. With the infinite wisdom of the ages and with my vision that sees far beyond the surface, I hereby recognize the eternal love between the two spirits before me and now pronounce you for the remainder of this lifecycle as husband and wife."

He brought his hands together from his sides, indicating that they should come together too. They embraced each other and kissed passionately. The priest dissolved as they lost themselves in the pleasure of kissing with their arms wrapped tightly around each other.

When Keith finally opened his eyes, he was looking straight into the eyes of the Sphinx. He backed up quickly in surprise and tripped over one of the legs. He fell down and the ground shook.

Kendra burst out laughing and went over to help him up, stepping over the giant legs of the Sphinx to reach him.

"My God, you could have warned me you were going to do that," he said, joining her in laughter.

The two of them walked to the great pyramid as giants, hand in hand. They stood looking at the not so huge pyramid and Kendra said, "I wish I could find out what's inside the secret chamber."

Suddenly they were standing 200 feet inside the airshaft in the Queen's chamber, looking at a small door with copper handles. Keith and Kendra were less than twelve inches tall.

"Keith! What are you doing?"

"You wanted to see inside the secret room? Let's go."

He shrunk them again until they were one inch tall.

"I love that you're so thoughtful, but we don't know what's in there, so we can't discover anything."

"Let's check it out anyway while we're here," he said, striding forward like a tiny man on a big mission.

They walked under the door and into the secret room that no one had been in since the pyramid was constructed.

"It's pitch black."

Keith conjured up a wooden matchstick and the huge sulfur tip ignited with a roar, pulling the air away from them. He held the long wooden torch out in front of him and moved it around, illuminating the small chamber.

In the center of the chamber there was an ornate gold stand supporting a small crystalline pyramid, alive with sparkling blue liquid inside.

"What is this?" Kendra asked, amazed that they were seeing anything at all.

"I have no idea. I knew the chamber was here because I watched a show on the Discovery Channel, but that's all I know."

Kendra watched the swirling sparks of light drifting around in the vibrant blue liquid and couldn't imagine what it might be. She turned to Keith.

"Okay, my dear husband and eternal lover. Where shall we go next?

"Wait. Before we go someplace else, I need to ask you something before I forget. I need to know something that only you and your mom would know so I can prove to her that we're actually in communication and spending time together. Can you think of anything that would work?"

Kendra was caught off guard by the question and couldn't think of anything right then. She told him she'd think about it, and she wouldn't forget. After they traveled to Stonehenge, Easter Island, the Rock of Gibraltar and Machu Picchu, she finally thought of something and told him at their last destination of the night – the dark side of the moon. Kendra had summoned Pink Floyd to perform because she thought it would be funny. While they were laughing in each other's arms at the silliness of their private concert, Keith's phone rang and he vanished, leaving Kendra alone on the moon.

She stayed for one final song before returning to her island, which she considered her home in the astral plane. Kendra cried softly as she listened to Pink Floyd sing about racing toward an early grave.

Thirty-eight

Keith awoke and was startled to see his room, and that it was filled with light, and he felt the full weight of his body pressing down on his bed.

Kendra.

He missed her already. He cursed himself for not turning off his ringer. He looked at his phone and saw that he had a missed call from Joanne. He sat the phone back down and let his head collapse back onto his pillow.

Against his will, his thoughts returned to the real world and his fears about how long Kendra would remain in it. He had barely begun to worry about Kendra's pending death when his phone started ringing again.

"Just give me a minute, Joanne!"

He pressed a button on the side of his phone and the ringing stopped. He needed to talk to her and tell her what Kendra had told him so she could finally realize that he really was seeing her every day and talking to her. He just couldn't do it immediately upon waking.

He closed his eyes and tried to clear his mind and think about how to very carefully and rationally explain to Joanne and Paul that he needed them to just hear him out. He knew they thought he was crazy and in denial, after his blundering attempt to relay his good news at Outback, but he really needed them to just reserve judgment and listen.

Laci started licking his hand and nudging it, trying to get his attention. He blew out a breath and gave up on concentrating.

"Okay. Fine. I'll take you out. Just a minute."

He realized he was stressed beyond endurance. He never got upset with Laci. She was doing nothing wrong, but here he was, irritated by her simple and routine request to go potty, and maybe get some food and water.

He bent over and let Laci lick his face.

"I'm sorry, girl. It's not you."

Talking to the dog made him realize he'd spoken very little lately to anyone, and it felt good to say something about his feelings.

"Kendra is going to die, unless I can stop it from happening."

Laci wagged her tail because Keith was looking at her as he spoke.

"You dumb dog," he said, laughing. "You have no reason at all to be so happy about what I'm telling you. If only you knew what I was saying. Now I think I know what they mean by, 'it's a dog's life.' You don't have a thing to worry about."

He picked up his phone and put it in his pocket, then went to get Laci's leash. As he walked her down the sidewalk, he remembered to check his voicemail. He dreaded what Joanne's messages would be about – killing off Kendra.

He saw that he was wrong about the second call. It was from Jared. He decided to listen to that message first. However bad things were at work, they couldn't compare to how bad things were in his personal life, so that was easier to face.

"Hey dude, I was just checkin' in with you and, you know, like, wondering if you knew when you're comin' back. Things are goin' well here – except, well, they're not. I can't do all the stuff that you do, and though Ronald just says you'll be back when you get back, I know that's just what he's sayin' out loud. Ya know what I mean? Like he's tolerating me bein' in charge, but he don't like it. He just don't wanna look like a prick on account of what happened to Kendra. Ya know? Well, I hope to hear back from you soon, and I pray to like, God, or whatever that you have good news. See ya, bro."

Keith deleted the message and realized that the mere thought of work wasn't something he could face right now. It felt like something from another world; from a previous life. He didn't want to hear about Ronald or Katie or Tom. He really couldn't care less, and trying to imagine himself actually being there and listening to their petty problems about their computer lagging, or the network being slow, or their inability to type a website address properly into their browsers and being bent out of shape about the stupid little things they didn't understand – the thought of it all just made him feel sick. He never wanted to go back. Not if his life didn't go back to normal, and that didn't look like it was ever going to happen.

The best he could hope for now was to continue being able to have astral time with Kendra. The time he spent in the dreamlike world with her was the only thing that felt real to him anymore. His waking life felt like nothing but an insignificant dream. He wanted to be with Kendra to the exclusion of anything else in life except for Laci. If he couldn't be with Kendra, he didn't want to be alive anymore.

When he got back to his house, Keith unhooked the leash and gave Laci a command that let her know she was free to run around, but could not leave the yard. The fact that it was a beautiful day seeped into his awareness so he decided they could enjoy it a bit longer as he sat on the porch and worked up the nerve to listen to Joanne's voicemail.

He looked down the street, appreciating the serenity of his neighborhood. Lawns were manicured, trees were shrouded in vibrant green leaves, and birds were singing and chirping. He looked back at his own perfect lawn and saw Laci wagging her tail and happily sniffing the grass that was neatly trimmed to the edge of the curb.

He suddenly missed Kendra on another level that hadn't even occurred to him before. Everything seemed so beautiful; he just wanted to experience it with her. He started to recall times when Kendra wanted him to do something with her but he was too stupid to abandon whatever it was he already had in mind and just do what she wanted. Like washing his stupid car, or trying to figure out the best way to invest the money his dad had left him. Those things could've been done at any time; any other time when Kendra wasn't asking to spend time with him.

Keith only realized he was crying when Laci came up to him and started licking tears off his face. He pulled himself out of the daze he was in and stood up. Inside the house, he spoiled Laci with her favorite snack treats and downed a bottle of water. He told himself he needed to move forward. He was wasting time by avoiding Joanne.

When he finally played the message he'd been putting off, it was anti-climactic. She had just said she needed to talk to him, and it was important. Steeling himself inside and resolving to maintain a calm and pleasant attitude, he called Joanne and asked if it was a good time to talk. Joanne covered the phone and spoke to someone else, then she said, "Now would be good if you can come over so we can talk in person."

He told her that he'd be right over, then locked the front door and walked to his car, feeling like he was heading toward his own execution.

Thirty-nine

When Paul returned from the dentist, Joanne asked the pastor to excuse her for a moment as she went to talk with Paul. She found him in their bedroom changing his clothes and asked him how things went with his tooth, then gave him a quick summary of her conversation with Dave. She finished by telling him that she was ready to move forward with letting Kendra go.

"I wanted to make sure that she would be going on to something better, Paul. And now that I know she will be, there's no reason to delay. We're just keeping her from a better afterlife."

"I'm glad your mind is settled. Is the pastor staying for lunch?"

"I suppose he will be. We hadn't discussed it. We've just been talking, and Keith is on his way over."

Paul breathed in deeply and looked up at the ceiling.

"Paul, I'm going to explain to him why it's in Kendra's best interest that we let her go, and he's just going to have to accept it. I think he'll be okay."

"Is he still going on with his crazy talk about seeing her every day?"

"I haven't really spoken to him since the restaurant. But he sounded just fine when I invited him over to have a talk."

"I'm in no mood for another scene with him – especially not with the pastor as our guest."

"Well, if he does start talking that way, we'll be in good hands with the pastor here to tell him that's impossible. I'm sure Keith wouldn't deny that when it comes to spiritual matters, a pastor is far more of an authority on such things than he could possibly be."

Paul sat on the bed and put on his sneakers and tied the laces without saying anything. He had put on nice clothes to go to the dentist and was now changing into more casual attire; slacks and a polo shirt. He was going to wear leather penny loafers but decided he would go totally casual in the shoe department despite the presence of the pastor. Maybe it would help him relate more to Keith a little.

Paul felt it was important to look your best when meeting people outside the house for nearly any reason. He was also raised to dress up whenever traveling by plane or train, regardless of the purpose of the trip. One of the things he disliked about Keith was that he went to work as a manager of the computers, as Paul understood his position, wearing nothing better than Levi's and a t-shirt.

"Don't you think so, Paul?"

Before he could respond, the doorbell rang.

"I'll get it," she said, and walked quickly to the front of the house.

Paul used the bathroom then went to the kitchen where he found the pastor sitting by himself with a pleasant smile on his face.

"Pastor Giddens. It's a pleasure to see you. I'm sorry I missed you earlier. I had a bit of a dental emergency."

"That's fine. I hope everything turned out okay."

"Good as new," Paul said, smiling and sliding a chair away from the table.

"Keith, I'd like to introduce you to Pastor Giddens from our church. Pastor Giddens, this is Keith Erikson. Kendra's fiancé."

"Oh. It's a pleasure to meet you, Keith."

What is he here for? Last rites?

Keith didn't like where this seemed to be going. He had expected it to be bad, but they invited a priest?

The pastor stood and stretched out a hand and the two young men shook.

"Please, take a seat, Keith. Are you hungry? I was just about to serve lunch. How about you, Pastor? Would you care for something? I hope you like egg salad. You like egg salad, don't you, Keith?"

Paul cleared his throat, raising his eyebrows at his wife. He thought she should stop talking so the gentlemen could have a chance to answer one of her questions.

"That'd be great, Mrs. Hodges. Thank you."

"I'd love a sandwich, if you don't mind. Thank you, Joanne."

Paul relaxed a little in his chair. Then he looked at Keith who sat down across from him and tensed up again. He didn't know what to say. He would've asked Keith how he was doing, but he feared the answer he might get.

"So…." Paul started.

Joanne was quickly assembling things on the counter to make sandwiches with one ear on the men at the table. No one was talking, and she felt the awkwardness even though she was the one person who had something to concentrate on.

"Who wants their bread toasted?" she called over her shoulder.

"That sounds good to me, Joanne," Dave responded.

"I do," Paul said.

"I know *you* do, honey," she replied, laughing more than the remark warranted. She dropped four slices of bread into the toaster, took four plates out of the cabinet and set them down, then turned around to face the table as she waited for the bread to pop up.

"So… how is your mother, Keith? Have you spoken to her lately?"

"No, I haven't. I guess she's okay." He thought of saying, "I've been spending all my time with Kendra, so I don't know how anyone's doing except for Laci," but he decided to wait until someone else brought up Kendra before he began discussing the time he'd been spending with her. He wasn't just going to listen to them say they were going to pull the plug on her, then thank them for lunch and leave. He was going to convince them that she was alive, and she was *well* - in a way. He had to.

"Do you have plans to visit her any time soon?"

"Um… not really. I haven't given it any thought. I've been a bit pre-occupied lately."

Keith would have preferred it very much if he had been able to come over, have a talk with Joanne and be done with it. He felt very uncomfortable in this pseudo-social setup. He had never felt comfortable around Paul for some reason he couldn't identify. Paul always made him feel like an insecure kid, and he hated that because he did *not* feel insecure in almost any other circumstance.

Now he found himself sitting at a table with Paul and someone from their church. What did Joanne call him – pastor? So this was definitely not a social gathering. They were here to talk about Kendra and nothing more. The sooner they could do that, the sooner Keith would feel better.

Keith's comment about being pre-occupied had left Joanne without a follow-up, so she turned back to the toaster and was startled when the toast popped up.

"Oh!" She raised her hand to her chest and the men at the table looked over at her. "I guess I wasn't expecting that. Well, I was, but I wasn't."

She quickly slathered egg salad on the bread, sliced the sandwiches and carried two plates to the table, then went back and retrieved one more.

"Aren't you going to eat?" Paul asked.

"Yes. I just wanted to get you all started first."

Paul sighed through his nose. It would have been more sensible for her to have made her sandwich too and seated herself so someone could say a blessing and they could all eat. Now what we're they going to do? Say grace while she stood there like a nervous hen?

"What's the matter, Paul?" Joanne looked at him with concern lining her eyes.

"I think it would be best if you joined us so we can say grace."

"Oh, you're right. I'll just be a second."

Joanne went back to the counter and made an egg salad sandwich in record time and promptly rejoined the men at the table. She took a seat at the table and looked at the pastor.

"Would you?" she asked.

"I'd be happy to," he responded, and he, Paul and Joanne closed their eyes. Keith looked down at the table.

"Heavenly Father, we thank you for this food and ask that You bless it and let it nourish our bodies. We thank You for bringing us together today and ask that You guide us and give this family strength and wisdom as they seek to learn Your will. And Lord, we are reminded that this world is a dangerous place. You never promised that we wouldn't experience pain, anguish, and all forms of human suffering. But you did promise us that you will sustain us, draw near to us, and work all things for the good. And whether you choose to heal Kendra on this side of life, or the next, please remind us that You are a God of redemption and sacrifice, as evidenced by your Son who paid for it all, and by whose name it is in which we pray, Amen."

Paul and Joanne said "amen" in unison. Keith remained silent. The pastor made "getting to know you" small talk as they ate, asking Keith questions about what he did for a living and how long had he lived in Tulsa. Keith gave brief, uninteresting answers. He answered politely that he worked in I.T. and he'd lived in Tulsa for a little over a year. He wanted to scream, "Can we talk about Kendra now?" He had never cared for small talk before, but now it was even worse since it was just a delaying tactic, or adherence to some kind of social rule that he didn't understand, as if they shouldn't bring up an unpleasant subject while eating.

Finally, they finished their sandwiches and Joanne asked if anyone wanted seconds. No one did except for Paul. Joanne gathered the plates, then made another sandwich for Paul and sat back down at the table.

Keith couldn't stand the thought they were going to continue avoiding the subject of Kendra. The fate of his future and his love life was on hold because of an egg salad sandwich.

"You said you needed to talk to me, Joanne?"

Joanne straightened up in her chair and pressed her tongue against her top lip as she looked around the table. She blotted her mouth with a napkin, more as a stalling tactic than anything else. Keith continued looking at her expectantly.

"Yes, Keith." She paused for a few seconds. "This isn't easy to say, and I want you to know that this is not something that we've decided on lightly and without giving it serious consideration, from every angle – which is why Pastor Giddens is here, actually."

"Okay," Keith responded in a neutral tone that said, "Go on."

"Since the doctors at St. Joan's have said that there's no chance for Kendra to recover, I believe – *we* believe, actually, that keeping Kendra's body alive artificially doesn't serve any purpose, and in fact, is keeping her from moving on to a better afterlife. You see, she can't very well go to heaven while she's still technically alive. But we all know she's not *really* alive, so… we're just keeping her in a sort of limbo." She looked to the pastor to see how she was doing with her explanation and if he might want to step in and take over since this was really his area of expertise. He smiled and nodded slightly.

"But that's incorrect, Joanne. Kendra *is* alive, and she's not in any kind of limbo at all."

The pastor cocked his head. He certainly hadn't expected Keith to say that. He thought the young man might cry or get angry. He thought his own presence was needed to aid with breaking the news to Keith of the final loss of his fiancé.

Paul had been watching Keith and Joanne as he ate. Now he put down his sandwich and said, "Not this again."

"I know you guys find it hard to believe that she's alive and that we spend time together every day. She and I talked about this and Kendra told me something that I couldn't possibly know without her having told me so I can prove to you that she's alive. You won't have to just take my word for it, okay?"

"Pastor Giddens," Paul said. "Would you please tell Keith that what he thinks he's experiencing is just not possible?"

"Keith, when you say that you—"

"Did anyone hear what I just said? I have proof that was given to me by Kendra, and you're just ignoring it and psychoanalyzing me. Don't you want to hear what she said?"

"Keith, I'm at a disadvantage. I'd like to hear what you have to say, but I'm just wondering what you mean when you say that you spend time with Kendra. Paul and Joanne apparently know what you're referring to already. Can you tell me what you mean? I understand that you can spend time with her at the hospital, but I don't see how she can talk to you when she's in a coma. Help me understand?"

"I know this will sound strange, but actually it shouldn't since you all believe in God, which means you believe in spirits. After all, what goes to heaven, if not your spirit? Obviously you don't think your body gets out of the coffin and flies off somewhere, right? It's the spirit that goes somewhere. So this shouldn't come as a shock to you that since Kendra has been in a coma, she's been coming to me in spirit form or whatever you want to call it, and we've been spending a lot of time together, hanging out, talking, and stuff."

The pastor looked thoughtfully at Keith. "And you don't feel that it's possible that these could be dreams you're having?"

"Absolutely not. People in dreams don't talk about the weird way that they've come together. Kendra and I talk about the state we're in and how we can do stuff as if it was a dream, but it's not. We're wide awake and we know that we're in this weird place where anything is possible. I know how crazy it sounds, so I just want to tell Joanne what Kendra told me that no one but she and her mom knows about, so they'll know I'm really talking to her."

Dave looked at Joanne. Joanne looked at Paul.

"Fine, Keith. Tell us what she said. Let's get this over with."

"That's a really nice attitude you have there, Paul. Your daughter asked me to relay something to your wife, which proves she's alive and well… and you just want to get it over with."

Keith had never spoken to Paul in a confrontational way before. He had planned on marrying Kendra and never wanted to do anything to create tension or problems with her family. He was surprised at what he had just said, but he also realized at the same time that it didn't matter anymore. He wouldn't be marrying Kendra and he was free to speak his mind.

"I shouldn't have to remind you that I lost my daughter in that bombing. Losing Kendra was the worst experience of my life. But denying it happened is not an option for me. I'm facing the real world. That's something you need to do too, Keith. Excuse me," he said, looking at the pastor. He stood up and calmly left the kitchen.

Keith saw that Joanne's eyes were watering and she was pressing her lips together to keep them from trembling.

"Joanne, listen. Kendra said that she was twelve years old when you took her to the dentist one day to have a cavity filled. She said it was the most embarrassing experience she ever had because she didn't realize that while she was sitting in the dentist's chair, she got her first period. And she was wearing white pants. She said she could've died when she realized that the dentist and his assistants saw the blood that had soaked through while she sat there for at least a half hour, oblivious to what was going on."

Joanne held her breath half way through Keith's revelation. She resumed breathing with a gasp, covering her mouth with one hand.

"Oh, God!" she cried out, and looked to the pastor for some sort of help.

The pastor was nearly stunned and didn't know what to think. "Is that what happened, Joanne?"

She vigorously nodded, then reached for a fresh napkin to wipe the tears from her eyes.

"Don't get me wrong, Keith, but certainly it's possible that she told you that before the accident, isn't it?"

Joanne hadn't thought of that, and her emotions flip-flopped. She had never believed that Keith was in communication with Kendra, but when he described what had happened at the dentist, she did believe. And now she realized the pastor was right, and she wasn't sure what to think anymore.

"Yeah, it's *possible*, but she didn't. She told me last night!"

"You understand that no one but you can possibly know that, but since it's something she could have told you before the coma, it's not evidence that she's communicating with you. But let's assume for a minute that she is. What does she tell you she wants?"

"She wants to live. She said, 'My parents are going to kill me.'"

"Oh no!" Joanne began to cry again. She felt that the pastor was not only not helping her through this ordeal as she had hoped, but he was possibly making the situation worse.

As interesting as Dave found this discussion, he knew he needed to comfort his parishioner.

"Can we have just a moment?" he asked, glancing toward Joanne.

"Sure. I'll go outside and get some air." Keith got up and went toward the front door. Dave scooted his chair closer to Joanne and spoke softly to her as he put his arm around her.

Forty

Keith wished he hadn't quit smoking. He hadn't smoked a cigarette since the month before he met Kendra, and he hadn't missed it after meeting her - until now.

He looked up at the leaves on the giant oak tree in the front yard and spoke to Kendra in his mind.

Are you here, watching this? I guess we didn't think about the fact that anything you tell me now, you could've told me before, so it's not working as proof.

He walked through the yard, aware of a variety of nature's fragrances; the freshly cut grass, the roses that lined the front wall of the house, honeysuckle, and even the bark of the oak tree. He kept his mind silent, listening, and wondering if Kendra could talk to him while he was wide awake and walking around.

He heard nothing. There was no telepathic message coming to him. He guessed that it wasn't possible and this would have to be a one-sided conversation.

About the only thing you could tell me now that you couldn't have told me before is anything that happened after the bombing. But that wouldn't do any good because your mom wouldn't know it either.

The situation felt hopeless.

The only way we could convince her would be if you talked to her.

He bent down and picked up a piece of quartz rock.

That's it!

Why he hadn't thought of it before?

You can talk to her, like they do on TV on those psychic medium shows!

Now he just had to convince Joanne to go along with such an idea. He wouldn't bother trying to convince Paul. He'd never agree to such a thing. But Joanne might.

He walked over to his car and took a piece of gum from the pack sitting in the center console, thinking of how he could talk Joanne into giving this a chance. He walked back under the tree and thought for a few minutes, then headed back inside.

When Keith entered the kitchen, he saw Joanne adding sliced lemon to a pitcher of iced-tea. She heard him enter and turned toward him.

"Keith, would you care for some tea?"

He thought it sounded good, but then thought of how it would taste weird with the gum he was chewing.

"No, thank you."

"I'm sorry I… lost it again. I can't tell you how hard this is for me to think about."

"I sorta know how it is, although I don't know what it feels like to be a mother. Obviously. But Joanne, have you noticed how I've been fairly happy every time you've seen me since Kendra got hurt? Does it even seem possible that I could be doing so well, with my fiancé – the girl I love more than life itself, lying in that hospital bed?"

Joanne came back to the table with two glasses of iced-tea, giving one to the pastor and taking her seat. She held her glass in front of her and gazed into it, considering what Keith had just said.

"It does seem odd. And it could be explained by you really being in touch with Kendra, or, and I'm sorry to speak so bluntly, but we may as well cover all of the bases, it could be that you're in very serious denial, dear."

Keith came over to the table and sat.

"You're absolutely right. Those are the two most logical explanations. Right?"

Joanne looked at Dave and asked, "Is it even a possibility, Pastor Dave? Could a person in a coma be able to communicate and have experiences as a spirit?"

"That's not something I could give a definite answer to, right off the cuff. I'd have to research pretty much everything the bible has to say about spirits, and since I'm sure it doesn't mention anything at all about being in a coma, I'd have to extrapolate from what it does say about spiritual experiences taking place independent of the body…" He trailed off, thinking about it and trying to recall such passages.

"What's your name again?"

"Dave Giddens."

"Dave, what do *you* think is possible – aside from what the bible says? I know Mrs. Hodges is like your sheep and you're the shepherd of the flock or whatever, and you want to give her sound biblical advice, but think about it. You already believe that when you die, you go to heaven. And it's not like your body goes to heaven, right? Your spirit goes. And when you arrive as a spirit, you can talk and do stuff just like you could with your body, right? So considering the things you'd say are already established facts according to the bible, doesn't it make sense that Kendra, being in a state that's *like* death, could be out of her body, but hasn't left for heaven yet?"

"That makes sense within certain paradigms. But there are also scriptural references to spirits simply sleeping as they await judgment, so Kendra could also be in a living sleep state, waiting… to pass on to the spiritual sleep state. Can I ask what your belief is about the afterlife, Keith?"

"I don't have a belief about anything. I just know that since this happened, Kendra has been coming to me and we've spent a lot of time together. And if the Hodges turn off her life support, then I'll lose her completely – more than I have already. And I thought of something when I was walking around." He turned to Joanne. "I realized that you're right. Kendra could've told me about having her period at the dentist while she was alive. She didn't, but you don't know that. So the best way to convince you that she's still alive as a spirit is if you talk to her yourself. We could meet with a psychic medium like on TV. You'd know if you were actually hearing from your own daughter or not. Wouldn't you?"

Joanne had been following the conversation between Dave and Keith but it was hard for her to just listen and think about the meaning of what they had been saying. To her, this wasn't just a theological discussion – it was her daughter they were talking about. It was impossible to remain emotionally detached.

"Oh, Keith, that sounds like it could be a good idea, but doesn't the bible forbid talking to mediums, Pastor Dave?"

Dave nodded solemnly. "Yes, I'm sorry, but that's true. There are several scriptures that forbid consulting mediums, wizards, necromancers, psychics, etc."

Keith wasn't ready to give up that easily. "Can you cite one? Maybe the context doesn't apply to this situation."

"Well, one that I can recall says, 'Do not defile yourselves by turning to mediums or to those who consult the spirits of the dead.' That clearly forbids consulting a medium, Keith."

"Actually, I don't think so. I was right. It's all about context."

"How so?" Dave asked, curious to see if he could actually be wrong about this.

"Kendra's not dead," Keith said, smiling.

"You know, I'll have to look up some passages, but I think you may have something there. It might just be a prohibition on talking to the dead – not just merely consulting psychics because they're psychics."

Keith was excited now. It didn't seem likely that he would have even gotten this far – especially not with a man of the cloth coming out on his side of the issue. He smiled at Joanne.

"So, will you do it? Will you give it a chance to see if Kendra can come through and talk to you personally and let you know she's really here? I know Kendra would love to talk to you"

Joanne felt her heartbeat speed up at the thought of actually talking to her daughter again. That was something she was sure had happened for the last time prior to Kendra's flight to Iraq. It would be a miracle if it could really happen. She could tell Kendra at least one last time how much she loved her and how much she meant to her. The thought of trying was also a bit terrifying. It meant hoping and believing and possibly being completely letdown. But if Dave didn't object and thought it might work…

"I think I'd like to hear what Pastor Dave has to say about it first."

Keith thought that was fair. It wasn't an agreement yet, but neither was it a refusal. He had made progress.

"So, Dave, if you can confirm that the prohibition is just on talking to the dead, do you think it's possible that Kendra could communicate to us this way?"

"I suppose it would be. After all, the bible wouldn't prohibit it if it was impossible to begin with. So it sounds to me like some psychics can really do it, and the bible disapproves. But when the person isn't dead? I wonder if there's even a psychic who would be willing to try."

"You just confirm for Mrs. Hodges that the bible isn't against it, and I'll find a psychic to do it."

They agreed, and Dave went to his car to retrieve his bible.

Keith drove home filled with optimism. He would begin his search for a psychic as soon as he got to his house. Then after he found someone and could mentally relax with having that out of the way, he needed to find Kendra and ask her if *she* thought she could do it.

He sure hoped so. Her life depended on it.

Forty-one

Laci was ecstatic when Keith walked in. He laughed and dropped to his knees so she could lick his face as he rubbed the fur around her neck. Then he let her out and filled her bowls.

He went to his computer and did a Bing search for "Tulsa psychic medium." The first two local business results had one bad review each, so he went to the third, and dialed the number. He couldn't believe it when the psychic herself answered the phone. He expected a voice-menu, or a secretary, or maybe even an answering machine.

He briefly explained his unusual situation, stating that he wanted a medium who could contact a person who was still alive, but in a coma. Could she do that?

"I don't see why not. A spirit's a spirit, right?"

"I guess so. I don't really know how this works, but I talk to her every day, so I guess it should be possible for someone else to."

"You're a psychic too? I'm confused."

"No, not at all. I just…"

Keith tried to think of how to explain without making it too complicated.

"I meet with Kendra when I'm sleeping. That's when we talk."

"I see. So you're meeting her on another plane. That's very interesting. So now you want to talk to her while you're awake? Is that it?"

"Exactly!" Keith was greatly relieved that there was someone who could understand the situation that to him, was still completely crazy and not very explainable. "So you can do it?"

"Sure. When do you want to come in?"

"I want to bring someone else, if that's okay. The thing is, I need to convince her mom that she's still alive and communicating, even though she's in a coma. Her parents want to turn off her life support, and Kendra and I are afraid once that happens, she'll end up somewhere else and we won't be able to see each other anymore."

"Don't you worry a bit. Bring her mother with you and we'll make sure she hears from your girl."

Keith wanted to kiss the psychic through the phone. He thanked her profusely and assured her that she couldn't possibly know how much this meant to him. He said he'd call back to schedule a session as soon as he confirmed with Kendra's mother.

When he ended that call, he made another one. Joanne confirmed that Pastor Dave couldn't find any biblical objection to what Keith wanted to do. Not specifically, anyway.

Keith was elated. He asked Joanne when would be the soonest possible time she could do it. She said anytime would be good, so Keith said he'd see if he could schedule it for that night.

After calling the psychic back and making an appointment for that evening, he called Joanne again and told her he'd made the appointment. He wasn't sure if he should offer to drive her or not. He couldn't imagine Joanne sitting in his car. That just seemed weird. So he asked her if she had something to write with so he could give her the address.

She wrote it down and said she'd see him there. She sounded really nervous, but Keith was counting on her keeping her word. He finally plopped down on his bed, intending to meet with Kendra and tell her what he'd accomplished so far. The rest was up to her now – her and the psychic.

Keith tried his standard relaxation techniques, but they weren't working as they usually did. His mind was abuzz with too many thoughts and he couldn't shut down his internal monologue.

What would Paul say about this? Would he forbid Joanne from going? What if it didn't work? Would they pull the plug on Kendra tomorrow?

By the time he finally got his mind to quiet down and quit racing around like a madman, and the first of the vibrations started, another vibration made an audible sound, followed by the ringing of his cell phone.

"Dammit! Why didn't I silence my phone?"

Keith opened his eyes and reached for his phone. "Hello?"

"Keith, is that you?"

He closed his eyes and shook his head.

"It's my cell phone, Mom. Who else do you think would possibly be answering my personal cell phone, *and* sound exactly like me?"

"Well, I never hear from you. Maybe I forget what you sound like."

Keith looked at the ceiling and sighed. The only person in the world he wanted to talk to right now was Kendra. If he had to come up with a list of ten other people he'd be willing to talk to, his mother wouldn't even be on it.

"Are you still there?"

"Yes. I am. I think that goes without saying as well. What do you want, Mother?"

"Keith, I'm worried about you. Tell me what's going on."

"What do you mean? Why are you suddenly worried about me?"

"I know this thing with Kendra must be tearing you up, and I think it would be best for you to be home right now. You need to be with family at a time like this."

Everything his mother said drove him crazy. He always had multiple mental responses that he had to restrain himself from verbalizing, and then come up with something civil to say.

You're right mom. My fiancé being blown up by a bomb is tearing me up. Being at home with you would add being driven totally insane to what I'm already dealing with. And when you say, "at a time like this," do you mean, those times when someone's fiancé is in a coma because they survived a terrorist bombing?

He could feel his blood pressure spiking. Every time he spoke to his mother, it was abundantly clear to him why his father had committed suicide. He really couldn't blame him.

"Thanks, Mom, but I don't think that would help at all. I'm fine."

"Keith, you are *not* fine. I know what you're up to."

"What the hell is that supposed to mean? You make it sound like I'm involved in a sinister plot, or I'm doing something illegal. What am I *up to*, for God's sake?"

"There's no reason for you to start cursing at me. I'm just looking out for you and trying to help."

Again, Keith wanted to scream in frustration. He took a long breath and let it out slowly.

"I am not cursing at you. I've never cursed at you and I resent the hell out of you accusing me of doing something I've never done."

"You just did it again!"

"I did not!" he yelled. "Using the word 'hell' is not cursing at someone. If I said 'damn you to hell,' *that's* a curse!"

"I didn't call to split hairs with you, Son."

"Oh for God's sake. Words mean things, Mom. If I asked you for a glass of water and you brought me apple juice, would I be splitting hairs if I complained that apple juice and water aren't the same thing?"

"I don't know what you're talking about now. I just want you to come home until things get better. And don't tell me you can't leave your job. You don't even need it with all that money your father left you, *and nobody else.* And you haven't even been to work in over a week anyway, so you might as well be here, where you belong."

Keith wanted to crush his phone in his hand. He didn't understand how she could do it. How she could drive him absolutely crazy in the shortest amount of time, and with no effort, or even any awareness that she was doing it.

His father had killed himself because of the hell she put him through, and then she brings up the fact that Keith was the sole inheritor in his will. As if it made any sense that his father would have left anything to her.

And how did she know he hadn't been to work? If she had called his job and asked about him... And then to tell him that he *belonged* at home with her. He was a grown man. He was taking care of himself. He didn't quit his job when he suddenly found himself with several hundred thousand dollars. He continued to work and be responsible and he lived off his salary. The only thing he blew money on occasionally was special gifts for Kendra. The money his father left him didn't even feel real to him. But he had definitely planned to use it for his wedding and to travel with Kendra after they got married.

Now he wanted to cry. His mother had succeeded in completely bringing him down, as usual. Now all he felt was the loss of Kendra in his life. He had to stop thinking this way. She wasn't gone. She was still there and she still loved him. Just the nature of their interaction had changed. He needed to stop thinking about her while he was upset.

"How do you know if I've been to work or not?"

"Keith, please. Let's don't argue."

He hated the way she talked and the way she avoided questions, and made non sequitur comments, and if he pointed out that she wasn't making sense, then *he* was the strange one. She was the most exasperating person he'd ever had the displeasure of speaking to. She was the reason he moved out the day after his eighteenth birthday.

"Yeah. Let's not. I gotta go. I'm really busy."

"Wait, Keith! Don't hang up. I'll tell you why I called."

"Oh. So you did have a reason. Okay. Why *did* you call?"

"I don't want you getting mixed up in this devil worship you're planning tonight."

That was Keith's last straw.

"Do you even bother to try coming up with words that actually apply to what you're talking about, or do they just need to be in the same fucking ball park? Devil worship? I'm not planning on worshipping anyone tonight, mother. Especially not the devil. That is one of the stupidest things you've ever said, and goddamn, have you said a lot of stupid fucking things in my life.

"Please explain to me how talking to Kendra through a psychic medium has anything at all to do with worshiping Satan. Do you think I'm going to draw a pentagram on the floor, light some candles and praise Lucifer, then say, 'May I please speak to Kendra, great Lord of Darkness?' Is that it, Ma? Tell me how I'm planning on worshipping the devil. I want to hear this."

"Keith," she said, sniffling. "I called you because I love you. I'm trying to protect you. And you abuse me like this?"

"Abuse?! You made a boneheaded, insulting, ludicrous statement and I merely asked you to explain. That's abusing you? Fine. I have a solution for you. Don't call me again until you're prepared to explain how talking to a medium is equal to worshipping the devil. You have no idea what you're talking about and I have more than enough to deal with already!"

He pressed End Call and lay back on his bed, focusing intently on his breathing and struggling to calm his mind and his body. It was going to take a long time to get into a relaxed state now. He was going to need Kendra's help more than ever to be able to meet with her. His mind was a mess and his thoughts were chaotic, jumping from one thing to another as he replayed things his mother had said. How did she know he was going to the psychic? Joanne must have called her. But why? It didn't make sense.

Forty-two

After an hour of trying to relax his mind and body, Keith was still nowhere near the state he needed to be in. He got up and took a walk with Laci, then came back and lay down again. He still had time to meet with Kendra before the appointment, if he could just calm his mind.

During Laci's walk, he had felt the familiar pull that told him Kendra was there and trying to nudge him over to her side. He smiled, knowing that she was there and trying to help him. But now he was failing her.

Then something occurred to him. If she was there and trying to bring him across, maybe she could hear him talk. He had never thought to ask her about that. It was worth a try. He cleared his throat.

"Kendra. Are you here?"

He felt awkward talking in a nearly empty room. Laci lifted her head from her paws and looked him.

"I feel like you're here right now, so I hope you can hear me. I made an appointment with a psychic and your mom agreed to go with me, believe it or not. I'm hoping you'll be able to reach the psychic and talk to your mom through her. Then she'll know that pulling the plug on you would be killing you, and she won't do it. I hope you can follow me there. You've got to try to do this. Okay, babe? I love you."

Laci stared at Keith while he talked. Keith wondered if Laci thought what he had just done was strange. But it should be just as strange to her when a human held a small metal and glass object up to the side of their head and started talking. Shouldn't it? But she kept staring at him.

"What?"

Laci barked, which was unusual. She almost never barked.

"Do you sense Kendra?"

Laci barked again.

"No way. You're not Lassie. I think we're both losing our minds."

The sun was setting as Keith followed the GPS directions on his phone to the psychic's address. It was in the north part of Tulsa and he hoped it wasn't in a bad area. The closer he got, the more run-down the area became. Then he turned onto a residential street with multiple apartment complexes. He double-checked the address he'd put in his navigation app to make sure he wasn't going to the wrong place. She hadn't mention that she worked out of an apartment. The address was correct.

When he pulled up in front of the apartment building that her unit should be in, he didn't see either of Joanne's or Paul's cars. He got out and located the apartment number that he had thought was going to be a business suite number, then went back to his car.

Joanne was going to be very uncomfortable here. There was graffiti on the walls, one car was up on blocks, another had four flat tires and a broken windshield, and a group of what looked like tattooed, Mexican skinheads were huddled in the parking lot, smoking and talking.

Keith sat in his car waiting. Twice, headlights turned into the parking lot, briefly splashing the building in front of him with light, but it wasn't until the third time that he saw Joanne pull in, driving her Lexus. He quickly got out and waved to her before she could change her mind and turn around toward the exit.

She parked, but left her engine running and she stayed in the vehicle. Keith walked over to her door and stood there looking at her. She rolled down the window.

"Keith? Are you sure this is the right place?"

"This is the address for her listing online. I'm sorry. I didn't realize it was going to be in the ghetto. But it shouldn't take very long. Let's just find her and we'll be out of here soon."

"Keith. I told Paul where I was going. I had to. And he called your mother. I tried to talk him out of it, but he insisted. I'm sorry. I had to tell him what I was doing."

Keith sighed. "It's fine. I talked to her. Let's go inside. I really don't feel comfortable talking out here."

They walked toward the building with Keith looking around alert and hyper-aware of his surroundings. He was glad for Joanne's sake that it was a downstairs unit. He didn't know why that should matter. She was in fine health as far as he knew, but it seemed to him that if the unit had been upstairs, it would have just made things worse.

They approached the apartment and Keith knocked on the door. He could hear a television inside turned up loud. After a moment, he knocked again, louder. The TV was suddenly muted and a few seconds later, the door opened about an inch.

"Are you the guy who made the appointment?" It was the voice he had heard on the phone earlier.

"Yes. I'm Keith, and this is my fiance's mother, Joanne."

The door opened the rest of the way and the woman gestured for them to come in.

"I'm Cassie, er, Cassandra. Please, come in."

They stepped into a small apartment with a worn out couch facing a large flat-screen TV. There were baby clothes and toys under the couch as if they had been kicked there in a rush to clean up.

Nobody said, "Oh, what a nice place you have," or any other social niceties. Keith and Joanne were filled with misgivings, but Keith was not even close to backing out. They had to do this.

"My office is being repaired right now, so I'm working out of my home for now. Please, have a seat." She gestured to the chairs at a small table on the far side of the room.

Keith cringed inwardly at the thought of Joanne sitting in her nice pants-suit on the grungy looking chair with torn fabric revealing Kool-Aid-stained padding underneath. He gave her an apologetic look.

Joanne sat in the chair to the right. Keith took the chair in the middle, and Cassandra took the remaining chair. Joanne was just about to rest her clasped hands on the table when she saw that if she did so, they would have rested on a few cold and wet Spaghettios.

"Oh. Let me get that," Cassandra said, quickly getting up and taking a few steps over to the kitchen sink. She turned back around and attacked the table with a dark brown sponge that might have been pink when it was new.

Joanne scooted back as if to make room for Cassandra as she wiped the entire table, smearing tomato sauce in places that could have theoretically been cleaner before her well-intended efforts. Joanne rested her hands in her lap and hoped this wouldn't be a séance type thing where they all had to hold hands.

Cassandra tossed the sponge into the sink, where it hit the top of a stack of dirty dishes and made a soggy ricochet onto the floor.

"I'll get that later," she said, drying her hands on her pants. "I told you it's fifty bucks for half an hour, right?"

"Um… no, but that's fine." Keith reached for his wallet. "Can you take Visa when you're not in your office?"

"I'm sorry, my Visa thing ain't workin' right now, but there's an ATM inside the liquor store just down the street."

Keith opened his wallet and was relieved to see it wasn't empty. "That's okay. I have cash. Do I pay in advance, or afterwards?"

"Cash in advance, and no refunds. Sorry. I can't guarantee results, because it's really up to the dearly departed on if they want to come through. I'm sorry, but that's the policy. You understand I can't go to all the effort and not get paid if the loved one ain't int'rested in comin' through, right?"

"I understand," Keith said, handing her three twenty dollar bills.

"If you want change, I'll run to the liquor store when we're done here. I don't like to keep cash in my home office. It's not the greatest neighborhood, if you didn't notice. My house is being remodeled at the moment, so I just found something cheap for the time bein'. You know how it is. It's costin' me a fortune. No pun intended!" Cassandra laughed, but it petered out quickly when no one joined her.

"That's fine. You can just keep the change. Can we start right away? This is more important to me than anything right now and I'm eager to get started, if that's okay."

"Sure. Sure. I unnerstand. I'll be right back."

Cassandra went past Joanne, turned into the living room and walked down a short hall. True to her word, she came right back, turning off a lamp in the living room as she passed back through. She set a candle down in the center of the table and lit it with a Bic lighter.

"This helps me focus my concentration." She quickly sat and began taking slow, deep breaths, lifting her head up on each intake.

Oh please, please let this work, Keith thought. But it was hard for him to believe it was going to.

"Give it back! Give it back! Mommmmm!!! Make him give it back!" The yelling was muffled, but clearly came through the wall dividing Cassandra's apartment from her neighbor's.

"Give it back to her right now, so help me God, or I'll bust your head wide open, you little shit. I've had all I can take from you two today!"

Cassandra opened her eyes and rolled them upward, saying, "Oh, those kids! If I had a gun…" She saw the horrified look on Joanne's face and Keith's stony expression and revised the direction of her sentence. "…I'd want to use it on myself. They can drive ya crazy, ya know?"

"That's it. Get in bed. If I have to get up, and drag you to your room, you'll live to regret it. Both of youze, in bed, NOW!"

"Okay, I think it's going to be quieter now. Just gimme a minute so I can get my concentration back."

Cassandra resumed the slow breathing and began to sway slowly, side to side.

"I'm feeling a presence. Is there someone here?" she asked in a higher pitch than she spoke in previously, and sounding like she was in a trance or an altered state. "I feel a woman's energy. A young woman. Is that you, Kendra?"

Joanne felt the fine hair on her arms rise as goosebumps spread from her arms to her shoulders. Keith thought he would feel Kendra's presence if she was there, as he usually did, but he wasn't feeling it at all.

"Kendra is with us tonight," Cassandra said in her spooky medium voice. "Kendra, I have two people with me who are here to talk to you. Your mother is here, and your boyfriend is here." She tilted her head as if she was listening intently. "Oh, he's your fiancé. I'm sorry. I didn't pick up on that."

Joanne was startled. When the psychic referred to Keith as Kendra's boyfriend, it seemed as if Kendra had corrected her. She believed her daughter would've really done that if she had been physically present.

Keith had more doubt than ever. He saw Joanne's reaction, but Joanne didn't know that he had already told the psychic that Kendra was his fiancé. She was definitely putting on a performance. He hoped she was just augmenting her real ability to contact spirits and putting on a little show for effect, but he began to fear that this wasn't going to go well at all.

"Yes, dear. I'll tell her. Joanne," the psychic drew out her name as if Joanne was not sitting two feet away from her and she too had to be reached across the spiritual divide.

"Your daughter has a message for you. She says that she loves you and she misses you, and she wants you to know that she's okay. It's very beautiful and peaceful on the other side. Angels are with her and she feels at peace. She's very happy."

"Kendra is in a *coma*. She's not dead, and she's not in heaven. There have never been angels with her." Keith was getting angry.

"You're right. She's not in heaven, but she can see the angels from where she is. The angels are just standing by in case she crosses over. This is the first time she's seen them."

Joanne thought of something that Kendra had probably never told Keith because there would have been no reason for it to ever come up.

"May I ask a question?

"Kendra, your mother has a question for you. Are you still with us?" She paused and listened. "Okay, I'll tell her." She took a breath and leaned back a little in her chair. "She is still with us, but her energy is growing weak. She'll need rest soon. It's taking a lot of *my* energy to maintain the connection. She wants you to hurry with your question before she has to go."

"Ask her what her grandmother's middle name is."

"Kendra, your mother wants to know, what is your grandmother's middle name?"

Kendra looked right at her and said, "Rose."

"I didn't hear you clearly, dear. Could you say it one more time?"

Kendra shouted, "Rose! My grandmother's name is Mary Rose, you fraud!"

Cassandra flung herself backwards suddenly, opened her eyes and breathed like she had just exerted a tremendous amount of energy and needed to catch her breath.

"She had to go," she said, panting. "I couldn't make out the name. I think it might've been something like Beatrice..." She looked at Joanne for a reaction. Joanne's eyebrows lowered as she looked at Cassandra. "Not Beatrice... maybe it was Elizabeth. They sound similar, ya know?"

Joanne's head was just barely moving left and right.

"I'm sorry. I couldn't make out what she said right before she left. She was already drifting off when she answered and I could barely hear her. But at least she was definitely here. Your daughter was with us tonight. Isn't that wonderful?"

Joanne looked at Keith. He asked, "Is that it? She had to go?"

"Yes. Sometimes they can't stay very long. It takes a lot of energy to be able to reach our side. And you know, it's very hard for them to get through if there's any negative energy around. And I hate to say this, but I felt a lot of negative energy following you as soon as you came in. I didn't want to say anything at the time though. I hoped it might be just a passing thing, but the spirits who came in with you are still here and they're very focused on you. That makes it hard for Kendra to reach us and stay for a long talk. The good spirits are just pushed away by the negative ones."

"Really?" Keith asked as he stood up and looked at Joanne, signaling that they were done here. It was time to go.

"We could clear the negative energy with just a few sessions, and then I'm sure Kendra could stay and talk with us for as long as you want. I specialize in clearing away negative spirits and cleaning your energy."

Keith started walking toward the door. Joanne got up and followed him.

"Thank you. I think that's all we need."

He opened the door and stepped outside into the warm, humid night.

"I could probably even clear the negative energy in just one session. It won't even take that long. I usually charge $400 for a energy clearing, but I'll give you a special deal. Just $200. Guaranteed to clear the negative spirits that are following you."

"Good night." Keith said, and walked Joanne to her SUV. He was relieved when he heard the apartment door slam shut behind him.

"Joanne, I'm sorry about that. I made a big mistake. I had no idea. Please let me find someone who can do this for real." He was going to tell her that he knew the entire time that Kendra wasn't even there, because if she was, he would have felt it, but he decided that might just make things worse. And then suddenly he felt it – the pulling thing that Kendra did, making him want to lie down as if it was an urgent need. Great, he thought. Now *I feel her. Should I tell Joanne?*

They reached Joanne's car and she pressed a button on her keychain fob.

"I tried Keith. I really tried. Look at where I am. You can't say that I didn't give this a chance."

"You did, Joanne, and I appreciate that. More than I can say. But I screwed up. I called the first psychic I could find. I didn't do research or take the time to look carefully for someone with a good reputation. Like you said, look at where we are. I was just in a rush to find someone. Let me find someone real. Someone respectable with a real business location."

Joanne just shook her head as she opened her car door. "I'm sorry, Keith."

So that was it. She was going to pull the plug. He had blown it by hiring a fake psychic. Now he felt that he had nothing to lose. He *had* to make her believe him.

"Joanne, wait! Kendra is here right now. I can feel her."

"Oh Keith." Joanne began to cry. "My heart breaks for you. It's already broken for myself and for Kendra, but honestly, it's breaking for you too now."

"Joanne, don't feel sorry for me. I'm the one who actually gets to talk to Kendra every night. I was hoping that you would have the pleasure of doing that tonight too. And you *can*. I just need to find someone who's really a psychic medium. I'm sure there's got to be at least one legitimate psychic in Tulsa. Let's just pretend this night didn't happen, and I'll make a new appointment with someone who can really put you in touch with Kendra. I wish I could talk to her while I'm awake, because she's here right now, pulling at me. She wants to talk."

"Keith. Please go home. I think it will do you good."

"I'm going to. And I'll be talking to Kendra right after I get there and lay down. She really wants to talk."

"I'll pay for the flight for you to go home. I'll even take care of Laci for you, whether Paul likes it or not. I'm really concerned about you, Keith."

Keith scrunched his eyes shut, gritted his teeth and sighed forcefully.

Fighting to hold back his frustration, he said, "I'll call you tomorrow, Joanne. Thank you again for coming out tonight. I'm going to ask Kendra to tell me something tonight that will utterly prove to you that she talks to me. Good night."

He turned and walked around her car and got into his. He waited for her to pull out, then he followed her until she turned to get on the expressway.

When he got home, he went straight to his room, ignoring Laci for the time being. He kicked off his shoes and lay back on his bed, exhausted from stress.

"Okay, Kendra. Let's talk. For real."

Forty-three

Kendra was just as frustrated as Keith was with the failure of the alleged psychic to communicate with her. Kendra could detect nothing about the woman's energy that made her different from any of the other people she saw as she flew around populated areas. Keith's energy was different somehow. She had always assumed it was just different to her because she loved him, so maybe she homed in on it or something. But now she wondered if he had something about him that made it possible for him to connect with her in and out of their bodies.

She followed him home and was eager to talk with him and spend as much time as possible together. If her mother was going to turn off her life support soon, every minute they had remaining was precious, and she didn't want any time wasted that could be spent with him.

She followed his energy pattern into his house and straight into their bedroom. She laid herself down beside him, patiently waiting for him to relax and reach the state that allowed him to cross into her dimension. She looked at the form she saw that was created by his unique energy combined with her memories, perceptions and expectations, and now she could see him more clearly lying there doing a breathing exercise.

As she waited, she tried to think of something she could use to convince her mom that she was here. Everything she thought of could be explained away though by her having told Keith about it when she was fully alive.

After a while, she noticed that Keith's energy was diminishing. He was fading away and becoming less visible to her. That meant he was putting out less energy and her construct subsequently had less solidity. He was falling asleep and going somewhere other than where she was. She was just about to see if she could track him when an idea came to her.

Keith had already had the best idea possible – a psychic who could relay what she said to her mother. Only a live conversation would convince her. She would know if she was talking to her own daughter or not. Kendra just needed to find someone who could really do it.

She flew up through the ceiling and continued flying upward until she was high above the center of Tulsa. She stopped and hovered, mentally closing her eyes and clearing her mind so that her sole thought was her intention to find someone who could sense her and communicate with her.

She turned in a slow circle, trying to see if she felt any kind of intuition or something that would guide her in any direction. As she looked around at the cityscape below her, she realized she was unconsciously mocking up its physical appearance.

She was seeing buildings and lights and cars and trees, traffic lights and power lines and so on. They didn't exist where she was. So she concentrated on not making these things appear. She imagined emptiness; an absence of cityness. She visualized everything she saw dissolving into flat, grey open space, as if she was erasing everything.

Now I need to see the energy from people. Strong energy. I need to see who can help me.

She looked at the large expanse of flat greyish-brown space below her and waited to see if anything would appear. She turned slowly in a circle and there it was. A soft amber glow began to pulse not too far away.

She didn't know if anyone or anything could hear her request, but she felt as though someone had helped her.

Thank you!

She shook her head to clear her concentrated image of nothingness away and to allow her automatic, subconscious construction of the city to reappear. She could still see the pulsing amber glow like a beacon in the night and she flew toward it, excited but nervous. She had never talked to anyone but Keith in this way, and she didn't know what to expect. Would the person think she was a ghost and be afraid of her?

She came to a stop in a nice neighborhood. The house in front of her looked well-kept and gave off a peaceful energy. She could imagine resting inside and stretching out on a comfortable couch, feeling lazy and happy. She imagined a cat, but didn't know why. She decided to go in for a closer look and to see the person with the warm amber energy glow.

She drifted in through the window pane at the front of the house and she saw a woman reclining on a couch with a book face-down on her stomach and a cat lying beside her. The cat raised its head and looked right at her with its piercing green eyes.

Hello kitty. Can you see me?

The young woman on the couch lifted her head and turned it to the side, listening, sensing.

"Is someone here?" she asked in the empty room. The cat meowed, still staring at Kendra. The woman pulled herself up into a sitting position and turned to see what her cat was staring at.

Hi. Can you see me – or hear me?

I hear you. Who are you? You don't feel like a Lost One. There's something different about you.

Kendra was excited and her vibrational rate increased, brightening her own energy glow.

I don't know what a lost one is, but I know I'm not lost. I came here to see you. I'm hoping you can help me.

What's your name?

My name is Kendra. Kendra Hodges. I'm sorry to just come into your house like this – I don't mean to be so intrusive, but I desperately need help. If you can't help me, I'm going to die tomorrow.

"Oh, wow. You're definitely not a Lost One. I'm Katana. You can call me Kat. Tell me what's going on. How can I help you?"

Thank you so much for not sending me away. The short version is that I was hurt very badly in a terrorist bombing and my body is at St. Joan's in a coma. My fiancé has told my parents that we spend time together every night, or whenever we can, but they don't believe him, so they're going to turn off my life support tomorrow. Neither of us knows how this all works, but we're both certain that once they pull the plug, I'll have to leave this plane and we won't be able to see each other anymore. I love him so much and I want nothing more than to just have more time together. We barely had a chance to be together before the bombing. And now, it's not the same, but at least we can still be together – on my side, at least.

"Okay, so he's not in a coma? He's still fully alive like me?"

Yes. And he did manage to talk my mom into seeing a psychic to prove that I'm really here, but—

"Ah... I see. That's where I come in. You need me to be a medium for you."

Well, yes, but I was going to say that we tried that tonight and it didn't work at all, so now I don't even know if my mom will agree to do it again, but Keith – that's my fiancé – was going to look for someone who wasn't a fake this time, and... well, I couldn't get through to him after the séance, or whatever it was, and so I went looking around and I found you. You have a really strong and beautiful energy. I picked it up from a mile away.

"I've never been involved in a situation like this before – in fact, I've never even heard of a situation like this. There's the Lost Ones, of course, but those are people who've died and don't know how to move on, or can't let go of someone or something here."

I guess you could say I'm not willing to let go of Keith yet either. I mean, I'm still technically alive, but I don't want to die yet and have to let go of him either. Does that make sense?

"I understand. It sounds like you two have a really special relationship. And you shouldn't have to leave him yet. You're still alive. Wow. What a really strange predicament you're in. You're like a living ghost. Have you encountered others like you – people who are alive, but running around spiritually?"

No. I sometimes feel the energy of what must be people, but I don't see them, and no one has talked to me. You might think I'm crazy, but the closest I've come to communicating with anyone other than Keith has been with some dolphins. I spend a lot of time with them. If it wasn't for them, I'd be alone a lot.

"Are you talking about real dolphins, or spirit-like dolphins?

Oh, they're totally real. I don't know how they can be there, because I know I'm the one who makes the ocean and my island appear right in the middle of Tulsa, but I've also gone to the coast and played with the dolphins there and it's no different. Their energy is exactly the same as the ones who appear in my made up ocean here.

"That is very cool, Kendra. And it actually doesn't surprise me. I've always suspected that there was something special about them."

They're really amazing. I can't even tell you how much so.

"I can just imagine it. So, how do we convince your mom that you're alive and not just lying in a hospital bed as a vegetable?"

I don't know, Kat. We may not even have another chance to convince her. After the session we tried tonight, she said to Keith, "I'm sorry, but I tried." Keith begged her to try again, but she just shut him out. Her mind is made up. She thinks Keith has literally gone crazy from losing me.

"I can see that," Kat said, nodding. "He must sound like a lunatic to her. Especially if she's not open to the possibility of the spiritual realm. Is she at all religious?"

She goes to church about three times a week.

"Ahh. You've really got your work cut out for you, girl."

Yeah. It was a small miracle in itself that Keith talked her into trying it once. My dad is totally against it. So now it's causing a problem between them. If Keith talks her into it again, it's going to make my dad even more angry at my mom, and at Keith too, who he's never been very fond of to begin with. So now I don't know what to do. I just don't want to die yet, Kat. I don't want to die tomorrow.

Forty-four

Keith didn't know where he was. He thought it was Syria, but it could've been Lebanon or Palestine for all he knew. The only thing he was sure of was they were out there, and they were armed, and every glance out the window of the dilapidated building he was in could bring a sniper's bullet into his brain.

He was trying to find a way out of the city, but it was a slow and frustrating journey. Everywhere he went, he saw insurgents. He had an assault rifle, but he didn't know if the safety was on or not, and he didn't want to find out via life-or-death confrontation, so he was trying to avoid the enemy.

He looked around the building and saw American candy wrappers and empty soda cans on the ground. The walls were spray-painted with a graffiti that was in a foreign language of squiggly lines that meant nothing to him. There was a stairway ahead on his left. He carefully made his way over to it, avoiding the debris in his path.

He quietly and carefully ascended the stairs, hoping to avoid any loose or squeaky boards. At the top of the stairwell, there was a door with no knob. He could feel warm air blowing through the hole where the knob should be, even though it was night. He ducked down and peeked out through the hole.

There was a sentry standing on the roof ten or fifteen feet away with his back to the door. He was probably looking over the edge for signs of Keith between buildings. Keith looked at his gun again to see if he could make sense of the safety switch. If he could be certain the safety was off, he'd shoot the sentry in the back. But he couldn't be sure, so he couldn't risk it. He decided to run at him as quickly as he could and push him over the edge.

He lifted the rifle by the shoulder strap and pulled it up over his head and gently placed it on the ground. He nudged the door just a tiny bit to see if it was going to squeak. It didn't, so he continued pushing it until it was almost all the way open. Now he could get a running start.

He counted silently to three and rushed at the sentry. At the sound of Keith's footsteps, the sentry turned around. He didn't have time to raise his weapon, but as Keith shoved him, he grabbed onto his shirt with both hands and pulled Keith over the edge with him.

They fell together toward the dirt yard below them and just before they hit the ground, they started moving forward, and then upward. Keith was glad that the man could fly, but he felt it was a very awkward situation now to be holding on to the man he had just tried to kill.

They flew higher than the rooftop they had fallen from and continued upward. Keith yelled over the sound of the rushing air, "Where are you taking me?"

The man swiveled his body around to face him and Kendra said, "Where do you want to go?" smiling mischievously.

Keith pulled the *keffiyeh* down from her head, revealing her long, wavy hair and smiled back at her.

"I can't believe it's you. How did you get here? What were you doing on that roof?"

Kendra laughed and brought them to a stop over the desert where there was nothing but an endless line of sand dunes beneath them, and a starry sky above.

"It wasn't easy, believe me. I concentrated on you and I found you, but I couldn't see you. There was some kind of wall blocking me."

"The one with the blood splattered all over it? I passed that hours ago. Have you been here all this time?"

Kendra laughed again and kissed him, spinning them both in a circle as she did so.

"No, silly! Not a physical wall. You know how we go to a place that's not exactly the same as the physical world? Well, you're not in that place exactly. It's someplace a little… I don't know… lower than that. You're dreaming, Keith. She kissed him again and laughed into his mouth. I've missed you so much."

"I missed you too." He remembered the séance, the apartment, and the fake psychic. "Tonight went really badly." She felt his energy turn grey. "Can you get us out of here? I don't know what the hell I'm doing in the Middle East."

"I can try. Close your eyes and clear your mind."

When Keith opened his eyes, he saw that they were on Kendra's Island. He instantly felt better; more relaxed. It was sunset here; her favorite time on the beach. He relaxed in her embrace and absorbed the feeling of love that washed over him.

Don't go! Keith, stay with me. We have to talk!

He looked at her and saw her and the beach super-imposed on their bedroom. She was in the middle of his nightstand. Laci was laying on a mix of carpet and sand beside his bed.

Damn! You're waking up. I found us a psychic. She's really cool and she'll help us. She totally reminds me of my cousin Beth. I was talking to her while you slept...

Keith opened his eyes. His body was warbling and his bladder was demanding to be relieved.

"Dammit!"

He got up and went to the bathroom, trying to keep his mind where it was just a moment ago as he relieved himself. It wasn't working. He could barely remember something about guns, falling off a roof and being on the island with Kendra. It didn't make any sense. Had he only dreamed of Kendra?

Forty-five

"Are you ready?" Paul asked, entering the kitchen from the hall.

"As ready as I *can* be. I think this will be the worst day of my life, Paul." Joanne was pretending to arrange freshly picked flowers in the vase on the kitchen table.

"I know, dear. It's a terrible thing. But the sooner it's done, the sooner we can really start to grieve. As long as she's there, artificially alive, we can't even think of her as properly gone. But the fact is, she *is* gone. We lost her that day in Iraq."

"I know. It's still so hard to know that she's breathing right now, but after we…."

"*She* isn't breathing. A machine is pumping air into her lungs. That's not the same thing."

"Oh, I know, Paul. But still, she's alive, no matter how you look at it, and she won't be an hour from now. And her own parents are the ones who are ending her life."

"Now, now. You have to stop looking at it that way. She was killed in Iraq, but the 'miracle' of modern medicine has kept her heart beating. All we're doing is putting an end to the artificial life that makes her a mockery of the daughter we had. She is not there. She never has been."

"Unless Keith is telling the truth."

"Please don't start with his insanity. That boy is in dire need of psychotherapy. You don't actually believe him, do you? That's what's making this so difficult, isn't it? You're holding on to a crazy thread of hope. You have to get that nonsense out of your head. Think of our daughter as she was. It's an insult to her memory to think of her as a ghost, traipsing around with Keith all night. I don't even want to think about that. I'll go bring the car out."

He kissed his wife on her cheek and left the room. When Joanne heard the front door shut, she spoke out loud.

"Dear Lord, please forgive me for asking this, but if there's any chance that You're going to answer my prayers, this is the time for it. I know You have Your reasons, but it is *so* hard to understand why You would take away my daughter, and my sister's daughter before her. It makes me feel like our family has a curse."

Joanne started to cry and fished in her purse for a small packet of tissues.

"I'm sorry. I know better than to question Your will, but this is so hard. If You could possibly see it in Your will to let my daughter live, I beg of you. In Jesus's name I pray. Amen."

She carefully blotted the tears on her cheeks, threw away the tissue, and walked slowly to the front door. She wished she were on her way to do anything but what she was about to do.

Keith woke up from a restless sleep that left him feeling more tired than he had been before he slept.

His mind was a blur and he felt a sense of urgency, but he didn't know what for. He reached for his phone and looked at the time. It was 9:14. Why did he even wake up? He had nothing to wake up for.

He sat up and put his feet on the carpet. Laci wagged her tail when Keith looked at her. An image came to him of Laci lying on sand and carpet.

Sand. The island. Kendra.

Memories of the night before flooded into his mind.

Oh shit! They're going to kill Kendra today.

He rushed to the bathroom. A minute later, he came back to his room and grabbed his phone. He went to Recent Calls and touched Joanne's name.

Joanne wondered if this was what true depression felt like. She stared out the windshield at the traffic on the expressway. Nothing that she saw meant anything to her. She had no thoughts running through her mind like she normally would. She wasn't thinking about where they were going, or why. She didn't care about tonight's Women's Bible Study. She didn't even care what Paul wanted for dinner. She felt like she was made of cardboard.

When her cell phone started ringing, it didn't even register in her mind what the sound was at first.

"Are you going to answer that?" Paul asker her, staring straight ahead at the traffic and driving only two miles over the speed limit.

Joanne removed her phone from her purse on her lap and touched the Answer button.

"Yes?"

"Joanne, where are you?"

"Hello, Keith. We're on our way to St. Joan's." Her voice was wooden. She spoke as if she were talking in her sleep, with no emotion.

Keith looked around for his keys. He held the phone with one hand and picked his pants up off the floor with the other. His keys were in his pocket. He ran to his car as he talked.

"Joanne, you have to give Kendra one more chance. She was there last night, and after that fake psychic failed to notice her, she went and found someone she could actually talk to. She found one, Joanne! Kendra can talk to you now. I just need to get the details from her. I could barely reach her last night. But she found someone!"

"It's too late, Keith. We're on our way. We tried. We really did. All that's left to hope for now is if God wants to grant us a miracle or not."

Keith was racing toward the expressway. He had to get there before it was too late. He didn't care if cops chased him all the way there. He was going to get there before them.

"Joanne, hang up the phone. He's just going to upset you."

"Keith, I need to go now. I'm so sorry." Some emotion crept back into her voice as she apologized.

Keith pulled onto the onramp and pressed the gas pedal to the floor, steering erratically with one hand.

"Joanne, don't go! Listen to me. Kendra really connected with someone. She said she was just like someone… oh, what was the name? I think she said the girl reminded her of Beth. Yeah, that was it. She said Beth was a cousin. But she never told me she had—"

A car slowed in front of Keith and he dropped his phone and grabbed the steering wheel with both hands, braking and veering sharply to his left around the car in front of him. He picked up his phone.

"Joanne. Are you still there?"

Paul grabbed the phone and threw it out his window.

"That's enough!" he said, gripping the steering wheel so tightly his fingers were white. "No more. Please, no more!"

Joanne was stunned into silence. Paul had never acted this way before. He was always so gentle and caring toward her. But now he was angry at her and he sounded like he was about to have an aneurism. She could see a vein pulsing beneath his temple.

"Joanne! Are you there? Hello? Hello?"

"I'm sorry, Paul. There won't be any more."

They drove in silence. Paul wished that Kendra had never met Keith. It was awful enough to lose his daughter, but to have a maniac think she was still alive and talking to him was just insanity. It was a cruel insanity.

Joanne felt sorry for herself and she felt badly about what she was putting Paul through. But then she remembered the last thing she'd heard Keith say. "The girl reminded her of Beth." They never spoke about Beth. It was too terrible to even think about. She couldn't believe that Kendra told Keith about Beth, but she must have. How else could he know?

As far she knew, they had never found the person who killed her. He was still out there somewhere. She hoped to God that he hadn't chopped up any other girls. She hoped he was dead, whoever he was.

She shuddered at the thought of Beth's murder. She did not want to think about it, ever. Especially not now, as she was on her way to end her own daughter's life. She felt that she understood a little better now what her sister's hell had been like. She pushed the thought of Beth out of her mind.

Keith was passing cars as if he were driving in a video game. He was coming up fast on a black Lexus. That couldn't be them, could it? He slowed just a little, thinking he saw the metallic looking fish symbol on the back of the vehicle. Two people inside. That could be Paul and Joanne. He slowed some more and changed lanes to pull up beside the car to see inside.

It was them! He fingered the button to lower his window.

"Joanne! Joanne!"

She heard someone shouting and turned to her right and saw Keith yelling to her. He looked completely mad with his hair sticking out in all directions and his eyes wild.

She lowered her window to hear him better.

"Joanne! Who is Beth?!"

Joanne shook her head at him and pressed her lips together. She did not want to think about Beth. It was the worst thing that had ever happened to her family. She couldn't even begin to judge whether Kendra's fate was worse in its own way or not.

"Please! Tell me who Beth is. Kendra has never mentioned anyone named Beth before, so it has to mean something."

Keith was so focused on getting through to Joanne that he didn't see the slow moving VW in front of him and he slammed into it without slowing. The Beetle slid sideways in front of him and his car pushed it. He saw the driver raise her hands to her head, shielding herself as she screamed.

Keith slammed on his brakes and his car was hit from behind. The Beetle was now going backwards, its engine screaming in protest. The three cars eventually came to a stop, blocking traffic in two of the three lanes.

Keith didn't move. He sat there with his hands shaking and his heart breaking, dying inside. He heard noises, but they didn't register as meaning anything to him. He heard voices, but they didn't matter.

Then finally one of the voices got through to him. He turned his head and saw a police officer bending down and looking at him.

"Sir, are you injured?" he repeated.

Forty-six

"Ma'am, are you sure you're okay? You don't look well."

"I'm fine. Thank you."

"Can I get you some water, or coffee?"

"Coffee would be nice. Just black. Thank you very much."

The L.V.N. said she would be right back, and walked out of the small meeting room they were in.

Paul was breathing out forcefully through his nose on each exhalation. He could not wait to put this day behind him. At least with Keith in that accident, he didn't have to worry about him barging into the hospital and making a crazy scene. He knew that was a bad thought and he should have some level of concern about Keith's well-being, but all he felt at that moment was a small measure of relief.

Joanne had insisted they pull over and make sure Keith was okay, but Paul drove on, assuring her he would be fine, and pointing out that there was nothing they could do for him anyway. They weren't paramedics.

Joanne didn't say anything more about it, but now it was her turn to be angry. She couldn't believe that Paul could be so callous. She knew he was upset with Keith, but still. He was their daughter's fiancé. And even if he wasn't anymore, he still deserved Good Samaritan treatment, just like any person. They had driven away from an accident that they had played a part in. If nothing else, they had a responsibility to stay there and inform the police about what had happened.

Joanne wondered if they had broken the law by leaving the way they had.

The nurse came back with two cups of coffee and set them on the table. Joanne reached for hers and wrapped her hands around the paper cup. It was so hot that it was burning her hands, but she didn't move them. She just stared straight ahead, lost in her thoughts.

Paul and the nurse talked, but Joanne just tuned them out. She couldn't quite say that she loved Keith like a son, but she certainly foresaw him as becoming her son-in-law, and she had looked forward to it. She couldn't wait to help Kendra plan the wedding.

The thought of a wedding was so pleasant, she got lost in imagining all of the things she would have done with her daughter, and then she imagined Kendra and Keith walking down the aisle. They would have made such a beautiful couple.

"Mrs. Hodges?"

Someone was repeating her name. She snapped back to reality and looked at the woman who kept saying, "Mrs. Hodges?"

"Yes, I'm here."

"You're being paged to the information desk."

"Oh. Where is that?"

The nurse gave her directions and Joanne excused herself and left the room, barely even curious about why she was being paged.

The man working the desk told her that she had a phone call and directed her to where she could take it.

When she picked up the phone, she said, "This is Joanne Hodges speaking."

"Oh, thank God! I was only supposed to get one phone call, but you didn't answer your cell."

"Keith, are you okay?" Joanne awoke from the spell of apathy she had been in.

"I'm fine. A little banged up, but I don't care. I'd gladly suffer far more if I could just convince you to give your daughter one real chance. If it's not too late…"

"Keith, where are you?"

"I'm in jail."

"For the accident?"

"Sort of, but not exactly. I'll explain when I get out. My bail is only a hundred dollars, but I can't bail myself out."

"I'll do it."

She got the location from Keith and asked the desk clerk if he could call her a taxi. Then she waited outside for a few minutes, then rode off in the back of a cab, saying, "I hope you'll forgive me, Paul."

Ten minutes later, Paul was sitting by himself in the meeting room. The nurse had left and told Paul to ask for her at the nurse's station when his wife was back and they were ready to proceed.

Paul shook his head and went to find out what was taking Joanne so long. When he saw the information desk, he went over and spoke to the young man who pleasantly informed him that the lady who had taken the phone call asked him to call her a cab, so he did.

No, he didn't know where she went. But one thing seemed odd. She had come to his desk looking like she was sleepwalking. But when she got off the phone, she seemed to be very excited.

"What do you mean, excited?"

"I don't know. Kinda like someone who was about to go on an adventure, or maybe about to do something they thought they shouldn't be doing, but looking forward to it anyway."

Paul thanked the man and walked to his car. He resigned himself to the madness that he could not put a stop to.

He didn't know where Keith was, but he had no doubt that Joanne did, and that was where she was heading.

Forty-seven

The cab was still waiting when Joanne and Keith walked out of the police station, as promised. She knew the fare was going to be outrageous, but she didn't care. Money meant nothing to her right now.

"Okay, Keith. Where is this psychic?"

"I don't know yet. I woke up before Kendra had a chance to tell me."

"Do you mean to tell me that it's in dreams that you talk to her?"

"Not normally, no. But last night I was having a dream and Kendra came into it. She ended it actually, and turned it into one of our regular visits. But I woke up and I can't talk to her when I'm awake."

"I'm sure I don't understand this."

"I don't either, to be honest. It's the strangest thing I've ever done. But I swear, it's also the most real thing in my life. I live for the time I get to be with her."

"How do we find this person now - the psychic?"

"I have to try to reach Kendra. If I can just relax somewhere and sort of fall asleep, I'll be able to talk to her."

"What do you mean, relax somewhere?"

"I guess we should go to my house. I lie down on my bed and act like I'm going to sleep, and that's when I see her. I know this sounds crazy, but it's really not. If we can find this psychic, you'll see. I promise you."

"I've come this far, there's no point in stopping now. Paul is probably going to divorce me over this."

"Don't say that. Let's go to my house and take it from there."

Keith gave the cabbie his address and then gave him his credit card when they reached his house.

"Would you like to watch TV while I try to do this?"

"Won't that disturb your concentration?"

"I suppose it might. I don't really know."

"How about if I walk Laci? It might be good for her and for me."

"That's a great idea."

Joanne and Laci walked down the steps and Keith ran to his room. He lay down and concentrated like never before on relaxing his mind and body. He breathed slow and put all of his attention on his breath as he visualized his body relaxing, inch by inch.

When he started to feel the vibrations, he had to force himself not to get too excited or it would bring him back to regular consciousness.

Kendra was there and waiting. As soon as she was able to make a connection, she grabbed onto the hands of Keith's energy body and pulled him up and out.

He came forward into her embrace and they tried to kiss, but just merged into each other's space.

They both laughed, filled with the same excitement and anxiety.

"We probably shouldn't waste any time switching to virtual physical form, huh?"

"You're right. As much as I would love to hold you and feel you close, I need to find out when the psychic you found can see us."

"Okay. Her name is Katana, and she goes by Kat. She's really sweet. You'll like her." She gave him enough information to be able to find her online. Then she asked, "Are you okay? I was there when you crashed. I almost had a heart attack. Or something."

"I'm fine. Just a few cuts and bruises. It was nothing. Hey. That reminds me. Who's Beth? I think that might be what got your mother to change her mind."

"I'll tell you later. It's not a good story. I haven't talked to anybody about her in a long time. And trust me, this isn't a good time."

"Okay. I'll take your word for it. I love you, but I need to call Kat and see if she can see us right away. Your mother just ditched your dad at the hospital to get me out of jail. We gotta do this as soon as we can before she comes to her senses."

"I know. Daddy's mad right now, but he's going to thank her for this later. Lay down and I'll try to help wake you up. I'll be with you the whole time. I'm not leaving."

"Okay. I love you. More than anything."

"Me too."

Keith lay down in the same position that he had lain down in just several moments ago.

"Okay. Do what you can do, babe."

He closed his eyes and waited. Kendra closed hers and imagined a bucket of ice cold water floating above Keith. She stared at the bucket and focused her energy and intention into it and then flipped it over.

Keith jerked awake.

"It worked!" He laughed with joy and relief. He went to his computer and easily found Kat's website. He clicked the contact link and entered her number in his cell phone. His day was going really well now considering how it had started. Kat answered and said she'd be happy to do an immediate and unscheduled session. She had been hoping to hear from him today. She told him her address and said she'd be ready when he got there.

Keith ran to his front door and looked outside. He saw Joanne standing on the sidewalk several houses down on her way back, waiting for Laci after she stopped to sniff a fascinating patch of grass.

Keith called out to them, and Joanne had to hold on tight to keep Laci from breaking free as she towed Joanne back to the house.

Forty-eight

"Well, at least this is a much nicer place than the last one." Joanne looked around the peaceful, tree-lined street where Katana's Intuitive Sessions was nestled between other residential houses that had been converted for business purposes.

Keith handed money to the cab driver, telling him to keep the change, and said, "Yeah, this is much better. I have a good feeling about this psychic. Especially since she was Kendra's choice."

Joanne just smiled lightly. She wanted to believe that, but was still in need of being convinced. They walked up to the front door and as Keith raised his hand to knock, it opened. He laughed at the attractive young woman standing inside the doorway.

"What?" she asked, smiling.

"I was thinking that's a nice demonstration of psychic ability – opening the door like that before someone can knock."

She laughed and pointed to the security camera pointed at the front walkway. "Nothing mystical about that, aside from wireless technology, which I'll never understand. You must be Keith and Joanne. Please come in."

As they stepped through the doorway, the first thing they noticed was a really pleasing aroma.

Joanne wanted to ask what it was, but she assumed that Paul wouldn't like it if she introduced something new.

"Can I get you a drink? We have Chai tea and Dasani bottled water."

"No, thank you, sweetheart. This is a very nice place you have here. Is this your home and your office?"

"This is just my office. I'm glad you like it. I've tried to create a very relaxing environment. It helps with the sessions."

"It definitely feels relaxing and peaceful." Keith looked around, trying to see where the session would take place. "Do you need to do anything before the session?"

"I'm ready whenever you are. Do either of you have any questions before we start?"

"Do I pay before or after?"

"After, please. I want to make sure you're fully satisfied with your session before you pay for anything."

Joanne and Keith smiled at each other briefly in joint recognition of yet another nice difference between this psychic and the last one.

"I have no doubt I'll be satisfied. I was referred to you by Kendra." Keith's smile grew wider. He was anticipating the outcome he'd wanted from the first time he had told Joanne and Paul that he was in communication with their daughter. They would now know for sure he'd been telling the truth.

"Okay, then. If that's your only question, shall we get started?"

Joanne nodded. Keith said, "Yes. I can't wait."

Katana led them down a hall and into what had once been a bedroom. The windows were blacked out and there was a small lamp in the room with something like a colorful scarf wrapped around it to block it from emitting any white light. Katana turned on the lamp then shut the door to the room. The soft light barely illuminated the room, making it appear as though the sun was well into setting.

Joanne appeared to be mildly spooked by the dim lighting. Keith was still smiling and eager to start. This would be the first time he'd heard from Kendra while he was wide awake.

In the center of the room there was a large, round oak table. Katana told them to sit anywhere they liked and took her own seat first so they could choose places closer or farther from her, as they liked. Joanne took the second chair on Kat's right. Keith took the second chair on her left, facing Joanne across the table.

"Do we need to hold hands or anything to help you get Kendra to come to us?"

Kat looked at Joanne and held back her laughter, but couldn't stop from smiling when she said, "That won't be necessary. Kendra got here the same time you two did."

Joanne's eyelids rose, revealing how startled she was. The hair on the back of her neck also rose. Unconsciously, she adjusted her hair and smoothed out her top, wanting to look most presentable in case Kendra really was there and could see her.

"Keith, you've been in regular contact with Kendra so if you don't mind, I'm going to focus mainly on letting Joanne talk to her."

"Right. That's perfect. I'd love to talk to her too, but if I don't talk to her right now, I definitely will later." He was bursting with happiness inside. If this worked, Kendra would get to live. He would be able to see her every day for the foreseeable future.

"Okay." Turning to Joanne again, she said, "I want to tell you how I'll be doing this. Kendra is here and quite ready to talk. In fact, she won't shut up." Katana laughed. "Rather than telling you, 'Kendra says,' or 'Kendra's answer is,' I'm only going to repeat whatever she says. I just want it to be clear that I won't be channeling or anything like that. Kendra won't be speaking through me, and I honestly don't know if that's even possible. I'll be more like a foreign translator, except for the fact that I'll be translating English to English. So, just talk as if you were talking to her, and I'll repeat whatever she says. Okay?"

Joanne nodded nervously, still a little freaked out about the prospect of talking to her daughter's spirit.

"Just feel free, whenever you're ready," Katana said, and leaned against the back of her high-backed leather chair, closing her eyes as she did so.

Joanne looked at Keith, pursing her lips, symbolically sealing them. Keith smiled, hoping to put her at ease. He leaned back in his chair and relaxed, closing his eyes; not deliberately mimicking Katana.

Joanne breathed in deeply through her nose and exhaled. She glanced up at the ceiling.

"Kendra. Are you here?"

"I am, Mom. And I'm so excited to have this chance to talk to you. I miss you so much! And I love you, and I miss Daddy too. Please tell him that."

"I'll try," Joanne responded with a shaky voice. She felt somewhat badly about not saying, "I love and miss you too." She wanted to, just thinking of her daughter, but she really didn't know if she could believe it was actually her.

As if she knew what her mother was thinking, Kendra said, "Mom, it's really me. I know this is hard for you, but just try to accept that I'm here. And I'm really okay where I am. I can do anything at all here. It's like being in a dream, but everything feels so much more real than a dream."

"What do you do there exactly?"

"Oh, Mom, you wouldn't believe the things I've done. Keith and I went to the moon and we went to Paris and to Egypt and— Oh, oh, oh! There are these dolphins I spend a lot of time with that are just the most amazing creatures in the world!"

Joanne's breath caught in her throat and she held a hand over her mouth. Keith opened his eyes and looked at her. She looked upset, like she was starting to cry. He cocked his head and looked at her. She looked back at him and shook her head.

"Kendra, my dear, sweet child. I've missed you more than I can say. Are you really okay where you are?"

"Yes, I am, Mom. Believe it or not. It's really fantastic here. How did you realize this is really me talking to you?

Joanne leaned down and picked up her purse and pulled out a tissue. She dabbed at her eyes and said, "Ever since you were a little girl and you were excited to tell me about something you'd done at school, or on a field trip, or anything that you came home from that you were excited about, you would rush to get it all out. Then you would realize that you had forgotten something really good, and you would interrupt yourself by saying, 'Oh, oh, oh! Your eyes would be wide open and you were just the cutest thing ever."

"She's laughing and smiling, remembering that, Joanne," Katana told her.

"Kendra, do you already know what the doctors have said about your chances for recovery?"

"Yes. I don't really have any."

"I need to know something. If we're not blessed with a miraculous healing, are you really okay with being where you are… and not… moving on?"

"I really am, Mom. I can do anything here. It's like living in a magical wonderland. It's just that…"

"What, dear? Is there something wrong there? Are you at risk from bad spirits or something?"

"No, no. Nothing like that. I was just going to say, sometimes, I'm lonely. But then Keith crosses over and it's the best time ever. We have a blast. I wish you could visit here too."

"I don't know about that, sweetheart, but if you're happy, that's all I need to know. You can stay there for as long as... Well, I don't know how long actually. But you don't have to worry about us turning off your support. I promise you, that is not going to happen, regardless of what your father thinks about this."

"That's a huge relief, Mom. Thank you. I'm sorry that I've caused trouble between you and Daddy."

"Don't you even think that! Nothing is your fault. I'll take care of him. This is just not something he knows how to deal with."

"Maybe you can bring him with you next time and he'll realize that Kat is repeating my words the way you realized it."

Joanne looked down at her hands resting on the table and shook her head. "I don't know about that yet. This is a lot to take in, even for me. But if I can come back and talk to you, I will gladly do so."

"I'm sure Kat would love to have a new regular client" Katana opened her eyes. "Okay, that was weird, talking about myself from someone else's perspective. Sorry to interrupt, but I'm not usually mentioned in my own sessions. This is new to me too. And yes, I would love to continue relaying for you, Kendra." She closed her eyes again, returning to her objective role of translator.

Joanne and Kendra talked for the rest of the hour-long session. Keith sat there, listening and beaming with happiness. The best outcome he could have possibly hoped for had come through for him.

Forty-nine

Keith refused Joanne's offer to pay for the taxi as she prepared to get out of the car. Keith insisted it was on him.

"I'll let you know how things stand with Paul after I've explained everything to him. It will probably be best if I wait until tomorrow though. This is not going to be an easy discussion. Not for either of us."

"I understand. I hope it goes well and isn't upsetting for either of you. And afterward, I hope he realizes I'm not crazy. Cuz if I am, then we both are."

Keith smiled at her as she opened the door. Joanne grabbed her purse by the strap, then shut the door, waved, and walked to her front door.

"Okay. Back to where you first picked us up. Thanks for staying the whole time. I really appreciate it."

"It's my pleasure." The cab driver turned in his seat and handed Keith his business card. "Call me any time you need to get somewhere. I don't mind waitin'. My kids is all grown and that's all I got now is lots o' time."

"Great. I'll call you tomorrow to take me on a one-way trip."

"Just one-way?"

"Yeah. I need to buy a car."

"Oh, okay. I hate to lose you as a customer, but I can sure take you to buy a car."

Back at home, Keith tipped the cab driver generously and looked at the business card to see if his name was printed on it.

"Thank you, very much, Lloyd. I'll call you tomorrow when I'm ready to go car shopping."

Keith went inside and took care of Laci, then went promptly to his room, certain that he'd be able to relax now and meet with Kendra. He already felt practically weightless now that he was no longer haunted by the fear of losing Kendra.

He breezed through his relaxation exercise and felt the pull from Kendra's side. She was helping him, and the vibrations came quickly.

As soon as he was on her side, they both changed from sparkly energy bodies into their physical-like forms, wrapped their arms around each other and jumped up and down in celebration of their victory.

"So, what do you want to do tonight?" he asked. "We should do something more amazing than anything we've done so far."

"I agree. But first, let's go tell the dolphins that I'm staying!"

They joined hands and jumped into the air and flew through the bedroom wall and out into Kendra's version of the world where the ocean was not far away.

When Joanne walked inside, she found Paul pacing in the kitchen and looking terribly worried.

"There you are!"

"I'm sorry I left like that, Paul. I really am. But I needed to do something and I was in no state of mind to argue about it. The only way I could do what I needed to do was to just leave and do it. I hope you can understand."

"Joanne, I don't understand at all. I'm afraid you're infected with that boy's craziness. But right now I'm just relieved to know that you're okay."

"Of course I'm okay, Paul. Why wouldn't I be?"

"I assumed your leaving had something to do with Keith, and in case you've forgotten, that young man caused a serious little pile-up on the freeway. He's completely lost his mind. Who knows what he might do next?"

"Paul, may I please have a hug?"

He came over and granted her request. She held him for a moment, then said, "We need to talk, but first I'm going to make some coffee. No, I lied. First I'm going to visit the ladies room, then I'm going to make some coffee. I'll be right back."

Paul made the coffee for her when she left the kitchen. When she returned and heard the coffee brewing, she smiled at him.

"You are the best husband a woman could ask for. Just remember how much I love you, because I really do."

Paul felt some of the tension he'd been feeling as he worried about Joanne disappearing from the hospital leave his body. He was still concerned though about the discussion she wanted to have with him, so he couldn't completely relax inside. He was sure it had something to do with a new plan that Keith had concocted. He'd already talked his gullible wife into a psychic medium, so he couldn't imagine what new craziness was in store for him.

Joanne made two cups of coffee and brought them over to the table and sat in the chair next to Paul's.

"Paul, you were right. I left the hospital to go see Keith. He was the one who called me when they paged me to the information desk."

"I figured as much. We should go see about getting you a new phone. I apologize for throwing it out the window."

"We'll address that later. Keith called because he wanted to take me to another psychic."

"Oh Lord. Here we go again." He didn't admit it, but he was relieved to hear that it was only a craziness that he'd dealt with already and it wasn't something new and crazier.

As Joanne told him the story of what had happened at Katana's office, Paul did very well at maintaining a neutral expression out of love and respect for his wife. When she reached the part where she knew that her daughter was really there and speaking through the psychic, Paul closed his eyes and pinched the bridge of his nose.

"Look at me, Paul."

He lowered his hand and looked into his wife's eyes.

"Do I look like I'm crazy? Am I behaving irrationally? Aside from acting so rashly at the hospital. That doesn't count. Right now – am I acting like a crazy person?"

"No, dear. But perhaps it comes in stages. I'm sorry. I just don't believe in any of this new-age, mumbo jumbo and I thought you knew better than to start believing in it too. I think you must be grieving and holding on to some hope of not having to let her go."

"Paul, I understand how hard this is, but do you think Pastor Dave is crazy too?"

"I still can't believe he went along with these shenanigans." Paul shook his head, dismayed at the mystery of how people he had known to be intelligent and level-headed had seemed to just go off their rockers.

Joanne patiently explained to Paul how she had been convinced that Kendra was talking through Katana. Then she told him about all of the things she and Kendra had talked about.

As she talked, Paul's heart broke as he saw the woman he loved lighting up with happiness and once again becoming the woman she had been before Kendra's terrible experience. She was truly happy again. All she needed was the perfect delusion. He had never been dishonest with his wife before, and he didn't want to be now, but if this was what it took to make her happy, for the time being, then he resigned himself to going along with it.

"I can't believe I'm saying this, but you've convinced me, dear."

"Really? Do you believe me now, Paul? Do you really believe me?"

"I do, honey. I believe you. I'm sorry I resisted it and thought you were just going a little crazy."

Joanne burst out of her chair and almost knocked Paul out of his as she embraced him.

Joanne saw Paul wipe a tear from his eye. She thought he was crying tears of happiness at the realization that Kendra was still alive.

Paul silently asked God to forgive him for bearing false witness, and he tried to forgive himself for being a liar with good intentions.

"You can come with me to the next session and talk to her yourself. Oh, Paul, she'll be so happy to talk to you! She asked me to tell you that she misses you and she loves you."

Dear Lord, what I have gotten myself into?

Fifty

Joanne was wakened by the sound of the bedroom phone ringing on her nightstand. She quickly reached over to the handset and lifted it out of the charging cradle before it woke Paul. She glanced at the clock, and in her sleepy mind, she thought that a phone call this early could not be good.

"Hello?"

"Hello. This is Natasha Stravinsky from St. Joan's Medical Center. I apologize for calling so early, but could I speak to Joanne or Paul Hodges?"

Joanne felt her chest constrict with fear. She quietly but quickly stepped out of the room and didn't respond until she was in the hall, heading toward the kitchen.

"This is Joanne speaking."

"Joanne, would it possible for you to come to St. Joan's at your earliest convenience. I need to speak with you and it would be best to discuss in person."

"Is this about yesterday – how I just left right as we were preparing to turn off her life-support?"

"We could discuss over the phone if that would be better for you, but I think in person is best."

"Yes, of course. I'll be there shortly. Will you need Paul as well?"

"It would be ideal if both of you were present."

"I understand. I'll wake him up and we'll come over straight away."

"Thank you, Mrs. Hodges, and I again, apologize for the early call."

As each of the Hodges performed their morning routines in their separate bathrooms, they wondered why they would be called in so early to discuss the aborted life-support termination.

It made sense to Paul that the hospital would not appreciate going through the planning and scheduling to end someone's life only to have the loved ones disappear. But did it have to be discussed this early? The sun was just now rising. Surely they could've waited until normal business hours.

Paul was sure that some administrator was upset with them and wanted this matter seen through to completion to free up a bed for another patient who needed it more than Kendra.

Joanne dared to hope that perhaps God had seen fit to answer her prayers and restore Kendra's brain to good health. If that was it, the hospital wouldn't be willing to recognize a miracle from God and would want to be "cautiously optimistic" about Kendra's improvement, making no guarantees that she would fully recover.

On the drive to the hospital, they kept their personal theories about the nature of this early call to themselves. Paul did not wish to voice his cynical pessimism about hospital administrators, and

Joanne didn't want to appear foolish and prematurely optimistic until it was confirmed that a miracle was indeed occurring.

After parking in the visitor's lot, they walked to the front entrance, passing a few police cars with lights flashing and several policemen standing around talking and drinking coffee.

At the information desk, they were given directions to a room where someone would meet with them. They took the elevator up and followed the colored directional lines on the walls to the right department and then into the numbered meeting room. A few moments later, a woman in a suit entered the room carrying a manila folder.

The woman introduced herself and Joanne recognized the Russian accent of the woman who had called her a short while ago. Joanne felt her hopes for a miracle deflate as she studied the woman's expression. She looked somber and professional, giving only the briefest of smiles as she said her name, but it wasn't a genuine happy smile. It was a polite, introductory smile.

"I apologize for calling you to come in so early this morning, and even more, I apologize for having not good news to deliver." Joanne leaned forward, her eyes clouded with fear. "Is best to not delay and just go forward."

Natasha opened the folder in front of her and flipped to the page she wanted. She read over something silently, then looked up at Kendra's parents and resumed speaking.

"At 5:20 this morning, Nurse Callaway was alerted at Station 3 by an equipment abnormality alarm in your daughter's room. Promptly she went to investigate the nature of the problem and found the life support equipment for Kendra Hodges had been removed from power supply." She looked down at the page again, then back up at Paul, then Joanne. "The nurse called for assistance. A technician arrived promptly and restored power to equipment and two doctors attempted to resuscitate the patient. The efforts of all involved were not successful."

Paul put a hand on top of his wife's hand which was resting on the table. He put his arm around her, pulling her close to him with his other hand.

"Kendra is gone?" Joanne asked, barely moving her lips.

"I'm sorry, Mrs. Hodges. Everything which could be done was tried, but yet, we did not succeed. It is our greatest hope that as you were prepared to terminate life support the morning of yesterday, then this is not too traumatic to be happening unplanned today."

"I can see how you would hope that. But the fact is that we didn't go through with it yesterday because we changed our minds. Didn't we, Paul?"

Paul nodded, but didn't mention that he was relieved that this entire ordeal was now over. He would not have to attend séances, pretending to be speaking to his daughter through a crystal ball or a Ouija board. He was greatly relieved that such an insult to his daughter's memory was no longer something he had to dread or be a participant in. They could finally grieve properly and accept their daughter was gone, and eventually try to move on and enjoy the time they had left together.

Joanne didn't want to explain why they had changed their minds. She knew how crazy it would sound if she tried to explain everything regarding the psychic.

"Poor Keith will be devastated when I tell him Kendra is gone. This is terrible." Joanne began to cry for the loss of the child she had just re-established communication with the day before. She had looked forward to regular talks with Kendra for as many years as she could.

"I'm sorry to say this, but I have yet more bad news. Keith Erikson was found on your daughter's bed with no vital signs. He also could not be revived."

Joanne was shocked. Even Paul's eyes widened at this news.

"What happened to him? Did he…"

"We cannot say yet with confirmation of facts, but security video shows a person who is looking like Keith stealing from a nurse's cart. We are thinking he took the syringe which was in his arm when his body was found."

"Did he overdose on something? Did he steal medicine too?" Joanne was distracted from her grief as she puzzed over Keith's apparent suicide.

"It appears that the syringe was empty. No drugs or liquid of any kind, as far as we can tell, but we await lab results to confirm."

"Then how…?"

"Our guess is he injected 8cc's of air into his bloodstream causing an instantly fatal gas embolism immediately after cutting the backup power supply to…"

"But I don't understand why. We had just agreed to keep Kendra on life support. That's what he wanted."

"Two letters were found in the room. One of them is addressed to you, Joanne. It is from Kendra, written by Keith. She explains why."

Natasha took a sheet of paper from the folder and handed it across the table to Joanne, who held it in trembling hands as she read it to herself silently.

Dearest Mother,

I want you and Daddy to know that I love you both and I want to thank you for the wonderful life you gave me. I had a great life and I appreciate everything you both did for me. I wouldn't have changed anything before the bombing.

After the bombing, I found myself in a lonely world. Before long, my loneliness would end up being blissfully but briefly dispelled by Keith's ability to join me in the place between life and death. But he always had to go back.

When we talked at Kat's, you asked me if I was okay with staying where I am and not moving on. Keith joined me after dropping you off and after celebrating and traveling to a few exciting places, we ended up talking about our future together. We realized that this is not the way people were meant to live.

I have not been alive, but I wasn't dead either. Keith was alive, but he only felt alive when he was with me. We agreed that this isn't really living, and there must be something that comes after this. After we die, we're still alive as spirits and it can't be that we're meant to hang around the earth having silly fun. There is no one else here but me – and my dolphin friends. So we must be meant to go on to something else.

Keith naturally wanted to come with me. We argued at first, but he convinced me that he had no life worth living on earth and he refused to live without me. We could either play every day in limbo, or we could move on, in love and together forever, as we had promised each other.

By the time you read this, we will be together and taking the next step in our journey as immortal beings. It's actually very exciting and I can't wait to see what's next. So please don't be sad for me. I've already been gone for weeks. Nothing has really changed.

If there's a way for me to find you or communicate with you again somehow, I totally will. Wherever I am, always remember that I'm alive and so is my love for you.

Thank you, Mom and Dad for being the best parents ever.

I love you!!!

Kendra Hodges, (written by Keith Erikson)

Joanne set the paper down and turned to Paul, holding on to him as she cried.

"I can come back later," Natasha said.

"No. Please stay. I'll be all right. You said there were two papers. What is the other one?"

"The second one is a will, also written by Keith. I suppose it is legal for me to reveal to you."

Natasha removed another sheet and slid it across the table. It was much shorter and Joanne read it without picking it up.

I hereby apologize to the wonderful staff of St. Joan's for any alarm or trouble I caused by turning off Kendra's equipment and leaving an extra body in her bed for the staff to dispose of.

I hope you will forgive me and also grant me one favor. Please send this letter to my attorney, Peter Fanning at his law office in Philadelphia. (See address below.)

Peter, thank you for looking after my financial situation and guiding me with how to manage and invest the money my father left me.

If you're reading this, then my suicide was successful. For what it's worth, I wasn't depressed or anything. I've never been happier. It's a long story. Joanne Hodges can explain if you're at all curious.

I need to dispose of my possessions, and there's one urgent matter.

I hereby leave my house and all belongings therein, as well as the money in my bank accounts and whatever investment funds I have to Jared Hopkins of Tulsa, Oklahoma.

To Joanne Hodges, I ask that she adopt and take care of Laci for the remainder of her life. As the object of Kendra's and my love, she is the closest we ever came to having a child, and I hope that she can serve as a daily reminder of Kendra's love for her parents and a testament of our love for each other and our desire to be together wherever we go from here.

Should the Hodges decline to take care of Laci, please put her up for adoption and use funds from my account to finance an ad to find a family that will love her and take care of her.

Thank you for everything, Peter.

Here's to life, death, and the magical state in between that we sometimes visit while we dream!

Keith David Erikson

Epilogue

Kendra could feel her mother's sadness as she watched her reading the letters. She had reasoned that since they had already lost her weeks ago in Baghdad, her death would not come as a heavy blow. But the finality of it was still a shock that her mother hadn't expected.

Kendra's sadness lowered her vibrational rate, and subsequently her energy did not glow as brightly as usual. The brightest emanation coming from her was where her left hand was holding onto Keith's right.. In that spot, their energy flowed into each other and magnified, increasing the glow.

Are you ready?

Yes. I've seen enough.

Do you think you'll want to go to your funeral?

No. This is sad enough. I don't think I could stand watching my funeral. I just wish I could hug them.

Try it. Maybe they'll feel your presence or something.

Kendra let go of Keith's hand and floated closer to her mother and wrapped her arms around her.

Joanne shivered and pushed both sheets of paper back across the table.

Do you feel anything?
No. Just her emotions. But nothing from trying to hug her. Other than that, I feel like someone is tugging at me, like they want me to go to them, but it's not coming from my mom. Do you feel anything?

Yes. Something is pulling me from…
Keith turned to his right.
…that direction – where that light is.

Kendra let go of her mother and turned to see what Keith was referring to.
That's it!

What's it?

That's where we need to go! Remember when I told you before I had a feeling like there was someplace I needed to go but I couldn't tell where it was. Now it's really clear - that's it.

I don't know what it is, but it sure is inviting. When you're done here, let's go check it out.

I'm done, Keith.
Kendra blew her parents a kiss.
I love you, Mom and Dad!
She turned and took Keith's hand in hers.

Okay. Let's go check out that light. It feels like a mix between your love for me, my parents' love, and the feeling of going home to a family gathering.

They drifted out of the room and toward the light, picking up speed as they went.

As the light enveloped them and circled around them, they began to see colors on the far end as if they were looking through a tunnel. There was grass and trees and a waterfall with flowers growing on both sides of a beautiful lagoon. At the end of the tunnel-like passage of swirling white light they could see two silhouettes that appeared to be standing and waiting for them.

Keith started laughing with delight.

That's my dad!

Kendra's energy brightened as she smiled inside and out, happy for Keith.

That's awesome, Keith! Who's with him…?

As she came closer, she recognized the other figure.

Oh my god! It's Beth!

Their energy bodies swirled around each other as they kissed briefly, glowing brighter than ever, then they separated and zoomed forward to the end of the passage where they transformed to their solid forms as they embraced their loved ones.

The End
###

About the author

Edward M Wolfe is a former investigative reporter and journalist who now writes fiction. His short story, "When Everything Changed," appears in the sci-fi anthology "Nascence," and his short story "Halloween Bully" will be published in the "Moon Shadows" anthology in the fall of 2014.

He lives in Tulsa with two human children, and two canine children.

Also by Edward M Wolfe

In The End: a pre-apocalypse novel

When Everything Changed

Devon's Last Chance

Ataraxia

Why Do Kids Kill?

Coming soon…

Return of the Gods

Equal Signs

Ascended Bastard – an autobiography